Provocation

by

Katja Desjarlais

This is a work of fiction. Names, characters, places, and incidents are either the product of the author's imagination or are used fictitiously, and any resemblance to actual persons living or dead, business establishments, events, or locales, is entirely coincidental.

Provocation

COPYRIGHT © 2022 by Katja Desjarlais

Cover Art by *Diana Carlile*

The Wild Rose Press, Inc.
PO Box 708
Adams Basin, NY 14410-0708
Visit us at www.thewildrosepress.com

Publishing History
First Edition, 2022
Trade Paperback ISBN 978-1-5092-4048-7
Digital ISBN 978-1-5092-4049-4

Published in the United States of America

"Don't do this, Rhys," Lis pleaded, jabbing her makeshift weapon at him while he stalked toward her. "Please don't make me do this."

She retreated back, scuffling her feet across the floor while he took long, leisurely strides her way. He half-heartedly swatted at the chair legs as they crossed in front of him, his bloodied arm swinging out sloppily.

He's toying with me.

Her calf hit the cool glass shower enclosure and she lifted her eyes to his, adjusting her grip on the chair. He was studying her, his oval irises watching her intently as she swung her weapon up and hesitated.

"Tick tock, flower child," he growled while he crouched in preparation of attack.

With every ounce of strength she could muster, she swung the chair into the glass, screaming and shutting her eyes tight as the shards began to fall and Rhys leapt forward.

Dedication

To Colleen. You know why.

CHAPTER ONE

Rhys leaned back on his elbows and adjusted his hips, his dark eyes locked on his phone as he contemplated his next move. His thumb hovered over the screen while his other hand ghosted distractedly through the colorful curls bobbing in his peripheral. Pursing his lips, he growled low in his throat and made his choice.

This shouldn't be so fucking difficult.

He'd done this tens of thousands of times.

Four moves later, he knew he'd screwed up.

"I'm deleting this stupid game," he grunted, increasing the pressure on Simone's head a fraction to correct her form when her rhythm stumbled. The Tender immediately righted her course, adding a quick swipe of her tongue in repentance.

The phone bounced off the mattress as he dropped it in frustration and lolled his head back. He needed a new game, a new app to fill the black spot on his screen.

Maybe Mahjong.

Looking down the expanse of his torso, he met the pair of scathing blue eyes watching him with open resentment. "You're doing great, angel," he muttered, patting around for his buzzing phone. "Focus on reining in that look of utter contempt when you don't have my complete attention. Think of something pleasant, like kittens or puppies. I'll be back on board once I check this message."

Honing in on the change in Simone's gaze, he

1

flicked his note application open. He would need to work with her on that tomorrow evening.

Ignoring Nichol's link to Lis's interview and Kaius's subtle reminder to watch his tongue when Audra arrived back on site, he pulled up the text he'd been anticipating and relaxed a fraction.

"Everything's a go," he stated as he fired off a reply. "All right, sweetheart. Now you have my complete attention, I promise."

****

At least her master will be going out with a smile, Rhys mused while he carefully covered Simone's sleeping form with her comforter. He flicked the lights off as he left her room, collecting her laundry on his way through the door. Scanning the main training area, he replaced the throw cushions on the sofa and loaded his arms with dirtied dishes and practice stakes before he locked the door behind him.

No sense encouraging Simone to use up her bloodlust prior to her sale.

While the kitchen sink filled, he checked over the fridge and pantry, making quick notes on what items the haunt's second-in-command, Nichol, would need to add to their upcoming deliveries. With Bianca on site again, he would need to double his orders for fresh fruit and salted meats. Returning to the sink, he began absently scrubbing the plates and cutlery, noticing Molly's selection of pink dish soap had replaced the depleted antibacterial yellow bottle Audra ordered in.

The pink shit definitely smelled better, even if it was essentially useless as a cleaner.

Leaving the kitchen light on in case Bianca had a midday case of the munchies, he strode through the empty hall of the Tender quarters toward his room. Running his fingers along the picture frames while he walked, he ignored the absence of heartbeats and steady breathing in the wing. As he entered his room, he tossed his phone on the coffee table and double checked the lock on the door. The black Egyptian cotton sheets were calling to him, beckoning him to get a few hours of rest before the shit rising toward the fan finally hit full throttle.

Fucking Tenders.

He stripped down to his boxers and stretched out across the large bed.

Maybe my exit from the Tender trade really is long overdue, he thought as he tossed his arm over his eyes to block out the light. The world was changing faster, vampire society morphing along with it. The need for trained courtesans specializing in vamps was no longer a priority while everything went to hell around them. Humans were gunning for them. There were traitors among their own species sharpening their stakes.

And between his timing miscalculation with Amy, his abject failure with Molly, his half-assed retraining of the Tramp Twins, and the future assassin asleep down the hall, he was definitely losing his touch.

And then there was Lis.

Fucking Lis.

If he lined up the hundreds of women he had successfully trained, rotated, and placed over the centuries, Lis and Bianca would be at the forefront of his achievements. Bianca Schumann, with her disarming beauty and refined tongue, came to him as royalty disguised as a runaway. He honed his methods to her obvious innate nobility, molding her mannerisms and skills to rival that of any blood-born queen.

Perhaps he should have paid more attention to quashing the rebellious side that brought her to his door.

Fuck it.

Her altruistic social warrior streak was his hauntmate Jagger's problem now.

But Lis. Fucking Lis.

That one stung.

He groaned and rolled onto his stomach, burying his face in his pillow.

"LAGOOOOOOOOOOOOON!"

He watched with concealed disdain as the sputtering yellow school bus pulled up alongside him, a long-haired asshole howling out an open back window.

Fucking hippies.

The driver reached over and wrenched at the door handle. "Hey, man!" he yelled over the din of music and shouts emanating from the bus, "You need a lift?"

He glanced down the empty highway and weighed his options. "You going north?"

"Salt Lake City bound. If you got some bread to add to the communal, come aboard."

Reaching into his back pocket, he pulled out his wallet and tossed several bills onto the foul smelling kid's lap as he sauntered onto the bus. He scanned the occupants, subtly scenting the air for the least offensive odors and gripping a seat back when the vehicle lurched into gear.

"LAGOOOOOOOOOOOOON!" the long-haired fuck-up in the back howled out again, setting off a chorus of hoots and echoes from the other passengers.

He flopped into the first available seat, straightening out his leather jacket and running a hand through his hair. As he adjusted his long legs in the cramped quarters, dirty-nailed fingers entwined in his and turned his palm up. "I can read this for you," a lethargic voice murmured, drawing his attention to his bench mate. She ran her finger up the center of his palm, blonde hair hanging in frizzy dreadlocks which swung with the motion of the bus. "Your lifeline," she muttered. "You're gonna live a long time. But see this break here? That's when your life changes, alters your destiny."

"Flake off, Janet," a sweet feminine voice called out. "You're gonna make this hunk bug outta here at the next gas up if you keep up the hokey shit. Come sit over here, man."

He disentangled his hand from the filthy fingers with a tight smile as he moved beside his new companion. "Thank fuck," he grunted, getting comfortable and shaking his hair into his eyes to hide his oval vampiric irises. Without glancing over, he accepted a thin joint and inhaled deep despite the nonexistent effect it would have on him.

"Janet hasn't showered once in all the time I've been riding. Says the dust of her ancestors is keeping her short lifeline at bay, or some shit," the woman commented, passing the joint behind her. "You been on the road long?"

Finally deciding to give his travel mate a once-over, a smirk formed on his face. "Just long enough, sweetheart."

Despite the facial blurring used by the networks to protect her identity, he had known it was Lis the second his ears picked up her voice. It was the hint of a Tennessee twang mixed with a midwestern lilt and the way she blended 'the' so seamlessly into the next word its presence was imperceptible.

He'd spent months reworking her enunciation before deciding it was easier to market her linguistics as a unique trait.

He did manage to break 'ain't' from her habits.

What the fuck had gone down at McConaughey's to turn his little flower child into the cold informant he saw tonight on the evening news?

Derry McConaughey purchased Lis for a favor and a song, the one dollar price tag a mere formality against the reprieve Rhys received from the Irishman's haunt.

It was, for Rhys, the deal of a century.

Turning onto his back, he stared up at the ceiling, absently scratching at his tattoos. He would have an hour from dusk to prepare for his call to the Los Angeles branch of the McConaughey haunt where Derry resided most of the year. With any luck, the old vamp already had a bead on Lis's location and was priming for an extraction.

And with his luck, Derry would be on the hunt for a full refund.

Fuck.

He swung his legs over the edge of the bed, gripping the mattress and running his options through his head.

He could shower. Maybe take an hour or two in the sparring room. Watch a movie.

Go for a run through the woods at peak daylight.

He dressed slowly and wandered out of the Tender quarters to those of the bloodslaves. Steeling his senses for the foul odors associated with this wing of the Kaius haunt, he hefted the door open and headed down the stairs.

"It's just me, Boy," he called out, his eyes scanning

the room for the tall blond vampire who was cloistered away from the others, his scent not one of their bloodline.

Most of the humans were sleeping, their schedules having long adapted to the night hours of their vampire captors. He walked between the cells, peering into each without much interest.

So much mediocrity, made more prominent by the navy track suit uniforms the haunt psychologist Audra had selected to provide a basic framework for the reestablishment of dignity."

He thought the unflattering identical outfits made the humans look more like bulk soup cans. Knocked over and dented. From a discount store.

Following a soft sloshing sound, he made his way into the storage room. Boy's back remained to him, tensing slightly when he entered the room. The mute male was carefully rotating the blood stock, pulling out the oldest bags and setting the newest in the back. Shoving his hands into his pockets, he watched Boy move meticulously through each of the freezers, the monotony of the work lulling his whipping mind.

"How many months' worth would you say we have?" he asked as Boy finished up the final row. "Nine? Ten?"

Boy nodded slowly, his attention off the freezers and on to the stack of syringe boxes.

"You and I will be in the same boat once we finish the shutdown of the Tender and bloodslave trades," he mused, making no move to assist. "Looking for work. Handing out resumes. I'm putting you down as a reference."

Silence.

He leaned against the door frame and crossed his

7

arms. "Care to join me in the sparring room for a round?"

Boy's blue eyes glanced toward him, obscured by his long hair. He placed a box of plastic tubing on the floor and began the trek through the bloodslave quarters. Rhys sauntered along behind him, running his hands along the cell bars as he passed by and watched the humans stir at the intrusion. The few who opened their eyes shuffled back, cautiously tracking his movements. With a quick flash of his fangs, their gazes dropped, arms and legs pulled further from his reach.

Boy paused outside the weapons room.

"Fists and fangs," he stated as he strode past, flinging open the sparring room door and pulling his shirt off. Boy followed suit and tossed his faded, ratty tee into the corner before joining him in the center of the floor. "Hit me with everything you've got, you old fuck."

CHAPTER TWO

It was well after sunset before Rhys made his appearance in the communication room. He flipped a chair around behind Jagger, straddling it as he smacked the hood from his best friend's head. Jagg's mate, Bianca, looked back at him in feigned disapproval before she reached up and began absently stroking the tattoos along Jagg's temples.

The haunt leader, Kaius, leaned back in his seat. "Since most of tonight's agenda revolves around you, Rhys, you have the floor."

"Nice of you to fucking join us," Nichol grumbled, whatever meticulous timetable he had set thrown to shit with his hauntmate's lateness.

"I promise it was worth it, Nicky," he drawled, tugging at the cuffs of his shirt. "I've got good news, great news, and just-fucking-stake me news. Which do you want first?"

Kai's grim stare was answer enough.

"The good news is that Lis has been located. The McConaughey haunt tracked her to a hotel in East L.A. Apparently the first channel to break the story also put her up in a room and is providing round the clock security," he opened.

Nichol nodded slowly, scrawling a quick note for himself. "Consistent with our findings," he agreed. "The story's been cycling every hour, but so far no others have come forth to corroborate her story. So you have that working in your favor."

Thank fuck.

He tugged at the fabric around his wrists, stretching it out in annoyance. This was why he hated long-sleeved shirts. "The great news is I have an eager buyer for Simone and will be delivering her tomorrow night."

"Who's the purchaser?" Bianca inquired, adjusting her position slightly to face him while ensuring Jagg could still read her red lips.

"Confidentiality clause is in effect," he lied smoothly, his millisecond hesitation long enough to draw Kai's attention. The haunt leader's arms crossed and he set his blue stare directly on him. But Rhys forged on, knowing his next revelation would overshadow his first two pronouncements and likely save him from being grilled too harshly. "As for the stake-me news, I spent the last two hours on the phone with the McConaughey haunt's new commander."

Nichol frowned. "Derry passed the reins over to Thomas?"

"No," he said slowly. "Derry's second eldest, Fallon, has stepped into his creator's role effective three nights ago. It seems Lis has been far busier than we thought. She got the poor old bastard in the chest with the handle of a rosewood kitchen knife."

"Damn," Jagg muttered, tossing an almost imperceptible glance at Bianca. "Derry was staked by his own Tender? That's gotta sting."

"Yeah, well, that's not what kept me on the phone," he stated calmly, rubbing his arm. "Fallon is seeking retribution and is expecting me at his door within the week."

****

Kaius Khthonios waited until his stern glare vacated the room, leaving him and Rhys to silently contemplate the implications of Lis's betrayal of both McConaughey and the species. His second oldest was surprisingly relaxed through the link they shared through their bloodline, the only emotions of any discernible notice being a pulsing discomfort and an annoyance which appeared to be tied to the tight fabric on his wrists.

"Perhaps you should remove it if it bothers you," he suggested, noting the broken threads appearing on the shirt cuffs.

Glancing over at the open door, Rhys stood up and kicked the door closed. He pulled the shirt off to reveal dozens of healing bite wounds and fading bruises. "Midday sparring sessions with Boy," he grumbled as he sat back down. "That silent bastard is way too fucking reliant on his fangs in the ring."

He appraised the damage. "It's unwise to go up against Boy without one of us present," he cautioned. "Next time, ensure Nichol or I accompany you."

"Next time," he scoffed as he leaned back in his chair and rested his booted feet on the table. "Next time will be in about fifty years. Forty, with good behavior." He lolled his head back, black hair flopping off his brow. "Holy fuck, Kai. The piper always gets paid, doesn't he?"

He placed a hand on his child's ankle. "McCon…Fallon Derry may be open to a negotiation. I authorize you to offer whatever sum meets his demands."

"He's not after retirement funds," Rhys grumbled, closing his eyes. "With this kill, I've directly or indirectly ended the top two of their line. I know I sure as fuck wouldn't negotiate with anyone who took out you and Nichol."

The top two.

He inched his chair forward. "What do you know of Thomas Derry's whereabouts?" he asked grimly.

One navy eye opened lazily. "I know I didn't like his look."

****

Rhys relaxed his jaw a fraction as the first telltale crack of a molar echoed in his head, the din bringing Nichol and Jagger back to the com room in record time. Kai's grip tightened around his neck, holding him flat against the floor.

"What the fuck! Watch the syste—" Nichol yelled, freezing in his tracks as he rounded the corner. "Kai."

Rhys held still as Kaius's hard blue eyes shifted from him and focused on Nichol. A long moment of silence blanketed the room until Kai nodded his head in an unspoken agreement with the eldest child. He sat back, releasing Rhys's throat with an aching slowness.

"Go," Kai ordered quietly as he stood. "You have responsibilities to wrap up before you leave for Los Angeles."

The ancient vamp exited the room, ignoring the ghosting pat of Nichol's hand on his back. Jagg extended an arm to Rhys, pulling him to his feet. "I'll be in the weapons room until the Bloodslave Release team arrives back on site," Jagger said softly as he took in the bites and bruises peppering his torso. "If you need anything from me or Bianca, come see us."

He nodded, snatched his shirt from the ground, and yanked it down hard over his head. "You don't need to hang around, Nicky," he muttered. "Show's over, computer's fine."

Nichol stood fast in the doorway, blocking his exit. "What was all that about?"

"Nothing."

Nichol ground his fangs, the freckles across his cheeks dancing with each twitch. "It's never easy for him, having to ride you so fucking hard," the old vamp stated. "Trying to stay one step ahead of whatever bullshit mess you've gotten into is made significantly more difficult when Kai isn't provided with the information he needs to find a way out."

"Find a way out," he scoffed. "Trust me, brother, when there's an exit clause, I'm the first to exploit it."

"Perhaps," Nichol mused. "But one of these times, you'll be up against a lot more than a few years in a pit. When we don't know the hows or the whys, it puts us at a disadvantage when we attempt negotiations. We all know you're the consummate fuck-up around here, and we've pretty much gotten used to watching you get hauled off every few decades by some pissed off ancient with a bone to pick, but frankly, Rhys, it's getting a little old."

His piece said, Nichol stepped to the side and looked to the back wall while Rhys strode past him and headed toward the Tender training quarters to begin preparations for Simone's transfer.

One thing at a time.

****

"In the future, select the two inch heel over the three. With that hemline, an inch is the difference between seductive and trashy. Add it to the pile and let's see the next one."

Rhys returned his attention to his Mahjong game,

ignoring the puff of exasperation Simone emitted as she turned back toward her room. Fourteen outfits in, and he was beginning to bore of the fashion show. With Simone's lithe physique and mile long legs, she could pull off a garbage bag and call it couture. It made his job easier, and easy was boring.

Like Mahjong.

The swish of a green skirt caught his eye, and he glimpsed up to see Simone had returned.

"Put that one away," he stated without further assessment. "Stick to the front of the closets. Nothing in the back will suit you."

"I like this one," Simone argued before schooling her expression and retreating to her room to select a more appropriate item.

"Same here," he grumbled, scanning the Mahjong tiles for a match.

No. Fucking. Way.

Rhys loped up alongside his hippie seat mate as she scampered barefoot across the parking lot, giggling, and sashaying along the pavement with the other women. He took hold of her arm, pulling her attention from the group and slipping a handful of bills into her hand. "Give this to the cashier," he stated firmly, calculating their proximity to Salt Lake City and the likelihood the urban center would have one of those new automated banking machines Nichol had gone on about a few years back.

No way in hell was he going to sit back and watch his future trainee beg for money from the group of slimy-looking men smoking outside the store.

She squealed and hopped in place before she took off after the others, waving the bills frantically. "Tell

Billy to fill 'er up and grab food!" she called out excitedly as she passed the money to the shaggy driver.

He leaned against the bus, observing the jubilant chaos ensuing from the meagre offering. Even in the dim exterior lights, the bright green chiffon skirt of his bench mate remained in his sights at all times, her thin ankles peeking out from under the filmy fabric as she wove her way through the pockets of fellow travelers. He knelt down and rifled through his backpack for any loose money, his focus held steady on the sylph.

With a little work, she'd fetch a king's ransom.

Pocketing the few bills he had left, he assessed his future acquisition. Her long, chocolate-brown hair fell straight down her back, held off her face by a thin braided rope decorated with mismatched thrift beads. The elasticized band of her lime green skirt rode low on her hips, the roped tassels of her makeshift belt swinging with every movement.

The underfed scrawniness apparent through her threadbare tank top would require immediate addressing.

He narrowed his eyes as he examined the woman's waistline, moving his gaze between her braless chest, visible ribs, and jutting hipbones. His experienced mind calculated an increased weight displacement of no less than twenty pounds, accounting for the narrow thighs likely hiding beneath the billowing skirt.

Make that a thirty pound minimum.

It was those incredible emerald eyes that would clinch a sale, though. Green-eyed Tenders were few and far between, their limited presence in the human population making them highly valued and rabidly sought after in the vampire one. This woman's eyes, with *their vitality and uncommon warmth, would make up for her other visible shortcomings.*

She would make a perfect addition to his sales line.

"Master?"

He held his gaze on his phone, pairing the final two tiles before he looked up and deliberated Simone's final outfit of the evening. "Spin," he instructed, examining the hang of the crepe fabric. "Bra off."

Simone's spine stiffened at the order before she complied, unhooking the garment underneath her dress, and shimmying it through the narrow dress straps. She turned back to face him, her expression a mix of expectation and resentment.

"Better," he muttered, placing his phone in his back pocket as he rose. The black dress hung unimpeded now, the perfect combination of allure and naiveté. "This is what you'll wear tomorrow night. If I can't erase the scorn from your eyes, we'll need to distract your buyer with your body. Pack the others and place this one on top, along with black flats. The rest of the night is yours."

A look of uncertainty crossed the Tender's face. "This is it?" she asked, her hands clasping nervously. "You're, what, done with me now?"

His head dropped a fraction, his shoulders rolling the tension out as he ran through the litany of things he needed to do. "Would you prefer if I stay until dawn?"

Of course she would.

Fucking Tenders.

CHAPTER THREE

"Fan-fucking-tastic," Nichol muttered under his breath as the news site refreshed, another breaking story taking center stage. "Kai, you better read this over while I fact-check the info," he said while he opened the article up on his main computer screen and angled it toward his hauntmate.

Kaius scanned the intel, his brow furrowed. "Corroborating source?" he inquired, wiggling the computer mouse, and inadvertently closing the browser.

"Here," he grumbled, passing his laptop over and taking back control of his computer. "Don't touch anything on there. Not even the screen."

Keeping his hands a deliberate distance away, Kaius read through the information while he continued to scan headlines and track social media trends. "I don't know what's worse," Kai muttered, "our enemies or our defenders."

He grunted in agreement.

In the wake of Jagger and Bianca's Lincoln attack against the Species Purifier group, Senator Green had risen to the forefront of the anti-vampire movement as a vocal—and influential—proponent of Deepfryers. His push for the glass enclosures armed with UV lights intended to fry a vampire in minutes filled his speeches in the Senate, becoming breaking news as more and more of his peers fell at his feet in the wake of public pressure. His Deepfryer legislation was gaining momentum in the government, its passing imminent as his colleagues pledged support on their social media accounts.

It had taken Nichol thirty minutes to establish Green's connection to a Deepfryer supplier in Hungary, bypassing the vampire traitor Kaspars Dovidas entirely for the pending transaction. The sale would be a financial windfall for the man once it was solidified, but despite Nichol's anonymous tips to the more liberal leaning news sites, the information was swept under the rug as rising fears of vampire attacks consumed the news cycle.

Two more votes and Senator Green's vision of a Deepfryer on the steps of every courthouse would become realized.

"Are the teeth really necessary?" Kaius huffed as he looked over his shoulder at the second tier news headlines. "These people look ridiculous."

He enlarged the photos and sat back. "How does it feel to be a Divine being, Kai?"

Kaius sneered, his expression alternating between disgust and awe while they compiled the pictures into a folder on the hard drive. Behind them, the hauntmates began noisily trickling in for their evening meeting. The sounds of chairs scraping across the floor and boots dropping heavily onto the com room table grated at his nerves while he wrapped up his research and spun his seat to face the others.

The youngest hauntmate, Dominic, was gesturing wildly while he spoke with Jagger about the first mission of the Bloodslave Release Program—BRP for short— with Louis periodically interjecting when Dom's exaggerations became too unbelievable. His hauntmate, Mickey, and Dominic's connected mate, Molly, were deeply engrossed with Molly's MP3 player, with Molly attempting to sell the vamp on a newly discovered band and Mick adamantly rebuking every pitch with detailed deconstructions of the guitar riffs.

Audra and Bianca stood behind their respective mates, Mickey and Jagger, their conversation centered on hotel room horror stories and their shared distaste for carpeted floors.

Boy took up his position in the corner, his empty eyes latched onto the floor while he wisely ignored the women.

When Rhys appeared in the doorway, bag slung over his shoulder and arms crossed, Nichol barked the meeting to order.

"First order of business," he opened, "is this."

He angled his computer monitor to the group, slowly flicking through the images he and Kaius had compiled.

"You have got to be fucking kidding," Mickey groaned. "Friends and Advocates for the New Gods? What dipshit thought THAT up?"

"Those dipshits," Kaius said, his posturing waning slightly, "are the faces of our most adamant supporters."

"Nope," Louis muttered. "No way am I going to be associated with that. Order me up a Species Purifier hat, man, cuz there's no way in hell I'm being linked to that."

Audra leaned closer, squinting her cat eyes. "What's on their teeth?" Nichol pulled up a webpage and dropped his head to his chest while the group scanned the document. Audra's laughter of disbelief echoed in the stunned silence. "Fake nails and eyelash glue? This is a joke, right?"

Jagger looked toward Bianca. "Tell Anton I'm out. I'm not leading any revolt supported by humans gluing fake nails to their yellow teeth."

"At the moment, this group is a harmless fringe element," Nichol stated, closing out the photos to redirect the group's attention. "However, I'll be monitoring them and their movements closely because they tie directly to the second item on tonight's agenda, the passing of the Deepfryers. We can expect the government to vote them into law within the week, with implementation following shortly after. Our good friend Senator Green is wading ass-deep through the sales end and stands to pocket around two hundred grand for each Deepfryer he brings over from a factory in Hungary."

"So he's figured out a way to cut out Dovidas and profit even more from this shit?" Dominic growled as Molly brushed his bangs from his eyes.

Molly's imprisonment and abuse at the hands of Dovidas had left a bubbling rage beneath the surface for her, Dominic, and the rest of the haunt.

"Not entirely," he replied, glancing to Kaius for permission to continue. "I suspect Green and Dovidas have resumed telephone communication within the past month. Unfortunately, I have no way of tracking those conversations." He pulled up an image on his monitor and turned it toward the group. "However, Green sent out this email yesterday. The receiver links to a dead end, but given the context, we can safely assume this is Dovidas."

The hauntmates scanned the message, their expression turning solemn.

"What's the'Reichstag fire'?" Molly asked.

****

Rhys stood against the wall as his hauntmates filed out of the room to begin their evenings.

"Watch your back," Jagger said quietly, patting his

arm when he passed. "Check in with me when you return tonight. I have some things I want to go over."

He nodded absently and pushed away from the wall. Nichol and Kaius remained at the table, their attention wholly focused on the computer. "I'm meeting Simone's buyer outside the Springs," he stated as he adjusted his pack. "Watch the Tender account for a deposit in about two hours and text me when it comes through."

Nichol immediately pulled up the haunt's accounts, selecting the one dedicated solely to the sale of Tenders. "There's no record of any holding funds," he reported, scanning the transactions.

Kaius locked his gaze on him. "Who's this buyer?"

"Someone who's paying an extra million for confidentiality," he replied, anchoring his feet to the ground, and returning Kai's stare. When the haunt leader finally looked away, he grabbed the keys to one of the 4x4s and left the com room to collect Simone. Nichol's hushed voice trailed down the empty hall, his tone somber as he assured Kaius Boy was already prepped to trail Rhys at a distance.

Might not be a bad idea.

He found Simone in her bedroom, suitcase at her feet. "All right, sweetheart," he grinned as he hefted her luggage under his arm. "Shall we?"

The Tender followed him silently while they made their way to the garage. It wasn't until they were speeding down the highway that she finally spoke. "You're using me," she stated with conviction. "You want me to take out my new master."

With his eyes on the road, he reached over to Simone and tucked a stray curl behind her ear. "Your master holds no illusions about you, angel," he said, resting his hand on her bare thigh. "I marketed you as a weapon. A beautiful, talented weapon capable of taking out vampires when the opportunity presents."

Her heart rate slowed slightly when his hand made contact with her leg, her gaze returning to the blackness of the fields running along the road. "What will it be like in his home?"

"Your accommodations are truly spectacular," he replied. "Large closets, a private bathroom, a caged terrace overlooking the grounds. You'll be on the same floor as another Tender and possibly a few other preferred humans."

"Another Tender?" Simone frowned.

He chuckled. "As I said, your purpose is truly unique. You, my little succubus, will be bait. Armed, lethal bait. It's highly unlikely your master will be making use of any of your other impressive qualities, which is truly a pity."

He drove the rest of the way in silence, his attention divided between the dark highway, the silent woman, and the headlights following them at a steady pace.

When the neon lights of a truck stop came into view, he began to slow the vehicle. "The buyer will do a visual inspection first, with permission," he said, pulling into the large, paved lot. "Once complete, he will move on to an open-palm physical assessment." Simone's blue eyes hardened. "Fix your gaze on a spot in the sky during the appraisal. It can be a little uncomfortable, but I'll be standing there to ensure he takes no liberties. This bastard is itching to get his hands on my final sale and won't dare fuck it up," he said with assurance.

"Until the transaction is signed off, do not, under any circumstances, speak. He may attempt to question you as a way to test your training. Don't fall for it. Until his signature hits this contract, you belong to me, and I won't be providing permission for interaction." He parked and pocketed the keys. "Remain in your seat until I have your bag. I'll escort you over."

With the luggage in tow, he opened Simone's door and held out his arm to her. The slight tremble in her hands was commonplace, as was the close proximity she maintained while they crossed the lot. The buyer was leaning against his car, his unlit position carefully selected between the multitudes of UV lights ringing the truck stop.

"Rhys Kaius," the vamp greeted, careful to avoid the visual assessment of his purchase prior to adhering to the formalities of the trade.

He crossed his arms and stared down the vampire as he took two steps away from Simone. "You have three minutes for the visual," he instructed. "One finger touches the product during that time, it'll be removed."

The vampire nodded tersely and began walking circles around the Tender, his eyes scanning her from top to bottom. Simone stood completely still, her focal point the shadow of a tall male on the outskirts of the lot.

"Ten seconds," he warned, smirking when the buyer straightened his stance immediately and stepped away. "You have three more minutes for a physical assessment. Flat palm only, same consequence for breaching."

When the first hand pressed to her hip, Simone's scathing blue eyes flashed to him, her animosity for him and his kind sparking before she muted it with a deep breath. He monitored the buyer closely, watching for any twitch of possession prior to the signing of the contract.

"How can I be sure she has the talents you claim she

possesses?" the vampire murmured as he moved away from the woman.

"Turn your back to her," he suggested. "Though I'd prefer you transfer payment first. Ash piles often leave their bills unpaid."

The vamp looked back to Simone warily before he pulled out his phone and tapped a quick message. His phone dinged moments later, the money transfer complete.

"Sign pages three and five," he instructed as he handed over the contract. "Initial beside clauses nine, twelve, and seventeen. Mistreatment outlined in clause nine will result in an immediate return of the product, with a financial penalty of no less than half the purchase price. Twelve covers defects in the product, so if she dies or becomes ill without external causation during the next two years, you can petition for a full refund. Seventeen is a no-trade clause. The Tender is yours and yours alone. You are not permitted to transfer ownership of said Tender without explicit written consent by myself or one of my line."

The pen stilled a moment, then signed the final page.

"Congratulation, Stojanovski. Enjoy your hybrid."

CHAPTER FOUR

Bianca stretched up on her toes to kiss Rhys's cheek quickly before she exited the weapons room, leaving him alone with his growling hauntmate.

"Relax," he chuckled, straddling a chair, and tossing a greasy rag at Jagg. "Women never forget their first vampire. It comes with the territory."

"You're such a dick," Jagger grumbled, catching the rag midair, and placing it beside his oils. "Simone's sale went through smoothly?"

"Perfectly," he replied. "With her gone, you and Bianca should consider moving into the Tender training quarters. There are five open suites, two common rooms, and easy access to the kitchen. I'll be posing the option at tomorrow's meeting before I head out."

Jagger nodded slowly, absently fiddling with a small throwing star as his expression hardened. "Heading out is what I wanted to talk to you about," he said quietly. "What are you expecting when you hit L.A.?"

"Best guess is fifty years in the cell," he stated flatly. "If Fallon manages to secure Lis prior to my arrival, he may insist I be the one to end her. I'll play it up and use that to pull ten years off my punishment."

Pushing his hood off of his head, Jagg leaned forward onto his knees and clasped his hands. "Kaius came around tonight asking if any of us had any information about Thomas Derry. Last time I saw him was over forty years ago when we passed through their haunt to collect those surplus bloodslaves he couldn't care for anymore. What the fuck did you do, Rhys?"

He went silent.

No way was he spilling the details to Jagger.

His hauntmate's head dropped. "Goddamnit, Rhys. At least fill me in on the Simone deal so I can be on the watch for any rising problems on that front. You have my word it won't leave this room."

He briefly contemplated how much to tell his hauntmate before deciding Jagger's benefit from the knowledge far outweighed the disproval he would receive in return. "I've sealed cooperation from Jackson Stojanovski for the time. Hopefully long enough for you and Bianca to use his network to filter intel about supporters and detractors."

His arms twitched as the discomfort at his tattoo sites resumed. Fuck, was it annoying. "Only thing is, don't go to his compound. Stay off the Stojanovski grounds and keep the others from there as well. Make use of his contacts from a distance and don't hold back on sending him the names of any problem vamps you come across. He's in possession of a phenomenal weapon now, and he's eager to use it."

"Goddamnit, Rhys. That's what you'd been doing with her in the sparring room," Jagg said, shaking his head. "Bianca warned me about Simone and I thought she was just being possessive. Fuck, Rhys. If she ends one of the Stojanovskis—"

Giving in to the itch, he rubbed the most insistent of his markings. "Feed him the names of species traitors to sate Simone's bloodlust, and she'll be too busy inadvertently working for us to contemplate taking out her boss."

"Every favor comes with a price," Jagg stated, his voice heavy. "How much will you end up paying when it eventually goes bad? Because it will, Rhys. Sooner or later."

"I'll have a good forty to fifty years in L.A. to figure that out. Now thank your older, handsomer, more virile brother for the intel bounty and suit me up for my vacation."

****

Tugging off his shirt, Rhys used it to wipe any lingering dust from the piano keys before sliding the cover closed. He glanced around the training room once more to ensure he hadn't missed anything before he wandered the hall to the laundry room. Pulling the warm sheets from the dryer, he headed to Simone's empty room to finish preparing it for its next inhabitants.

Jagger and Bianca would definitely take him up on the offer, the lure of the kitchen's proximity overpowering any reservations the Former Tender-turned-Official-Hauntmate still carried about her time in the Tender quarters. Mick would probably use the option to lure Audra from his own cramped bunk. Dominic and Molly would likely jump at the chance, but he suspected Kaius would tie their move to Mick's to ensure Dom's hunger and moods were sufficiently monitored by the empathic vamp.

With Simone's room adequately cleaned, he made his way back through the quarters, leaving the kitchen light on for Bianca's inevitable midday foraging. He toed off his socks and tossed his backpack onto his bed. A few shirts, cargos, and socks were stuffed into the bag, with boxers added once he remembered the dampness of the McConaughey cells. Packing complete, he turned on the shower to maximum heat and stepped under the strong spray.

"Where've you been all day?" the green-eyed nymph called out over the crowd as she flitted toward him. *"And where did you find a shower?"*

He ran his tongue over his newly clipped fangs. "Walk with me, sweetheart, and I'll show you."

The woman flashed a dazzling smile and ran toward the bus, yelling for him to wait for her.

Like he had anywhere better to be.

Tossing her threadbare bag over his shoulder, he led her away from the racket in the park and toward the quiet suburban home where he had holed up during the day. "What's the plan tonight?" he asked as a van filled with revelers chugged past them. "Looks like everyone's gearing up for something."

"Only because the greatest band to ever come out of L.A. is playing The Lagoon tomorrow," the woman squealed, clapping her hands in excitement. *"The singer is...oh god..."* She fanned her face as she feigned a swoon.

He chuckled and escorted her up the walkway to the house, pulling the keys from his pocket and opening the door slowly to listen for any signs of visitors during his absence. "After you," he bowed, propping the door for her to enter.

"Is this your house?" she asked as she glanced around the dark rooms.

"A friend's," he replied casually, locking the door behind him, and flicking on a few lights. *"He's away for the weekend."*

'Friend' was a loose term. 'Away' also lent itself to a broad interpretation. 'A meal stuffed behind the

washing machine in the basement' was more accurate, but significantly less socially acceptable.

"Bathroom's at the end of the hall," he said, handing the woman her bag. "Take all the time you need."

"Thanks, uh…" She frowned. "What's your name, anyways?"

"Rhys."

Her warm smile lit those incredible, profitable green eyes. "Nice to meet you, Rhys. I'm Lis."

He rinsed the shampoo from his hair and slicked it back from his face.

Fucking Lis.

He could still bring up her exit from the bathroom that night. The billowing green skirt and tattered tank were replaced by a strapless floral dress grazing her bare feet as she walked. The ruffle across her bust and the oversized cinched belt at her waist gave the illusion of the curves he knew she'd have with a few months of good meals. Her freshly scrubbed face and long, wet hair had instantly taken his mind to potential clients with a penchant for perceived purity.

For him, the vision sealed Lis's fate.

With one ear open for any movement in the Tender quarters, he collapsed face down onto his bed.

It was too fucking quiet.

Bianca wouldn't be rising for a snack for another hour or two and the rest of his hauntmates were likely down for the day. Rolling onto his back, he stared at the overhead light until his eyesight blurred slightly from the brightness.

"Doesn't that hurt?" Lis whispered as he wielded the needle with expert precision.

He glanced up at his spectator, pleased to see her pull another banana from her satchel and open it. A simple search of his 'friend's' home had yielded a virtual bounty of food and an acceptable pittance in cash, both of which he collected without hesitation. "Hurts like a bugger," he gritted out, returning his attention to the narrow upward swirl of the loop. "Could you pop that vial open for me again?"

Lis's nimble fingers quickly uncapped the lid and held it steady for him to pull more mercury into the syringe. "What kind of ink is this?" she asked as she slowly swirled the tube around.

"Japanese import," he grunted as his design crossed an older tattoo. "Don't spill it."

She sat quietly, watching the painstakingly slow process with fascination. The mayhem of the park continued to grow behind them as more and more vehicles arrived on site and added to the increasing din of noise and the bevy of odors traveling on the winds.

"You can head back if you want," he suggested, an unintentional snarl escaping when he crossed another old line. The presence of his first human audience hadn't bothered him when he began the tattooing, but as more searing mercury was injected under his skin, his precarious control over his reactions to the pain was slipping. A low growl started to reverberate continually in his chest while he focused on outlining a thicker section. "Go," he instructed gruffly. "I'll find you once I'm done."

She glanced over to her fellow travelers and rose to her feet. Expecting her to leave him in peace to complete the marking, he stilled his needle and waited. The familiar sensation of the mercury seeping into his veins dispersed the fire throughout his body, eliminating the single focal point and igniting every nerve. He closed his eyes and concentrated as the agony gave way to numbness.

A warm body pressed against his back, one thin arm snaking past his ribs and steadying the open vial for him. He opened his eyes and refilled the syringe, determined to close the newest loop decorating his bicep. He returned his attention to his work, Lis's voice murmuring assurances in his ear while she gently stroked the nape of his neck.

Rolling sluggishly onto his side, he reached into the top drawer of his bedside table, rifling through the mess carefully until his fingers hit their target. With precision aim, the small velvet bag holding a syringe and a vial of mercury landed on top of his pack and he settled back in the bright room for a few hours of rest.

CHAPTER FIVE

As Rhys stood in the doorway offering up his Tender quarters to his hauntmates, Kaius quietly siphoned the streams of doubt clogging the room. Mikhail's shoulders dropped infinitesimally as the overpowering uncertainty disentangled into manageable branches, relieving some of the intensity. The others listened silently to Rhys, nodding slowly but refusing to lift their gazes to him as doubt gave way to resignation.

"I'll touch base once I hit L.A.," Rhys said, hefting his bag onto his shoulder and plucking the keys to one of the haunt's 4x4s from the wall before he turned his back and strode down the hall.

His emotional stream was steady, determined, and calm.

Unnaturally calm.

A manipulated serenity.

Jagger was first to respond to Rhys's leaving, a quick shake of his head preceding his exit from the room as he jogged toward the garage stairs, Bianca hot on his heels. Mickey was next, his hand clasped around Audra's while he led her after his brother. Molly's hushed whispers of concern propelled Dominic to his feet and the pair followed the others, Louis and Boy reluctantly joining the procession.

Nichol's attention was held by the meticulous, unnecessary wrapping of the cords peppering his work space. "You'll regret this moment," Nichol finally muttered, opening a drawer, and placing the wire inside. "I'll respect your decision to wash your hands of him, but I do so only to present a unified front to the others. There's already enough dissension in the ranks, enough uncertainty. That, I understand."

Nichol kept his back to him, his head dropping slightly. "You've done more for Rhys over the centuries than most creators would have. Negotiated away fortunes. Relocated to adhere to conditional sentences. Indebted your strength and name in exchange for reduced punishments. That, I also understand. We all understand it. But frankly, Kaius, he's our brother. My only brother for close to six centuries." Nichol turned, hazel eyes locking on him. "You groomed him to be everything I wasn't. He's your experiment in vampire perfection. Everything he is represents your own failure."

Nichol returned to his cords, carefully untangling and untwisting them with purposeful movements.

Kaius watched his eldest child for a moment, watched the tendons of his neck flex as he ground his teeth. "Go topside," he finally ordered, noting the speed in which Nichol dropped his work. "Wish him safe travels from me. Remind him to maintain contact. And tell him everything we have is his to negotiate."

With a quick bow, Nichol's heavy boots echoed down the hall.

He leaned back in his chair and stared blankly at the wall, cinching off the strands of his children incrementally to allow Mikhail time to adapt to the withdrawal and pick up the slack.

A failed experiment.

The first night he saw Rhys on the deserted streets

33

of a small Welsh hamlet, he had known he would be his. The man's long black coat accentuated his unusual height while he strode confidently through the narrow roads, turning a blind eye to the plague-ridden bodies lying outside the doors of the infected households. His wide-brimmed hat shadowed his face in the scant lamp light, flickering in and out of view as he moved swiftly through the quarters.

He had followed the man from hamlet to hamlet over the next few months, Nichol reluctantly joining in to assess the potential of his future hauntmate.

Armed with leeches, scalpels, and arsenic, the man moved across the overgrown countryside, attending to the wealthy until they inevitably met the same fates as the peasants. Some nights, the man remained in the houses of the deceased long after their bodies were left on the streets for collection. On those nights, Kaius and Nichol would move in close enough to observe as the man filled his belly and pilfered trinkets and coins for his purse.

"He's a thief," Nichol spat, his hazel eyes narrowing in disgust while he perched precariously on a sturdy branch.

Kaius smiled, the hint of silver in his fangs shimmering in the faint moonlight. "He's a survivor," he volleyed, adjusting his position slightly to gain a better view.

"Unscrupulous," Nichol retorted.

"Resourceful."

Nichol went silent, drawing from seven centuries of experience alongside his stubborn creator. He returned his full attention to the man carefully easing his way through the drawers of a chest.

The physician's hat and black cloak lay on the contaminated bed, the soiled blanket a stark reminder of its owner's final hours. The used scalpels sat soaking in a small bowl beside the door, their blades awaiting the man's nightly sharpening. His hand bypassed several items of obvious value, favoring cinnamon and simple gold chains over saffron and the more elaborately jeweled rings which would fetch higher prices at the waning markets.

They would also fetch higher scrutiny.

"He profits off the misfortune of others," Nichol ventured, his voice a whisper in the silent night.

He cocked his head and assessed his future child. "He is a survivor in a land of death, providing a fleeting light of hope amid the relentless despair. A bauble or two is a small pittance for that mercy."

Over the centuries, Rhys became known throughout the vampire community for what he was: Il Medico della Peste. A Plague Doctor. A Scourge.

****

When Molly's prolonged hug wasn't met with a possessive growl from Dominic, Rhys knew, in the eyes of his brethren, his fate was finally sealed. His hauntmates stepped forth solemnly to wish him luck on his journey, their gazes never quite aligning with his own. The women were less stoic, Molly's onyx eyes tearing up when she finally released him, Bianca's full lips holding no hint of a smile. Even Audra's attempt at a colloquial handshake saw her hand trembling slightly when she extended it, her studious scrutinizing replaced by concern while her cat eyes flickered between him and Mick.

It was fucking depressing.

Jagger held back while the others filed past him down the stairwell silently, the heavy boots of the vamps punctuated with the soft tapping of the women's heels. Except Molly. Even amidst his own preemptive eulogy, the thumping of her runners on the cement sent quivers of irritation through his skull.

With a wry smile, he tossed his bag into the vehicle before he walked over to Jagg. "You're all going to feel like absolute jackasses when I return," he warned. "And if any one of you has sex in my room, I'll fucking know. So don't."

Jagger rolled his eyes. "No you won't. You never did before."

"I knew," he retorted. "I'm just too much of a pervert to care." When his younger brother cracked a grin, he pulled a folded paper from his pocket and handed it over. "I wrote down the names and contact info of a few haunts who owe me. Not all are based in North America, but every one of them would serve as adequate bolt holes if you need it. Pass it on to Nichol and Kai for me?"

Jagg nodded, tucking the note into his cargos. "Text me. When you get there, if you run into problems, anything. Just leave me a trail at least. Names, locations. Yeah?"

Fucking. Depressing.

He leaned against the car as Jagger's boots echoed in the stairwell. Another set was advancing, climbing the steps quickly and heavily.

The precision of the gait gave Nichol away long before he rounded the corner.

"Ahoy, comrade," Rhys drawled, crossing his arms. "I take it you've come to pay your last respects, too?

Maybe pass on condolences from Kai? Did you at least bring flowers? None of those other cheap-asses did."

Nichol's jaw flexed. "I've come to remind you to use whatever we have to negotiate your way out of whatever mess you created. Kaius's orders."

"Duly noted." He opened the driver side door and dropped into the seat. "You gonna move?"

Nichol placed his hands on the hood and stared at him intently, his hazel eyes narrowing. "I'm going with you."

Turning the key in the ignition, he adjusted the height of the seat. "You aren't going anywhere, and we both know it. I appreciate the offer, Nicky, but I work a hell of a lot better alone. You come, I'm in the hole for a century. Minimum. Or beheaded on sight. On my own, I stand a fighting chance."

Nichol refused to move. "You take unnecessary, impulsive risks detrimental to your existence."

He cocked a brow. "But at least I won't have to negotiate for anyone else's existence."

The elder vamp's freckles danced across his cheekbones as he ground his fangs. With a sharp rapping of the hood, Nichol stepped to the side and bowed his head a fraction. "Survival is the end game," he stated while Rhys closed the door and cracked the window. "With survival comes freedom."

"Maybe for you," he retorted, pulling out of the garage and into the night.

CHAPTER SIX

"I can't believe this place is still standing," Rhys muttered to himself, squinting against the neon signs peppering the gas station's windows. He shrugged off his heavy leather jacket and adjusted his hold on the fuel pump as he catalogued the changes the building had undergone in the past fifty years. Throwing the jacket into the back seat, he topped up the gas tank and sauntered into the store to pay.

"Pump three," he stated absently, half-heartedly scanning the busy truck stop for a flitting sylph in a long green skirt.

Not that he thought she'd be there.

"That'll be eighty-one fifty," the man replied, nose wrinkling slightly as he looked down at the cash. With deliberate care to avoid contact, the clerk pulled the money from Rhys's grasp and focused his attention on the next customer in line. "Still owe a dollar fifty."

"I gave you a hundred," Rhys said, reaching toward a display and tossing two milk chocolate bars onto the counter. "Add those to the bill."

The clerk's eyes narrowed. "I only counted four twenties. You want those, it'll cost you another three forty-eight."

He stared the man down as a voice interjected behind him.

"I only saw four twenties, too. You're holding up the line."

Removing another bill from his pocket, he tossed it onto the counter. "Bag the bars."

"We're outta bags."

Fucking assclown humans.

The clerk plunked his change onto the counter, leaving it just out of a comfortable reach. Pocketing the chocolate, he eyed the money. With a lightning swipe of his hand, he sent the bills and coins flying across the floor, a sneer crossing his face when two humans instinctively bent down to retrieve it for themselves.

"Pathetic," he snarled as he walked out the door, leaving the money to whomever dove fastest.

He had just opened the car door when a voice called over to him hesitantly. "Hey. Are those them registry tattoos the government is making y'all get?"

He glanced up at the young man, noting his hesitant approach. "No. Why?"

The kid shifted his weight, keeping a healthy distance. "They're just kinda cool-looking. Real intricate." He rolled up his own sleeve, showing a scrawny arm covered in brightly colored ink. "I got a thing for tattoos."

Despite the limited light, his enhanced vision could see the imperfections of the lines the guy was showing off with reserved pride.

They weren't atrocious.

Pushing his sleeve back down, the young guy shoved his hands into his pockets and glanced around the lot nervously. "Could I maybe take a better look?"

He stepped closer, angling one arm into the light. "One wrong move and I snap your fucking neck. Got it?"

The kid's eyes widened. His lips drew into a tight line as he contemplated his options. Rhys stood patiently

39

until the young man took the two strides into his space. "The news says vamp tats hurt like a bitch," the kid muttered as he lowered his head closer to examine his arm. "Like, way more than normal inking does because of the mercury they use. These are really fucking cool."

Turning his arm slowly to allow for a closer assessment of the lines lacing his inner arm, he remained alert for any wayward movement. "You won't come across many of us who have these," he offered up. "Not voluntarily, at least. I know of one other in Europe, but he's a fucking masochist. Time's up."

The kid straightened up, hands fisting in his pockets. "Thanks, man. That kind of precision is impressive. I… yeah. Thanks for letting me take a look. And for not, you know." He grinned and feigned a neck snap before jogging back to his vehicle, unaware that Rhys could hear every word of his giddy description of the encounter to his awaiting companion.

Damn right, I have big fucking guns, he agreed internally as the kid's vehicle pulled out of the station. Revving his engine, he followed suit and went in search of shelter, tossing the useless chocolate bars out the window.

****

"What's the matter? Are you all dead out there?" the wiry frontman hollered into the crowd, shocking the few rambunctious revelers into silence.

Rhys lifted a lighter in solidarity.

He, too, had expected a little more anarchy and debauchery at the touted performance, given the tales he had heard on the bus ride over. So far the only thing akin to anarchy he had observed was the chanting and whistles coming from the motley crew he arrived with.

And he was pretty sure the only debauchery occurring was in the thoughts of every guy who had a bead on Lis while she danced and bounced in a pink miniskirt and the polka dot bikini top he casually suggested she throw a jacket over.

The jacket was currently slung over his own shoulder.

"What did you come here for anyway?" the singer demanded as he skulked across the stage, his stalking gait eerily similar to Boy's. The man's eyes locked onto Lis momentarily before they lifted to Rhys's unblinking glare. With a smirk, the singer broke into another song and the Utah crowd resumed listening politely to what Lis had described as the music act of the century.

He was as impressed with the frontman's Concho belt as he was with the quality of the music. The links flashed in the light as the lead vocalist moved, the hypnotic, serpentine contortions almost preternatural in their intensity. Combined with the haunting timbre of his voice, he wondered briefly if Kaius would be interested in adding to their haunt.

"He's a god," Lis breathed as the song ended, her back tight against him and her face turned up toward the performer.

"He's an asshole," he replied as the singer launched into another tirade toward the audience. "I can respect that."

A bony elbow dug into his ribs and the band went full tilt into another song, sending Lis and her companions into a frenzy of excitement. Glancing around, he noticed several attendees quickly exiting the venue, their faces pinched in displeasure. Returning his attention to the pixie shimmying and swaying against

41

him, he adjusted his stance to hold balance as the song ended and his bus mates became strangely invigorated with every interjected insult hurled their way from the irate performer.

With a final flip of the bird, the singer stormed from the stage, followed closely by his band. Lis's green eyes tracked them, her face falling in disappointment when it became obvious her idol would not be returning. She held her position long after the rest of their crew had wandered off, making their way to the bus to regroup.

"We should head back," he finally suggested, not overly anxious to return to the foul smelling bus and its loud inhabitants but eager to figure out his next stop.

Lis blinked, her gaze finally leaving the stage. "This was it," she muttered. "To see him, to be in the presence of greatness. Now… I don't know where to go now. I have nowhere to go now."

He waited until the cart of squealing kids passed by him on the funhouse track before he uncrossed his legs in the cramped space. The motion-activated monster shielding him from view snarled and clawed into an empty room, the canned voice echoing in the chamber and grated on his nerves.

The thing hadn't shut up in nine hours.

When he pulled into the parking lot shortly before dawn, he'd been impressed by the evolution of The Lagoon, its packed rides and plethora of twisting roller coasters illuminated with thousands of lights a far cry from his memories of decades earlier. With under an hour until dawn, he vaulted the fence and crept around the grounds in the shadows until he came across the haunted house with its sealed interior caverns. It was there he made himself comfortable throughout the day, entertaining himself with a scathing internal dialogue about the patrons traveling through the room.

CHAPTER SEVEN

"When did Sin City become another goddamn fun park?" Rhys groused, side-stepping a stroller with two sleeping infants. The mother scanned him slyly, eyes widening when he winked and flashed a fang.

"I'll take the husband and children off her hands for an hour or two if you want a go at her," his host offered.

Glancing back to appraise the woman from behind, he snorted. "Way too much effort, Vicente."

Wolfgang Vicente chuckled and motioned toward a small stairwell concealed among a garish display of neon lit palm trees. "I'll make sure to let my staff know you're looking for maximum satisfaction with minimal exertion. Lazy fuckin' sot, you are."

They descended the steps, nodding at the two human security guards blocking undesirables from breaching the heavy iron club door. The offensive lighting and tinny music of the Las Vegas strip was replaced by candle-lit sconces and a bass-heavy live band. He followed Wolfgang through the throngs of humans and vampires, staring down anyone who dared hold his eye.

"Make yourself comfortable," Vicente said as he led him into a private screening room. "I have to make an appearance on the floor to ensure no one's screwing me over." He grinned when a new woman took the stage. "Any requests?"

He reclined on the sofa, putting his booted feet up on the ornately carved coffee table as he assessed the dancer through the two-way mirror. "Mix it up. I trust your judgement."

Wolfgang bowed as he exited, closing the door, and leaving him alone.

The stripper lacked rhythm, her gyrations a distractingly half-beat off. He pulled out his phone and picked up an abandoned game of Mahjong while he waited for his meal and entertainment to arrive.

Wolfgang Vicente was a scoundrel, a conman, and a cheat, but he knew how to treat his most influential clientele. One of the first vampires to settle in the West, Vicente was Rhys's main Nevada contact. He was a vamp who understood his rank in the North American power arena, one who knew which asses to kick and which ones to kiss.

The door opened slowly behind his head, the scent of three AB-negatives and one O-positive filling the room. He finished his game, watching his phone screen light up with cheerful graphics to celebrate his win before he acknowledged the humans.

"Come on over," he called without glancing their way. The group walked quickly into his view and stood to await instruction.

He scanned them slowly, his mind instinctually cataloguing the tiny imperfections that would require addressing had the humans been entering his training rooms.

The blonde's left knee should be bent slightly at all times to hide the slight bowing of her legs.

The tall brunette's hair is parted too far to the right for her face shape.

The scar on the thigh of the shorter one is easily concealable with a longer negligee.

The man's hands should remain in view at all times. He's way too big to feign meekness.

But it was a good mix. Vicente did well.

He sat up and stretched his long arms across the back of the sofa as he used his boot to nudge the table into a better sight line. "How about we try the O-negative and the blonde on the table. Make it interesting but keep the noise down. You," he said, pointing to the taller brunette, "Can you dance? I want my view of the stage replaced by a woman who knows what a fucking down-beat is."

The women complied quickly, moving into position with ease.

He watched with mild interest as they began putting on a show, dividing his attention between the women and Mahjong. After his third loss in a row, he set his phone down in frustration and leaned back, glancing over at the man who was standing silently in the corner of the room.

"Might as well take a seat," he called over, adjusting his position slightly to provide more room on the sofa. As the large guy plunked himself down and leaned forward with feigned attentiveness, he returned his focus to his phone. "Don't have to fake it for my benefit, man," he muttered, scratching at his arm, and glaring at a Mahjong tile. "Want me to have Vicente send up a few beers?"

The man relaxed slightly. "Thanks, but there's a strict sobriety policy during work hours," he replied, his dark eyes more focused on Rhys than on the naked women splayed before him.

"Makes sense," he grumbled absently, reclining back again restlessly, and shoving his phone into his pocket.

Mahjong and Solitaire were both on his shit list.

He attempted to refocus on the women writhing on the table, struggling to turn off his training mind in a half-assed endeavor to turn on the rest of him.

The cheap tattoo on the ass of the blonde was atrocious.

A movement in his peripheral caught his attention. He tracked the human as he stood, moved directly into his line of sight, and dropped to his knees, raising his thick wrist in offering.

Whatthefuckever.

****

Rhys slung his bag over his shoulder and leaned against the car, pulling out his phone to fire off a quick text to Jagger before strolling up to the doors of the McConaughey mansion.

Derry mansion, now. Oops.

Show time.

A heavily-tanned bleached blonde greeted him, her miniskirt half a size too small, creating an unattractive line across her thighs.

"Rhys Kaius for Fallon," he stated, striding past the woman into the opulent front hall. "Be an angel and let him know I'm here."

He stretched out his senses, unwilling to be caught unawares by his host.

He could make out seventeen distinct voices trickling through the halls, conversations running the gamut from utilitarian to inane. As he scented the air to determine how many of McConaughey's line were present on the grounds, he wrinkled his nose in distaste. The house reeked of alcohol and chemicals, a smell amplified with every sub-par human passing through the reception room while he waited.

The place was a goddamn flop house.

He detected Fallon Derry's lilting accent approaching from the west long before the vamp appeared in the reception room. Tightening his hold on his backpack, he planted his feet firmly on the hardwood.

"I didn't think you'd actually show," Fallon sneered as he entered the room flanked by four younger members of his line. The vamps spread out in an attempt at intimidation, their nearly identical features and sizes creating a mildly impressive visual.

McConaughey had definitely had an image in mind when he selected his haunt additions.

Fucking puppies.

He smirked, ignoring the intentional stab at his honor. He held Fallon's stare while tracking the smooth movements of the others moving behind him. "We doing this here?" he inquired casually, hooking his thumbs in his belt loops. "If so, you might want to roll up the area rug. Tripping hazard."

Fallon grinned humorlessly, his dark brown eyes holding Rhys's with sniper precision. "I think this discussion might be better suited downstairs."

Without waiting for his acknowledgement, Fallon turned his back to him and strode down the hall, a purposeful display of confidence in his younger hauntmates' strengths. With a fangy grin toward the young vampires closing in on him, he sauntered after his host.

****

Jagger instinctively swayed closer to Bianca's hand as her fingers grazed his cheek.

"Why don't we call it a night?" she suggested, her

blue eyes tinged with concern. "We can finish compiling the contact list tomorrow."

He pulled the tiny woman onto his lap and nuzzled her neck. "I'm good," he murmured, tightening his grip on her hips. "I just forwarded his message to Nichol. Now it's just a waiting game to see if Rhys can worm his way out of this."

Bee leaned back, her hands tangled in his hair. "Then let's get busy doing something a little more fun," she offered coyly, adjusting her position, and sending a jolt of lust through him.

He trailed his hand up her smooth thigh, perfectly willing to be distracted from his worry for his brother. As Bianca hopped off his lap, he settled into his chair in eager anticipation of one of her sultry strip-teases. When she began to walk out of the weapons room, he frowned.

"Where're you going?"

Bianca's hands went to her hips, a pose he had quickly learned meant he wasn't to argue. "We're going to get the jump on Mick and Audra and start moving our things into the biggest room in the Tender quarters. I want the one with the jetted tub."

****

"Swanky," Rhys commented as Fallon led him through a heavy steel door and into the deceptively luxurious cells in the lowest levels of the haunt. Looking past the steel bars and cement floors, he noted each of the four cells was outfitted with a small desk, a chair, and a bed adorned with plush linens and soft pillows. Against the back wall of each containment was a small secondary room, one half bricked in for privacy and the other half encased in glass.

He cocked a brow. "A tad voyeuristic," he said,

noticing the shower head and drain located inside the glass enclosure.

Fallon grunted and motioned for one of his hauntmates to open the cell door in the back corner of the quarters.

He stood his ground and crossed his arms. "I take it negotiations are over?"

"Haven't even started," Fallon replied casually. "Hands on the wall."

Fallon was a good two centuries younger than him, but when flanked by the others in his bloodline, the chance of emerging from an attack with his head intact was slim.

Though three-on-one would be doable.

He dropped his bag and turned to the wall, placing his hands high. Two of the Derry vamps approached him slowly, their skittishness over patting him down inadvertently revealing their youth.

"You probably don't wanna touch that," he chuckled, pushing his pelvis forward as one of them ventured too far while checking his cargo pockets. "You don't know where it's been."

The vampire snarled, yanking his hand back quickly and landing a boot on his calf muscle. He winked and dropped his arms as he strode into his new accommodations.

Fallon Derry observed the show, his dark eyes glinting when the cell lock engaged. "I'll ensure Kaius Khthonios is made aware of your incarceration," he called over his shoulder as they retreated from the quarters. "We'll begin negotiations once a few ducks align."

He rolled his eyes and draped his long arms between

the bars. "If you kids need any help extracting Lis, I may be persuaded to be of assistance."

Fallon paused and looked back at him, a smirk on his face. "Already done. But thanks for the offer, old man."

As the steel door to the quarters slammed shut, he wandered over to his new bed and sat, unlacing his boots, and shoving his socks in the toes before he reclined back, tossing an arm over his eyes as he contemplated his situation.

Could be worse. No rats. No cockroaches. Decent thread count on the sheets.

The soft padding of feet placed him on alert. He lifted his arm and glanced over to the adjoining cell. "What the hell did you do to your eyebrows, baby?"

"Hey, Rhys," the quiet voice replied.

He stalked toward the bars dividing the two enclosures, narrowing his eyes, and crossing his arms as he assessed his fellow cellmate. "What the fuck? Is that a fucking tongue piercing? Why. The fuck. Is there a goddamn hole in your tongue, Lis?"

CHAPTER EIGHT

Lis dropped her eyes from Rhys's intense gaze, clasping her hands behind her back instinctively as her trainer stood silently on the other side of her enclosure.

"Oh, no you don't," Rhys chastised sharply, stepping closer until her bowed head could see his bare feet. "Drop those hands and look at me just like you looked into those fucking cameras, Lis."

The contempt in his voice drew her shoulders in slightly, a move that didn't go unnoticed.

"Fucking look at me," he hissed, slamming his hands against the bars.

She flinched back at the assaulting sound, tears welling up as she forced her shoulders to square and her hands to drop to her sides. She lifted her gaze to his, her stomach knotting at the shark-like coldness his navy eyes held for her.

The minutes dragged out as he stared her down, his only visible movement a slight involuntary twitching of his biceps until he finally shook his head slowly and turned away.

As he walked back to his bed, her feet propelled forward, her fingers gripping the metal bars. "Rhys?" she quietly called to him, unsure what she wanted to say, but knowing she wanted to say something. To say anything to eliminate the disappointment crossing his features before he put his back to her.

He lay down and slung his arm back over his eyes,

his knees bent to accommodate his long form on the bed.

"Rhys, I—"

"I didn't give you permission to speak," he muttered, angling his face away from her.

She was dismissed.

She retreated to her own bed and crawled under the heavy duvet for her second night of imprisonment.

Rhys will know what to do.

Until his cold eyes rested on her, it was her mantra as she had dug herself deeper and deeper into the mess that found her locked in the cells of her own home.

Rhys will know what to do.

Because Rhys always knew what to do.

Lis looked around the parking lot anxiously, her hands gripping the straps of her bags. "I'm not sure about this," she whispered as Rhys expertly connected two wires together, revving the convertible's engine to life.

He tossed a sly grin her way and adjusted the driver's seat to fit his long legs. "Moonlight's burning, baby," he called to her, patting the passenger seat. "You aren't going to leave me hanging now, are you?"

With a final glance around, she threw her bags alongside his in the back and climbed in. "What if we get caught?"

"We'll get out," he smirked, tearing out of the lot and onto the street.

Her heart pounded as the stolen vehicle picked up speed, hitting the highway out of Salt Lake City and barreling toward Denver. She angled her head to keep an eye on the rear view mirror, half-expecting the police to be in hot pursuit as he pushed the convertible's speedometer higher and higher.

"Relax, sweetheart," he purred, one arm casually draped over the steering wheel. "We'll make Rock Springs tonight, and by this time tomorrow, we'll be smooth sailing into Denver."

She looked out into the blackened fields. "So where will we be staying?"

He chuckled. "My...dad...has a big place. You'll have your own space. Like a little apartment."

Content with the knowledge she wasn't going to be spending the foreseeable future sleeping in cars or on the sofas of strangers, she relaxed into her seat and closed her eyes. "And you think your dad'll be cool with me working for you guys?"

"Oh, angel," he grinned, "he'll be thrilled."

****

Rhys listened for Lis's breathing to even out before he stood and began pacing the floor.

Her incarceration in the adjoining cell was no accident.

He turned slowly, examining the room for the locations of the cameras he was certain Fallon had on site. They were easy to find, their slight electric hum giving them away.

Cheap bastard. Nichol would've tweaked that shit into silence.

Once he pinpointed the recording devices, he examined the sight lines of each, searching for the blind spots in each cell.

One pointed at his bed.

One aimed at the desk.

Another monitoring the cell door.

The fourth trained on the glass shower.

Sick prick.

Scanning the hall running the length of the quarters, he noted only one other camera meant to scan the comings and goings through the steel exit door.

He peeked into the enclosed bathroom space, ensuring Fallon hadn't slipped a recording device into there as well. Finding it empty, he returned to the center of his room and mentally mapped out the dead spaces.

The bathroom.

Two square feet in the front right quadrant.

One foot left of the desk.

His recon work complete, he spun the desk chair around and straddled it, locking his attention on Lis.

The moment her traitorous voice had made it on to the evening news, her fate had been sealed. No amount of facial blurring would save her in the vampire world now. One word in the presence of vampires, and her death was assured.

But by whose hand?

He narrowed his eyes, watching her sleeping form for any indication of what had steered his pretty little hippie so far off her path.

She still slept with her fists tucked tight under her chin.

Fallon's capture and subsequent imprisonment of her was intentional. A mere vengeance kill would have been simpler, cleaner. A sniper shot. Poisoning. Even a break-and-enter with a draining would have left fewer loose ends. With kidnapping came investigations, and with investigations came unwelcome public attention into the highly secretive haunt society.

Fallon wasn't after a clean break.

Keeping her alive in the Derry haunt for mere revenge was counter-productive. She would never be released to assume her role again, never be trusted to live untethered. The expense and hassle of housing and feeding her for the next four or five decades, only to have her succumb to old age, made little sense. She could not be held for restitution, nor could her release be used in bargaining for increased wealth or favors.

Lis's situation was definitely more precarious than his.

He scratched at his arm, deep in thought.

It was highly likely Fallon intended to use her against him in some way, perhaps through physical punishments or psychological ploys. If he eliminated her early in the game, Rhys could potentially simplify his own sentence negotiations and save her a lot of pain.

After all, she was nothing more than a dead woman walking.

He contemplated the quickest, most efficient death he could provide.

Draining her through her wrist was too time-consuming and would definitely be interrupted once the camera picked it up.

The width of the bars wasn't enough for him to get the grip he'd need to break her neck without her complete cooperation.

The same went with strangulation.

Fuck.

He ran a hand through his hair and stood, replacing his chair quietly before reclining back onto his bed.

Fucking Lis.

The Kaius haunt was eerily silent as Rhys led Lis through the bunker halls toward the Tender training rooms. He ran his tongue along his filed fangs, listening for any signs of movement before he opened the door leading to the brightly decorated quarters.

"It's so pretty!" she exclaimed as she took in the artwork adorning the walls. "Is this where we'll be staying?"

He ran a finger along a picture frame, grimacing at the five-year dust buildup. "Fucking Neanderthals," he grunted in disgust at his hauntmates' inability to maintain a basic standard of cleanliness in the absence of him and his Tenders.

Next time he faced jail time, he'd make sure he had two well-trained women on site to ensure the haunt didn't fall apart.

Opening the door to the training quarters, he motioned for her to enter. "Your room is right through there," he stated, tossing his bag into the corner. "We'll do a quick grocery run tomorrow night, but you'll have to make do with canned shit until then."

"I can wait," she called over her shoulder as she walked into the larger of the Tender training bedrooms. "Wow! This place is gorgeous!"

He watched her skip around the room, skimming her long fingers over the luxurious bedding and tracing the ornate carvings of the redwood dresser. Her green eyes twinkled in the dim light, her excitement over the beauty of her surroundings a rare experience for him.

"Check out the bathroom," he grinned, eager to hear her reaction to the jetted tub and wrought-iron mirror.

"I...oh, wow! Rhys! You have GOT to check this out!"

He sauntered over to the doorway, stretching his arms up over the frame. She was crouched at the sink, eye-level with the array of expensive perfumes and lotions. "Those are all for your use," he stated, smirking when she squealed and pulled the collection onto her lap. One by one she opened the bottles, inhaling deeply and cooing over her favorites.

"Your dad must be loaded," she breathed as she meticulously returned each bottle to the counter.

"We do all right," he chuckled. "I'm going to grab you a bite to eat and get you settled in before I head to my room for the day."

Her brows knotted as she looked up at him from the floor. "Is it...will you be close?"

He stared down at the pixie who was currently wearing a full pout tinged with nervousness. He had intended to spend his first night home hanging with his brothers, catching up on the gossip, and, if time allowed before sunrise, hitting the city for a quick feed and fuck.

He dropped his head for a moment before accepting he'd be planting his ass on the couch instead.

Fucking Lis.

CHAPTER NINE

Lis's soft footsteps were easily ignored until the sound of rushing water drew Rhys's attention.

"Lis," he growled, rising from his bed, and yanking the duvet off. "Toss this over the glass." He threaded the comforter through the bars into her enclosure, crossing his arms and hardening his expression as she approached cautiously.

"It's not that big a deal," she muttered, head bowed as she collected the blanket.

"It's exactly that big a deal," he snarled. "There's a camera aimed at the glass. Despite the severity of your crimes, recording you while you shower is nothing more than an obscene act of depravity."

She paled as he spoke. "It'll get wet," she whimpered, glancing toward the steel exit. "And I already showered once, when they brought me in."

He grit his teeth, a back molar cracking as he did so. "The blanket will dry. Make it fast before they come down."

As she scurried to her shower and threw the comforter across the glass wall, he stalked to the door of his cell. Testing the strength of the bars, he stretched his senses past the rushing water, determined to provide her with enough warning if one of the Derry's made their way into the quarters before she finished. The scent of cheap soap and shampoo filled the cells as the heat of the steam began to warm the cool underground air.

His gaze flickered between the exit and her enclosure. "Fix the blanket," he barked out, noticing the weight of the water was pulling the fabric toward the floor. She was quick to react, her hands pushing the comforter back over the glass before she was exposed.

"I'm done," she called out to him as the water shut off. A few moments later, the comforter fell to the ground and she emerged, her hair twisted in a towel and another wrapped tightly around her bosom.

"From now on, you bring a change of clothes into the bathroom," he instructed, averting his eyes as she knelt to pull a small bag from under her bed. "The only privacy you have is in there. The less time you spend in an uncompromising position, the better."

Once she was dressed, she collected the blanket and tentatively approached the bars separating their cells. "Last night they came down around midnight with food," she offered up, pushing the blanket back into his room.

"And how much of the meal did you put aside?" he demanded, tossing the wet comforter over his own shower door.

Her brows furrowed. "Well, none. There wasn't much."

He stormed over to her, gripping the bars. "From now until the time Fallon or myself snaps your neck, you'll stash the least perishable item from every meal. Use the drawer of the desk and be fucking subtle about it. Am I clear?"

"Yes, sir."

He stepped back, pushing his hands into his pockets. "Go sit on your bed, back to me."

Moments after she obeyed, the steel door creaked

open and Fallon strode in with one of his carbon-copy younger hauntmates. He scanned the cells quickly, his eyes resting on the wet comforter.

"Lis," Fallon called out, meeting Rhys's stare. "Pass your laundry into the hall. Seamus has your dinner."

Lis dropped her clothes through the bars, carefully maneuvering the paper bag of food through the narrow opening. She retreated quickly back to her bed, far from the male's reach.

"Your creator has been notified," Fallon stated. "A generous financial offer has been put forth for your safe return."

He stood motionless, refusing to react.

"I rather enjoy having a direct line to Kaius Khthonios," Fallon continued, his voice conversational. "I don't believe I waited more than three rings for my calls to be answered."

"Let me know when you're down to one," he replied flippantly.

Fallon's thin lips tightened for a moment, the only outward sign of his flaring temper. As he moved to leave, Rhys took a step forward.

"And expect any negotiation to include all footage you've obtained of Lis prior to my arrival," he warned.

Fallon's shoulder blades twitched slightly before he disappeared behind the door.

He remained still, listening as Fallon and Seamus's footsteps disappeared into the main floor of the haunt.

"You didn't have to do that," she said quietly. "I'm never leaving here anyways."

He continued to stare at the exit. "My decision has nothing to do with you," he muttered, examining every inch of the door for weakness. "It's merely a matter of principle."

She ate quietly, the rustling of the paper bag periodically breaking the relative quiet of the room. At the sound of the desk drawer being shut tightly, he finally ended his assessment of the exit. "Was your meal sufficient?"

"More than enough," she replied. "I stored some, but the bag isn't even half empty. Didn't they bring you anything?"

Didn't they bring you anything.

He lowered his gaze to her neck as Fallon's intentions for her became clear. "Nope."

****

Kaius tossed his phone onto the table in frustration, ignoring Nichol's grunt of disproval over the rough treatment of the electronic. "Fallon Derry is a blight on the name of his creator," he snarled. "Place another two million into the account."

With a few key strokes, Nichol completed the transaction. "If he didn't nudge on seven, do you really think nine's going to do it?"

He leaned back and glared at the phone. "He's dangling Rhys's freedom like a carrot," he growled. "I don't believe he has any intention of honoring a deal. He's merely toying with us. How old is he? Five? Six hundred? Fucking child."

Fallon had first made contact five nights earlier, an impersonal text informing him Rhys was being held indefinitely. Since then, the phone had rung shortly after midnight every night, with each call ending with the same statement.

I'm sure you can do better than that.

Three million.

I'm sure you can do better than that.

Seven.

I'm sure you can do better than that.

He had even placed his pride on the line, offering the young vamp the full support of the Kaius haunt in all endeavors for the span of a century.

I'm sure you can do better than that.

He slammed his fist into the wall, earning little more than a frown from Nichol. "What does he want? Break into his records and put the feelers out. I want all financial statements, all dealings, and all alliances within the week."

Nichol crossed his arms. "Fine. But if your name, your strength, and your money didn't cut it, that leaves Fallon's reputation. He's now the haunt leader of one of the top reputed haunts in North America. At his age, a show of force is necessary to establish himself as both capable and worthy of the position. He doesn't want to barter. He wants to win. And Rhys's head is a highly coveted prize."

****

Rhys smirked as Lis's head tilted a fraction, just enough for her green eyes to surreptitiously peer behind her.

"I thought you said we shouldn't be caught in an uncompromising position," she called over the steady beating of the water.

Rinsing the shampoo from his hair, he arched his head back into the stream. "I said YOU shouldn't be caught in an uncompromising position. If Fallon walks in on me, all he gains is a good look at the strength that'll eventually end him."

She turned around completely before realizing her

error, a blush rising on her cheeks as she quickly righted herself. "You know you're being taped," she reminded him coolly. "He knows you're taunting him."

"Taunting him. Tempting him. Hard to say which one motivates me," he retorted, turning off the water and grabbing a coarse towel.

"I can't believe I once thought you were gentlemanly and debonaire," she huffed with feigned indignation.

"And I can't believe I ever gave you that impression," he retorted, pulling his cargos up over his hips. "You can actually face me now, sweetheart."

Her hair was pulled up high on her head, the strange rose gold color of her ponytail swinging with her every movement.

And drawing his eye to the smooth skin protecting her jugular.

Fallon's visits to the prisoners had continued like clockwork for the past ten nights. Sometimes Seamus accompanied him, sometimes one of the other Derry vamps, but every drop-in had unfolded much the same as the first.

A large paper bag stuffed to the brim for Lis.

A small pile of neatly washed and folded laundry.

A vague threat to Rhys.

A flippant reply.

And a noticeable absence of blood.

His hunger had yet to rear its head, his over-indulgence in Vegas keeping his appetite at bay.

But it wouldn't last.

Past imprisonments had taught him he had twenty more days before his strength began to wane. Another month before he became consumed by thoughts of feeding. By the end of the third month, Lis would be little more than a nameless snack.

But those calculations were based on imprisonments where the only energy he expended was opening or closing his eyes in a cramped box.

"Incoming," he warned, pulling his singlet over his head as the steel door opened.

She retreated to the back wall of her enclosure while Fallon and Seamus sauntered into the hall.

"You wound me, Lis," Fallon purred rapping his fingers on her cell bars. "You used to offer your wrist to me as quickly as you offered it to this asshole last night."

He stepped forward. "She was denied."

"Intentions, Rhys," Fallon replied smoothly. "Even the best can fall flat. Which reminds me, your haunt leader sends his regards."

He held his ground as Fallon stood within his reach. "Let me know when he sends a cake and file."

Fallon grinned, his fangs on display. "Seamus, grab that laundry and let's head topside. I'm in the mood for an A+ tonight."

The slamming of the door echoed against the cement.

He could feel his irises elongating as he began pacing the floor. "Get over here," he hissed to Lis, storming to meet her at the bars. "If you ever offer your wrist to me in here again, I'll drain you of every last fucking drop and relish in the stench of your decomposing body. Am I making myself really fucking clear?"

The color drained from her face as he booted the bars in frustration.

Seamus had arrived empty-handed.

CHAPTER TEN

Jagger's blade flew through the air and embedded in the oak wall.

"Two weeks is a huge breach in protocol," he seethed, stepping aside to allow Nichol room to move. "We should have a written agreement on file by now. Can't we blacklist Fallon for this?"

Nichol's knife landed within inches of his. "If this was you or me, blacklisting would be an effective strategy. But Rhys? There's a chance a public denouncement of Fallon Derry throughout the vamp world would provide more support for him than for us."

He pulled the knives from the wall, running a finger across the blades to remove the dust. "Derry McConaughey's death is compounded by whatever circumstance led to Thomas's end. Advertising Rhys as a bloodline eliminator won't reflect well on any of us."

He pushed his hood off of his head. "So how long do we wait this out? Is the standing financial bid contingent on proof Rhys hasn't been ended?"

"Mick and Kai are monitoring him the best they can," Nichol assured him. "If anything was to happen to Rhys, we would know."

"Not good enough," he growled.

****

The clank of the steel door sent a visible jolt through Lis.

"How much do you have left?" Rhys asked coldly,

turning his back to the woman, and placing his laundered clothes on the desk.

"Not much," she replied, her voice completely devoid of emotion. "A few crackers. A cookie. One muffin."

He nodded slowly, processing the information and implications. "Finish it tonight," he instructed. "Then a quick shower, and into bed. Energy conservation is necessary until the next meal arrives."

If the next meal arrives.

The past six nights had seen Fallon and Seamus come and go without a scrap of food for Lis. And with her stash depleted, he was hitting a wall.

Starving Lis was counterproductive to starving Rhys.

Something else had to be in play.

And he was banking on the cameras.

Fallon had to have seen something to indicate Lis's suffering would punish both her and Rhys. Perhaps they had interacted too casually once. Spoken too freely.

Something was feeding Fallon's actions.

He glanced over at Lis's blanketed shower. "Slipping again," he warned before returning his attention to the wall.

Fuck.

****

Rhys waited a good twenty minutes after Lis's breathing evened out before he unfolded himself from the chair in her room. Ensuring the training rooms door was locked, he made his way through the quiet haunt in search of his brothers.

"No fucking way," he grinned as he wandered past the weapons room in his quest. He stood in the doorway,

watching Jagger's back as he took aim at the target. When the blade embedded deep in the wood, he called over to him. "Jagg. Hey. Jagger?"

His brother ignored him, pulling another knife from his pocket, and sending it cleanly through the air. He stepped into the room and smacked Jagg's back. "What, not even a hey-how-are-you?"

Jagger flinched slightly before he turned to him, a smile spreading across his features. "When the hell did you get out?" he asked, tossing his remaining weapons onto the work bench.

"Me?" he scoffed, turning to lead Jagg out of the room. "When the fuck did you get here?"

Jagger caught up with him, his heavy boots thumping through the halls.

"Jagg. How long have you been in Denver?" he repeated as the pair wandered through the haunt halls toward the communications room. "Holy fuck, Jagg. How lo—"

"The others should be back within the hour," Jagger interrupted. "They went into town to hunt."

He grabbed Jagger's arm. "Jagg. When did you get here?"

Jagg's ice eyes fell to his lips. "Sorry, man. Could you repeat that?"

Fifty fucking years. He had been kept in the dark about Jagger's deafness for almost five decades while Jagg remained overseas. Maybe if Kai had opened his goddamn mouth earlier...

He moved quietly to the door of his cell, one eye on Lis's sleeping form as Fallon entered the quarters.

"She seems more tired than usual," Fallon mused loudly, stirring her momentarily before she resettled in her bed.

His lips tightened across his fangs as he took in the small pile of laundry in Seamus's hands. "What will it take?" he asked, his navy eyes locking onto Fallon. "Name your price."

Fallon's brows rose in false surprise. "What precisely are we bartering for?" he inquired, a slow grin spreading across his face.

Impudent fucking child.

"I want her fed nightly," he ground out. "No games, no restrictions. Enough to maintain her current weight."

Fallon nodded thoughtfully as though considering his words. "Why? The sooner she dies, the sooner you feed. And, perhaps, the sooner you're freed."

Bull-fucking-shit.

As Fallon continued to wait expectantly, his mind leapt back to his final conversation with Nichol. *But at least I won't have to negotiate for anyone else's existence.*

That plan was turning out really fucking well.

"With the death of her Master," he began slowly, "Lis's ownership has reverted back to me by default as detailed in the contract McConaughey signed. Therefore, until her punishment is officially carried out and restitution for her actions has been agreed upon by you and myself, her well-being and actions rest in my hands."

Fallon smirked. "Of course. Well, Rhys Kaius, let's just add the price of her feeding to the tally, shall we? We'll be back shortly. With food, of course."

He waited until the footsteps disappeared into the main haunt before he swung his desk chair around and sat. "You can stop pretending," he muttered, staring at the ground.

Lis's blankets rustled as she sat up. "You shouldn't have done that," she whispered, glancing at the camera pointed her way. "Now he can add anything he wants to your sentence."

Scratching at the most insistent tattoo, he looked over at Lis as she stood and wandered over to her cell door. "He already has his price in mind," he stated. "Nothing I do from here on out will change it. The same goes for you. Now get the fuck away from the door and stay out of reach."

Seamus entered the quarters alone and walked dangerously close to Rhys's cell, a large paper bag in hand. He waited until the male carefully wedged the sack into Lis's cell and began to walk away before he leapt over his chair and slammed his body full-force into his cell bars.

Seamus's startled reaction drew a fangy grin from him. "Just a little reminder not to become too complacent around me. Survival 101."

As the vamp retreated angrily upstairs, he took up residence on his bed. "Don't gorge yourself," he called over to her. "You know it'll make you sick."

"I don't feel too well," Lis moaned, curling herself into a ball on the passenger seat of the convertible. "I'm never eating again."

Rhys chuckled and slowed his speed, unwilling to risk a sharp turn with an overfed woman. "Perhaps next time one burger will be enough."

She groaned and rolled her head back, looking at him with pitifully wide eyes. "You should have stopped me," she whimpered. "Do they always stay open that late?"

"The owner and I have an agreement. He knows I

dislike leaving the house before sunset," he replied, shifting gears as he hit the highway. "It interferes with my badass reputation."

She laughed, stretching out and rubbing her concave belly. "So when do I get to meet your family? Are they around tonight?"

He ran his tongue over his clipped fangs. "Yeah. I might bring them by later."

The drive home was silent, with the exception of Lis's periodic moaning over her overeating. As they pulled in to the garage, he jumped from the car, his ears tuning in to movement coming up the cement steps.

"Wait here," he instructed, tearing down the steps and stopping Nichol in his tracks.

"Jagger said you were back," Nichol greeted. "Long time, Brother."

"Yeah," he said, glancing over his shoulder to ensure Lis wasn't heading his way. "I'm going to need you to bug out for a few minutes. There's a new trainee topside and I don't want to spook her."

Nichol crossed his arms, his eyes narrowing. "The one I scented in the halls? Why would she be out with you tonight? Shouldn't she be contained in the training quarters? Where did you take her?"

He ran a hand through his hair. "I wasn't exactly expecting to pick up a new one on my way back home," he grumbled, hiding his fangs from Nichol's inspection. "She was hungry."

Nichol's hazel eyes scanned him for a moment before he stepped back. "She doesn't know."

"Not yet."

Turning back toward the haunt bunkers, Nichol called over his shoulder. "You have five minutes. I'll ensure the others aren't visible."

He lifted his arm from his eyes. "That's enough," he warned Lis. "Have a shower, wait an hour, and you can have a bit more."

She huffed and pushed the bag from her lap. As he pushed his comforter through the bars, she yanked it from his hands and glared at him. "I'm. Hungry."

Join the fucking club, sweetheart.

****

Lis ran her brush through her hair slowly, untangling days of neglect as Rhys continued to pace the length of his cell. Four nights of good meals had left her feeling stronger, more alert, more aware of her cellmate.

And he wasn't doing great.

The night her first meal arrived, he monitored her closely, his navy eyes noticing every bite, every twinge, every movement. He sat up well into the day, watching her while she alternated between sleeping and eating, reassuring her the meal did not mean his death sentence.

She wasn't convinced.

By the third night, he had gone all but silent. He paced his cell, pausing periodically to test the strength of the steel bars before his jaw would set and he would resume his smooth stalking across the small space. Muttered instructions would break the silence, as though he suddenly remembered she was present and was obligated to ensure she ate and slept on schedule.

Now, as his dark eyes fixated on the cement floor, he sat straddling his chair and absently scratching at his tattoos. She watched as the skin of his bicep scored and healed in a gruesome, lulling repetition. Rhys appeared oblivious, his attention consumed by the pattern of the tiny cracks of the concrete. His bare feet traced the fractures, as though searching for any weakness he could turn to his advantage.

Lis emerged from her bedroom, her freshly washed hair leaving a cool, wet streak down her back. As he had for the two nights prior, Rhys was lounging on the sofa, his bare feet hanging over the armrest and his hands tucked behind his head. Her eyes drifted toward the strip of exposed skin below his shirt hem, biting her lower lip as she caught a glimpse of the V-cut of his hips.

"Hey, baby," he greeted her, his eyes closed. "Stop staring at me like a lech."

She could feel a blush rise in her cheeks and she averted her gaze instantly. "I wasn't staring," she grumbled as she crossed the floor and knelt at his side. "What're we doing tonight? Am I finally going to meet your brothers?"

He reached his arm toward her and gently pulled her head to his shoulder. "Soon," he promised. Again. "Are you happy here?"

"Of course," she replied quickly. "It's beautiful. I'm probably being spoiled for anything less," she laughed. "Everything's so lavish and expensive. It's almost like being a—"

"Kept woman?" he inquired, his voice devoid of humor.

Frowning, she lifted her head. "Well, yeah. But not really, I guess. Because I'm not—"

"My woman."

She sat back on her haunches. "Well, yeah."

His eyes remained closed, his arm returning to its place behind his head. "Would you be interested in the position?" he asked, one eye opening and lazily scanning her. "Full cupboards, clean bedding, a safe haven. Though you'd be surrounded by myself and my brothers, and I've been told in the past that we tend to be rather brutish."

Her eyes flitted around the living room and its elegance. Fresh flowers sat on the piano. A bowl of fruit had been placed on the coffee table. A deliciously handsome man with a scathing sense of humor and peculiar, yet intriguing, brand of honor stretched across the sofa.

"What's the catch?" she questioned, the hesitation in her voice belying her interest in the offer.

He smirked as he swung his legs around, caging her between them. He tilted her chin up as though appraising her features. "Well, baby," he grinned, exposing a pair of long viper canines, "I'm going to give you two choices."

Lis crossed her legs as she examined Rhys's profile. "Would you really have sent me to the bloodslave quarters if I didn't agree to train as a Tender?" she called over.

The rhythmic scratching stopped as he lifted his eyes to hers. "Of course, angel."

She nodded slowly. Of course he would have. "Why me?"

"Why not you?"

Rolling the metal ball in her tongue out across her front teeth, she waited.

"Put that fucking atrocity back in your mouth," he muttered, swiveling his chair to face her. A strand of black hair dropped into his eyes as he crossed his arms over his chest and pursed his lips. "Aside from the repairable physical imperfections, you had an impressive number of marketable attributes. I knew you'd fetch a good price, and I was right." He pushed up off his chair and walked over to the shower. "Lovely chat, sweetheart," he called over, yanking his shirt off. "You should probably pretend to look away now."

CHAPTER ELEVEN

Fucking Lis.

Nichol stared at his computer monitor, his teeth gnashing together as he flipped between different tabs. Her face was still on every news report across North America, completely unmarked by any blurring filters. He sat back, mentally comparing the Lis of fifty years ago to the woman flashing across his screen.

What the fuck did she do to her hair? It was the color of his damn phone.

Half of the news sites reported her disappearance two months earlier as a kidnapping, the other half countering with the claim Lis voluntarily returned to the underground Tender trade.

Neither was optimal.

And the speculation was keeping her green eyes front and center of every news site.

He turned to his hauntmates, rotating the screen for them. "I haven't been able to establish a definite timeline," he opened. "Her disappearance aligns with Rhys's arrival in L.A., but I've found no evidence he participated."

Jagger flipped a blade between his fingers, scanning the images on the computer. "Does it matter? I think we can assume Lis is on site with Rhys, in the McConaughey haunt. If they wanted her dead, she would have been killed on site. Extraction to kill later is a waste of time and resources and runs too many risks."

"And does THAT matter?" he tossed back. "Lis put herself in this situation and dragged Rhys down with her."

Mickey leaned forward, one hand on Audra's knee. "It matters if she's used against him. I know it's been a long time, but Rhys was pretty indulgent of Lis. I'm not sure he could sit back and watch if she was being harmed. And since Fallon's gone silent on negotiations outside of the weekly reports, I think we can assume he's compiling some ammo. Lis may be part of it."

But at least I won't have to negotiate for anyone else's existence.

He glared at the table, wracking his brain. "What has Rhys historically done when Tenders have gone rogue?"

"Put them down," Kai replied. "Or authorized masters to do it. He may have some of the paperwork in a file somewhere in the training quarters."

"Good," he stated with finality. "Lis is a non-issue from here on out. If she was on site, Rhys would have had the sense to end her before she could become a bargaining chip. Agreed?"

With a slow nod from the group, he closed the internet tabs and began reviewing the bloodslave data.

****

Fifty-eight nights.

Rhys sat on the cold cement floor, draping his bleeding arms over his knees, and staring through the bars.

Lis.

Lis's favorite flower is the daffodil. Yellow daffodil.
Lis dislikes any chocolate that isn't milk chocolate.

Lis's favorite musician is Janis Joplin. Mercedes Benz. Bobby McGee.

He forced himself to remember Lis's time at the Kaius haunt, back when she was his pretty little pixie. He pulled up visions of her sashaying down the halls with her long skirts and filmy blouses, of her teaching another trainee how to weave a floral crown, of her bare feet hopping through the kitchen while the radio blared.

But there were more.

He knew there were more laying just out of reach, squeezed out by the rising hunger slithering through his mind and body day and night.

His hand rose to his arm, freezing when he caught sight of the amount of his own blood staining his fingers.

Resisting the searing itch, he slowly stood and entered the brick bathroom to wash the mess off before Lis woke. The cool water did little to tamper the growing burn of his tattoos, their intricate swirling patterns resuming their precise lines as the water began to run clear.

He caught a glimpse of himself in the small mirror.

Rabid fucking dog.

His irises were completely ovaled, blackened slits giving him a feral, hungry look against the increased paling of his skin. His fangs lay long over his lower lip, slicing cleanly against his skin as he moved. Straightening his back and rolling his shoulders, he wet his hands and ran them through his hair to tame the few strands flopping forward.

Barely fucking better.

The increase of the steady heartbeat in the next cell alerted him to the female's waking.

Lis. Not the female. Lis.

He leaned against the brick wall of the bathroom and fought the urge to scent the air. It had become part of their new nightly ritual, him hiding out like a goddamn coward while she showered, dressed, and waited for Fallon and Seamus to arrive. The overpowering odors of her soap and shampoo were enough to temporarily drown out her B-negative blood during the evening hours when he needed to be as cognizant as possible.

So he waited.

The heavy thumping of Fallon's boots down the stairs was his cue to vacate his makeshift bolt hole. With a quick check to ensure Lis had taken her place at the back of her cell, he stood in the center of his enclosure and watched the steel door open.

"Evening, lads and lassies," Fallon greeted cheerfully. "Seamus, hand our lovely lady her laundry and meal."

He eyed the newspaper in Fallon's hand as it entered his cell and dropped to the floor.

"You know what to do," Fallon stated, pulling his phone from his pocket. "State your name and date, make sure I can see the headline. Go."

Without breaking his stare he scooped up the paper and scanned it before turning it toward Fallon's phone. "Rhys Kaius. October 1."

Holding position until the footsteps of the vamps retreated out of earshot, he brought his chair up to Lis's bars and sat. "Don't come closer," he warned gruffly as she advanced. "Tonight we'll start with elocution before we move on to Spanish. Until that contraption in your tongue is gone, French is on the back-burner."

****

Lis looked expectantly at Rhys, certain she nailed the pronunciation and conjugation. When he didn't respond, her heart clenched.

"The elephant is walking through the African savannah."

Lis scrunched her face momentarily before parroting Rhys's words back at him.

"Thelephant isswalking through thafricans avannah," he echoed. *"The elephant is walking through the African savannah. Do you hear the difference? Each word is completed before the next is begun."*

Lying back on the rug, she rolled her head back and forth in frustration. "You don't speak that clearly normally. Why should I?"

"Because while you're going to be the lady of some lucky vamp's haunt, I'm going to remain nothing more than the mangy tramp who found the rose among the thorns. Now sit up and speak sweetly about that damn elephant."

"Rhys?" she ventured, uncrossing her legs, and swinging them over the edge of her bed. "Rhys. Did you—"

"Fight," he interrupted, his eyes locked on the cement wall behind her. "When they come to remove you from your cell, you need to fight them off. Make as much noise as possible. Maybe one of the humans above will hear." He trailed off, nails digging into his arm.

She frowned and tilted her head. "Rhys, I don't think I'm ever getting out of—"

"I would do it during the day," he muttered. "Catch us off-guard." He stood up and began pacing the floor. "Only one vein opened, though. Makes no sense to weaken the prey too much prior to the hunt. Where's the entertainment in that? Over too fucking fast."

Rising to her feet, she began walking slowly toward their shared bars. "Rhys," she whimpered, "you're starting to freak me out."

He stilled, the muscles across his back flexing against his singlet. "There isn't a single scrap of wood in this place," he said quietly as he returned to his chair. "They're starving me for a reason, Lis. Within the next week or two, I'm not going to recognize you." He chuckled humorlessly. "As it is, I can't remember your whole name despite writing it out a million times in your sale documents."

"Lis Bruckner," she replied softly.

"Right. Lis Bruckner." He nodded to himself, as though attempting to catalogue the information back into his mind. "When I hit that state, I suspect Fallon will put you in here. With me."

"Oh," she breathed with relief, "you're worried you'll weake—"

"I'm going to drain every drop from your body," he responded coldly. She took a step back as he leaned toward the bars. "I can hear each pump of your heart in this room," he said, his voice low. "It echoes off the walls day and fucking night. Right now, it's gone up an extra eight beats a minute. That's eight more beats I have to fight past every goddamn minute you're alive."

He stood, stalking forward until he reached the steel divider. His hands gripped the bars. "I watch your every move," he murmured, his blackened gaze fixating on her throat. "Every time you open your eyes to watch me during the day, I know. Every time you stop yourself from approaching me, I know. Every time you pass within reach of these bars, I know.

"You nicked yourself on your right leg with a razor three days ago. There's one drop of dried blood on the floor of the shower. You bit down too hard on that fucking barbell in your mouth yesterday morning and scratched your gums. Every fucking move, female, and I know. I know, and I've resisted. But the next time you tiptoe within my reach, I promise you I will fucking end you. Am. I. Clear?"

Her calves hit her bed as she backed away from the snarling vampire, her hands shaking while she wrapped them around herself.

****

The woman's shivering amplified her scent in the enclosed quarters. Rhys's knuckles tightened on the steel, half willing it to break, half ensuring it wouldn't. His threats had sped her heart rate, the thumping of her pulse jackhammering into his skull.

The woman.

Lis.

Lis was repulsed by the word 'mauve'.

He dropped his head and pushed off the bars. "When they get you in here," he said, his voice graveled with the effort to control his rising bloodlust, "use this chair. With enough force, it'll break the glass of the shower and provide you with weapons. A fighting chance. A clean slice across my throat will weaken me quicker. Might buy you enough time to remove my head entirely. That should work."

Her deep, shuddered breath momentarily pulled him back from the edge and he tuned in to her voice. "I won't do it," she whispered. "I know you won't kill me. I know that."

"I would do it now if you took five steps my way," he spat, his fangs slicing his lip and drawing blood. "Don't over-estimate your value to me, or any other vampire. You're nothing more than an aging show pony."

CHAPTER TWELVE

Kaius rolled onto his back and stretched out across his bed as Rhys's hunger pulsed in the forefront of his mind.

Again.

Throughout his two thousand years, he had witnessed the evolution of punishment and revenge in vampire politics. In his early years, wronged vampires ended their offenders without hesitation, leaving the more paternal of creators to piece together the circumstances surrounding the deaths of their children and often resulting in bloodline-eliminating haunt wars.

Around the time of Nichol's turning fourteen centuries ago, the tide began to change. Early civil wars among the minuscule population saw a dramatic decline in the number of haunts, and the extinction of the species loomed on the horizon. Vampires inhabiting adjoining territories started to negotiate, to establish more definitive protocols for dealing with those who committed offenses. As the centuries passed, the unwritten agreements between haunts morphed into documented negotiations and became widely accepted as law.

Rhys's head remained attached to his body solely because of this.

"Five years," the ancient stated, his heavy accent exposing his Mediterranean roots. "A starvation cycle appropriate for the male's youth, confinement with

minimal mobility, and an agreement to return the perpetrator to his haunt within seven days of his date of release. Will you sign?"

Kaius placed a staying hand on Nichol's shoulder as his eldest moved to argue.

"I will," he responded, extending his hand for the contract. "At two decades, Rhys may go no longer than four weeks between feedings. I expect renegotiation should you feel he requires added physical punishment."

"Of course," the ancient conceded. "Five years from this date, your child will be released back to you, Kaius Khthonios."

Two of the ancient's hauntmates flanked Rhys as he entered the room, shoving him roughly to his knees in the presence of their creator. Kaius rose, standing over his youngest child in resignation.

"You've been granted a lenient sentence," he said quietly as Rhys flashed his fangs at his guards. "Nichol and I will be relocating closer to ensure frequent updates regarding your condition." He looked over to the ancient, who merely nodded his assent as he turned away from Rhys and led Nichol from the haunt.

"This is—"

He silenced Nichol with a hard look, sending a small pulse to Nichol's mind to reinforce his message. As they untethered their horses and began the long trek back to their haunt, he became acutely aware of the increasing distance between himself and his youngest.

"We won't make it before sunrise," he called to Nichol, glancing at the moon's position. "We'll overnight in the caves up ahead."

Nichol altered the direction of his horse without a word, the grinding of his teeth a steady beat in the darkness as he dismounted and began scaling the small incline to the caves, his eyes averted from his creator at all times. Kaius followed behind his eldest, pausing to assess the tight caverns for optimal protection from the rising sun.

"There are laws," he stated quietly as the light peeked over the horizon. "If Rhys cannot learn respect for those laws from me, perhaps it's better he learn it at the hands of another."

"He spilled no blood," Nichol ground out, propping himself against the cool rock. "What he took was a pittance compared to the wealth of that haunt."

He hunched over his knees, carefully sealing Nichol's resentment and Rhys's fury from his thoughts. "What he took," he corrected, "was not his to take. Furthermore, it was both unnecessary and unneeded. We're wealthy enough in our own right, and his actions called into question my ability to lead an affluent, successful haunt."

"So your pride was hurt?" Nichol spat. "Rhys won't last five years in a cell."

"It isn't my pride at stake when Rhys behaves as such," he huffed, tired from the mental exertion required to keep himself from inadvertently channeling the negative dispositions of his children. "It's our name. Our safety. It's the leg we stand on when we cross hostile territories. It's the reputation we hold across the land. Never underestimate the value our name carries when facing those who are older or stronger."

The gnashing of Nichol's teeth continued as the male mulled over his words. "He'll go mad in there," he muttered. "The confinement will destroy his mind."

He lowered his gaze. "Rhys will find a way to

survive. He always does."

Kai glanced down at his phone, pulling up Rhys's latest update and freezing the image on his screen. Despite the absence of a formal contract, Fallon had provided weekly—albeit brief—updates of Rhys's physical condition. Coupled with his link to his second-oldest, it was easy to surmise Fallon's preferred punishment was a looped starvation not unlike those Rhys had experienced numerous times in his long post-life.

Rhys bore no physical damage, no evidence of flaying or dismemberment. Lis's offense aside, if Rhys was directly responsible for Thomas Derry's end, the Kaius haunt had little sway in the decisions Fallon made. By rights, Fallon could easily call for Rhys's head. As others rightfully had over the years.

He shifted, his bed groaning slightly under his weight.

Perhaps it was time.

He couldn't save him. Centuries of cushioning Rhys's fall was culminating in Fallon Derry's cells, and he needed to step aside for the protection of the rest of his haunt.

Rhys's survival lay at Rhys's feet alone.

****

"The orchestra opened with Offenbach's *Barcarolle*," Lis stated, her hands clasped behind her back. "The orchestra. Opened. With Offenbach's *Barcarolle*. The orchestra opened with Offenbach's *Barcarolle*."

She paused, allowing time for correction before she continued.

"I prefer baked bread at breakfast over buttered

biscuits at tea time. I prefer baked. Bread. At breakfast. Over buttered. Biscuits. At. Tea time. I prefer baked bread at breakfast over buttered biscuits at tea time."

Another carefully timed hesitation to ensure any errors were processed and examined.

"My jaw's beginning to hurt," she huffed, alternating between pursing her lips and grinning widely. "Let's move on to posture."

Rhys's forearms rested on the stabilizing horizontal bar separating their cells, streaks of dried blood intermingling with the intricate patterns adorning his arms. As she leaned into the shower to grab a bottle of shampoo, a rumbling purr erupted from him.

"Come closer," he growled, the stray strands of black hair hiding his predator irises.

She smiled his way, steadying the bottle atop her head before she began to cross the floor.

Eight steps.

Slow turn.

Eight more.

Turn.

She rose to her tiptoes, her fingers framing the bottle to ensure it didn't topple as she steadied her balance. "Three-inch heel," she reported, repeating her trek, and returning to her place. She lowered herself slightly, wobbling a fraction. "Now two-inch."

She walked the path over and over, mimicking the heights of different footwear while Rhys's eyes followed her progression, the blackened slits tracking her when she passed just out of his reach.

"Your hair," Rhys purred, his hands gripping the bars as he pulled his body tight to them. "I want—"

"You're right," she interrupted with false cheer.

"It's dry enough to brush out, isn't it?"

She replaced the shampoo bottle and grabbed her brush, crawling onto her bed as she continued to converse with her trainer. "I know silks and satins are considered luxurious, but I find them cold. I really don't think anything can beat the softness and warmth of a quality cotton."

Rhys smirked, his entire stance a seductive invitation as his gaze raked over her. "Soft and warm?"

With a sigh, she set her brush down, crawling under her covers as the small tremor of impending daylight passed through Rhys. "Good day, Rhys," she said softly, turning away from the animalistic growl coming from the adjoining cell.

****

Lis opened her eyes, rolling over to check on Rhys.

He stood exactly where he'd been every night and day for the past week, his arms draped into her enclosure and eyes fixated on her throat.

The slight deadening of his gaze was the only giveaway he was resting.

Rhys.

It.

For three nights he spewed elaborate, spiteful venom at her, his elongated fangs scoring his chin and creating small trails of blood running down the column of his neck. He booted at their shared bars while she slept, startling her awake and sending her scrambling to the furthest corner of her enclosure. He taunted her with horrific fantasies while she showered, painting visuals which turned her stomach and sent chills through her body.

But it was Rhys.

Every snarled, contemptuous insult and insinuation was carefully crafted, aimed at burrowing deep into her mind and erasing every memory she had of him, replacing them with disgust and fear.

It was effective until dawn broke on the fourth day.

Lis stared at the cement wall, fighting to block the horrific image Rhys was describing as he paced the floor. Her eyes stung with tears, the onslaught of the past days wearing her already-frayed nerves.

When he finally silenced, she lay still and listened as he collapsed on to his bed, the springs creaking under his weight.

"I can't do it anymore," he whispered, his voice cracking.

She remained motionless, her blanket fisted tight under her chin.

"I'm fucking losing it," he murmured, a low growl echoing in the quarters. "The female. The female likes... she likes..." He paused. "Need to keep her away. Scared and ready and away."

She pulled her feet up tight to her body.

And so, for the past two weeks, she had resumed her Tender training under Rhys's ovaled gaze. At first, he would interject a small correction here and there, a quick flash of recognition crossing his face before his expression turned predatory again.

It had been six nights since she had last seen a flash of Rhys.

Now he stalked her while she moved, speaking only in an effort to coerce her toward him, toward his grasp. His arms were stained with his own blood as he tore violently at his tattoos, shredding his skin while the silver undertone of his fangs shimmered in the artificial light.

Her eyes drifted to the glass shower, snapping closed when Rhys's hands flexed toward her.

CHAPTER THIRTEEN

Lis eyed Fallon warily as he dropped bag after bag into her enclosure. He tossed a fangy grin toward Rhys, who had become violently agitated with the other vampire's presence. As Rhys snarled and slammed his shoulder into his cell door, Fallon stood just out of reach and laughed.

"I'll return at nightfall," he said, shaking his head as he turned to leave. "I expect you to make good use of everything in there."

Following Rhys's former pattern, she waited until she was certain Fallon had returned to the main haunt before she walked to her door and collected the packages. Dumping them onto her bed, she sat back and sighed. "Lucky you," she called over her shoulder at Rhys, who had resumed his position at their shared bars. "Looks like Fallon wants me all dolled up and pretty for you." She paused, thinking back to her days at the Kaius haunt. "I recall you telling me once you get violent when your meals are unappealing. Maybe some lipstick will tame the beast."

She sorted through the clothing first, holding up each piece for his approval. "Derry bought this for me to wear to a club opening on the Boulevard. I spent the entire night remembering your words. *Sequins are the diamonds of aging harlots.*" She assessed the dress with a discerning eye. "So many sequins."

His head tilted a fraction.

"And this," she continued, holding up a black lace gown. "This I wore to a movie premiere. Derry thought it was very vintage Hollywood. But it was about half an inch too long, and I tore the hem within the first twenty minutes." She held up the damaged gown for Rhys's inspection. "He ripped the entire bottom inch off in the bathroom to even it out. Can you see his fang marks on the side seams? He chewed through them like a dog."

Rhys growled, his eyes locked on the offending dress.

"Right," she said, hastily shoving the garment back into the bag. "You can probably smell him on there." She lifted the final gown fanning the skirt out. "I bought this shortly before…well, it's never been worn. You like?"

She held the dress high in the air, the emerald green of the chiffon skirt billowing around her lap. "It's a little loud, but I felt like a fairy princess in it. How could I resist?"

As she carefully set the gown at the edge of her bed, he grunted. "Yes."

Nodding slowly, she continued to rifle through the items, recognizing most of them from her quarters in the upper levels of the haunt. "The smell of this hair dye will probably stun you back into your right mind," she muttered, reading the box of the rose gold hair color. "It's practically vampire-repellent."

****

If she ignored the steel bars and the snarling vampire staring hungrily at her, Lis could almost pretend she was above ground, preparing for a night out. Her chestnut hair roots were gone, the rose gold color Derry had once found both fascinating and perplexing cascading over her shoulders. She had touched up her dark-tinted brows, making good use of her charcoal eyeliner to accent her green eyes.

But without her lipliner, her upper lip remained thinner than she liked in spite of the shimmering light pink lipstick.

She glanced over at Rhys, briefly envying his full lips before he caught her gaze and snapped his fangs at her. "Stop that," she chastised, sitting primly on her bed in anticipation of Fallon's return. "You'll get those damn things in me soon enough, I'm sure."

****

Rhys's feral snarl woke Lis moments before one hand descended on her mouth, another pinning her arms to her body and dragging her off her bed. She kicked her legs instinctively, her screams of protest held on her tongue. With Fallon and Seamus blocking the entrance to her cell, she knew one of the younger hauntmates was the one pulling her across the floor.

"We don't want her damaged, Liam," Fallon stated, stepping aside to allow them through the opening. "Lis. Stop thrashing. You'll tear that stunning dress."

She glared at Fallon before flinging her head back and cracking Liam in the jaw. While the vamp cursed and tightened his hold, Fallon approached.

"Look over there," he murmured, pointing toward Rhys's cell. "Liam, assist Ms. Bruckner."

Liam adjusted his position, yanking her head to the side.

"The more you fight, the more you spur on his predatory side," he continued, crossing his arms, and narrowing his eyes. "The transformation from cultured vamp to savage beast is intriguing, isn't it? One night, Rhys Kaius is the curator of vampire society's most valued possessions. The next," he paused, gesturing at Rhys as he stood motionless in the middle of the cell, arms covered in dried blood and black slits completely replacing his navy irises, "he's a rabid animal."

She struggled fruitlessly against Liam's grip, unable to get her footing as he held her just above the floor. Seamus moved to unlock Rhys's enclosure, one eye on Fallon and the other on Rhys.

"Ready?" Seamus asked, holding the key inches from the lock.

Fallon nodded, pulling two flashlights from his pockets as he did so. When Rhys took a step back, she frowned. The lock snapped open and Seamus swung the metal gate open while Liam lifted her higher and walked her toward the opening.

Fallon forgotten, Rhys charged the door, his blackened eyes focused entirely on her throat. A flash of light ripped across his chest and arms, charring a strip across him, and stopping him in his tracks. A second beam scorched across his body, forcing him to retreat a fraction.

UV lights.

She screamed insults against Fallon into Liam's hand, horrified at the amount of damage done by such an innocuous tool. She bucked against her captor, kicking backwards in the hopes of making contact with his shin as he hauled her into Rhys's cell. Liam dropped her unceremoniously onto the floor while Fallon kept Rhys at bay with a steady beam of light.

"He's igniting!" she yelled, scrambling to her feet as the cell lock clicked closed. A small tuft of smoke rose from Rhys's chest while Fallon held his position.

"You're not that lucky," Fallon replied cheerfully,

the light flicking off as the sound of retreating boots echoed in the chambers. The heavy steel door slammed closed, leaving Lis and Rhys alone in his cell.

****

Inhale.

Focus.

The stench of his own burnt flesh overpowered the enticing B-negative blood which taunted him for weeks. He used the searing pain of his burns to direct his concentration to the present, to the deliciously appealing package standing immobile five steps away.

Five steps and no steel bars away.

He tilted his head, observing the meal as she straightened her spine and scanned the room, exposing the rapid throbbing of her jugular.

Fear.

The word ricocheted through his mind and dove into his core, gnawing at his resolution to hunt, to conquer and sate the hunger pulsing through his body. Ignoring the strange sensation, he stepped forward slowly, closing the distance between himself and the tempting banquet now watching him warily. Her heart rate was slowing, the palpitations no longer echoing the thrum of cornered prey as he closed the gap another step and scented the air.

Daffodil.

He stilled, narrowing his eyes at the female crouched in defense, her skirt gathered in her hand.

Mercedes Benz.

His burns weren't healing. The pain bursting through him with every movement centered his thoughts, provided him with a beacon for his fading cognition. Ignoring the escalating pain radiating from his tattoo sites, he turned his attention to the burns, to the charred strips crossing his body. Grounding himself in the purity of the agony.

Lis.

****

Rhys stumbled backwards and Lis instinctively stepped forward.

"Back!" he growled, his bare feet moving heavily away from her. Snarling, he crossed his arms, and dug his fingers into his own skin. "Chair."

She hesitated, the brief glimpse of Rhys momentarily erasing the weeks of the feral animal he'd become.

"Now!" he roared, booting his bed with his bare foot, and collapsing the metal frame.

With a shriek, she scrambled to the chair, spun on the spot, and angled it toward him. Adrenaline pumped through her body as he lunged at her, stopping just short of the chair legs she flung in his direction.

"Don't do this, Rhys," she pleaded, jabbing her makeshift weapon at him while he stalked toward her. "Please don't make me do this."

She retreated back, scuffling her feet across the floor while he took long, leisurely strides her way. He half-heartedly swatted at the chair legs as they crossed in front of him, his bloodied arm swinging out sloppily.

He's toying with me.

Her calf hit the cool glass enclosure. She lifted her eyes to his and adjusted her grip on the chair. He was studying her, his oval irises watching intently as she swung her weapon up and hesitated.

"Tick tock, flower child," he growled, crouching in preparation of attack.

With every ounce of strength she could muster, she swung the chair into the shower enclosure, screaming and shutting her eyes tight as the glass shards began to fall and Rhys leapt forward.

She expected the sharp sting of fangs sinking into her throat.

Expected cleanly sliced wounds on her skin as the glass fell atop her and onto the cement, clinking at her feet.

Expected the metallic scent of her own blood to fill her nostrils.

What she didn't expect was his large body tackling her to the ground, covering her as the glass shards rained down around them. His tattooed arms twitched with tension while the last of the shower enclosure collapsed and shattered across the floor.

She held her breath, keeping her head on her knees and holding her balled position. She was completely vulnerable, a vampire twice her weight and a hundred times her speed pinning her down. She felt him shift slightly and she prepared for the inevitable bite.

****

Four glass shards were sunk deep into his back muscles. The discomfort provided Rhys a third centering point of focus, another thread to grasp while his fangs hovered excruciatingly close to the woman's skin.

Lis.

He chanted her name in his head while he remained wrapped around her, grappling along the cement for a piece of glass large enough to inflict damage. When he found it, he ran his fingers along the edges, searching for the bluntest side. Using his free hand to grip her arm, he brought the glass to her hand.

"Now," he grunted, the scent of his own blood intermingling with the alluring scent of Lis's. He scanned her as he rose to his feet, noting the small nicks bleeding on her arms.

The moment she was freed of his weight, she sprung to her feet and turned, brandishing the glass weapon. Fresh wounds opened across her feet when more shards embedded themselves into her skin.

As she launched herself at him and the scent of her blood overtook his senses, he had one final rational thought.

Good girl.

CHAPTER FOURTEEN

Rhys unhooked his fangs with a snarl as the UV light slashed across his face and seared his skin. The beams continued to cross over him and he dropped his meal to the ground, retreating to the corner of his cell. A low growl of warning emanated from deep inside him as the vampire wielding the light came into sharp focus and a ray burned a hole straight into his sternum.

Fallon Derry.

His vision expanded, the pinhole precision of the hunt no longer needed while his prey lay in a heap on the cement.

His prey.

Lis.

Refusing to look at her, he stared down Fallon while the hole in his chest began to smoke.

"That must be some potent B-neg," Fallon grinned, wiggling the flashlight in his hand to increase the area it damaged. "Stand back while Seamus and Liam get our girl fixed up."

Fallon flicked the light off as his hauntmates unlocked the cell and ventured in, approaching Lis cautiously. He remained still, holding Fallon's stare and tracking their movements in his periphery. The heftier of the vampires hoisted her unceremoniously onto his shoulder, allowing her feet to scrape across the glass-covered floor as he did so. Rhys took a step forward and was met with two beams across his abdomen.

"I think we've seen enough failed heroics for one night," Fallon warned while he slowly retreated to the far wall.

Once Lis and the vampires were safely through the door, Fallon booted it shut and snapped the lock closed. "Into her cell," he called over, bending down to open a box at his feet. One by one, he removed a dozen blood bags, easing them into Rhys's enclosure. "I was impressed with the shower trick," he stated conversationally. "I must admit, I believed you would be too far gone to recognize her by the time we put her in there."

He ignored the blood bags piled on his floor. Seamus and Liam had lain Lis on her bed, Seamus's sleeve rolled up as he prepared to open a vein for her.

"The whole predator-prey thing is entertaining, but predator-predator? Now that was an unexpected—and highly entertaining—turn of events," Fallon continued, waving the unlit flashlights around. "She got you pretty good before you took her down. Could you maybe tilt your head up, let me see how deep the glass went?"

He remained immobile, his attention wrapped around his injuries as he ground himself against the hunger still raging against his rational mind. Fighting the urge to scent the air while Seamus's blood dripped into Lis's mouth took what was left of his meagre willpower.

"Ah, well," Fallon sighed dramatically. "I suppose I can re-watch the footage later. Liam, has she stabilized?"

Liam nodded, Seamus rolled his sleeve back down, and they exited Lis's cell.

"A nurse will be down shortly to hook up an IV," Fallon called over his shoulder as he hefted the empty box under his arm and followed his hauntmates out the steel door. "We want to get our girl back on her feet as quick as we can."

He descended on the bags of blood moments after the heavy door slammed shut. One by one he tore at the thick plastic, hooking his fangs in the corners before devouring the contents. Slightly aged. A bland A-positive. But by the seventh, he could feel the sharpness of his mind returning to a clarity he hadn't experienced in over a month.

The approaching footsteps alerted him to the arrival of the nurse before the door opened. He rose from his crouched position and crossed his arms uncomfortably over his burnt chest, scanning the young nurse clumsily depositing his medical supplies into the narrow hall.

"I'm, uh, here to do a transfusion," the man stumbled, his eyes widening as he got a good look at Rhys's blood-drenched body. "Mr. Derry sent me."

He continued to stare while the nurse fumbled with Lis's lock, tangling his IV stand in the cell bars. The man approached her quickly, kneeling at her side and checking her pulse against his watch.

"58 beats per minute," Rhys stated. "Up from 52, steady for eleven minutes."

The nurse jumped slightly at the sound of his voice. "Thanks. I'm going to—"

"What you're going to do," he interjected, "is be very fucking thorough." He walked to the shared bars, draping his arms over the metal in a familiar pose. "I'll be watching."

The young man worked quickly and efficiently, running the IV line with expert precision, and carefully assessing her surface injuries. When he reached across her still form to roll her over, Rhys snarled.

"There's no fresh blood," he growled. "You'd be wise to step back."

The nurse hesitated a moment, then released her gently and turned. "Stepping back is counterproductive to the whole 'thorough' instruction, wouldn't you say?"

His eyes narrowed at the smart-lipped kid. "I'll be thorough, you be useful. There are no more external injuries requiring attention. I'll allow you to assess for internal damage, but her vitals have strengthened and are stabilized. You won't find anything."

"*Allow me*," the young guy mimicked under his breath as he pulled a chair up to the bed and began pressing gently along Lis's ribcage.

He ignored the jab and watched the nurse tap along her stomach and hips. Once he was satisfied with his findings, the man packed up his supplies, checked the IV line, and exited the cell.

"I'll be back in an hour to change the bag," he grunted as he fought the lock closed. "Want me to pull those pieces out of your back before I go?"

"Unwise move, reaching into the cell of an unknown vampire," he warned, stalking toward the nurse.

The young guy hoisted his bag onto his shoulders and grinned. "Yeah, well, I'm the only medical professional on site. You eat me and your cellmate's going to have a rough time. I'm banking on you not being a total dick. Turn around."

He obeyed with a smirk, backing against the bars slowly until his spine was in reach. "The bottom one has a nasty hook facing up. If you could... fuck... all right, you got it."

One by one, the glass fragments were unceremoniously yanked out and handed over his shoulder. By the time the nurse patted him reassuringly on the back, there were five large wedges piled in his hands, one more than he'd mentally catalogued when the hits first came.

"See you in a bit," the guy called as the door closed, and he sat back on the floor to polish off the last of the blood bags.

****

Rhys's hand froze when Lis's heartbeat increased slightly again. He sat back on his haunches while she muttered incoherently for a few moments before resettling, her pulse dropping as she fell back into sleep. Once he was certain she was out, he leaned over and resumed his careful clean-up of the former shower enclosure.

Over the past thirty hours, her waking had become more frequent while her body recovered. The nurse came and went periodically, ignoring Rhys's updates, and assessing her vitals for himself before disappearing back upstairs. Twice, the young guy brought coolers of blood bags, leaving them in reach for him while he changed IVs and checked Lis's pulse.

He had emptied each one, his own injuries knitting together at a decent pace with the constant supply of nourishment. The bone-deep laceration across his throat Lis had achieved right out of the gate was little more than a red welt now thanks to his uncontrolled taking of Lis's strong blood, and even that was fading to pink as the A-positive did its job.

With the largest of the glass shards piled in the corner of his cell, he was focused on clearing the floor of the last of the slivers. His clothes were stiff with dried blood, his newly healed skin tight under the filth covering his body. When the cement ground was free of glass, he turned on the shower and stood fully clothed under the hot water.

Lis smiled up at him, her knees hooked on the back of the Queen Anne chaise and her brown hair splayed across the rug.

"Comfortable?" he inquired, cocking a brow at her position.

"Very," she retorted, waving a book at him. "I had this textbook in my high school Home Economics class. Why would you have a copy in here?"

He plucked the book from her hand and flipped through it. "I picked it up a few years back, thinking it might be informative. It's a good primer on decorum but lacks the necessary financial and legal information Tenders require. The title's misleading."

Long legs swung up and over, narrowly missing the coffee table as they landed. She stood up and stretched. "I love the dizzy feeling I get right after I stand," she grinned, closing her eyes. "It's the same feeling you get when you spin around really fast."

He tossed the book onto the table and watched with amusement as she swayed slightly on her feet. "It's probably good for you to be reading up on proper decorum. Your skirt is still upside-down."

Her arms dropped and she quickly checked her clothes, those arresting green eyes narrowing when she realized he was teasing her. "I'm plenty decorum'd," she stated haughtily, tossing her hair back. "What I'm not is socialized. When am I gonna meet the others? You keep promising. It's been months!"

He walked around the table, wrapped his arms around her, and pulled her onto his lap as he sat. She relaxed against him instantly, her head dropping to his shoulder while he absently stroked her hair. "Eventually," he finally answered.

"Not good enough," she grumbled. "My psychological need for interaction is lacking, and I'll never reach self-fulfillment without it."

He chuckled, tightening his hold on his trainee. "Have you been reading that Maslow psychology book again?"

"Maybe. Now when?"

"Soon," he replied, leaning back and dragging her along with him. "Now shush."

A strange calm drifted over him when she hummed in contentment and began tracing the grey lines on his upper arms. He flexed in response, smirking when he felt her cheek lift in amusement against his chest. Her finger dug into his bicep until he relaxed again and she resumed quietly following the loops and swirls of his tattoos. When her tempo slowed, he would flex his muscles again until she poked him into submission and her nails would once again trail over his markings.

It was almost soothing. If he found anything soothing.

But Lis was right. He couldn't hide her down here forever.

It was time.

And he found that knowledge anything but soothing.

He peeled his singlet off and hung it on the tap before yanking his heavy cargos down and kicking them away from the drain. The water was turning cooler, pulling him from his daze and reminding him to check Lis's stats.

Heart beat steady.

Breathing regulated.

Scent… still an unappealing mix of Seamus Derry and unknown B-negative donors.

He turned off the shower and shook the heaviest water drops from his hair before leaning nonchalantly against the back wall and waiting patiently for Fallon Derry's inevitable return.

CHAPTER FIFTEEN

Kaius schooled his expression as Jagger leapt forward and pinned Molly's arms to her sides.

"You have GOT to stop doing that!" Dominic yelled from behind a tree. "One of these days you're going to sludge me!"

Jagg grabbed the crossbow out of Molly's hands and engaged the safety. "It was a good shot," he said calmly. "But next time, do your celebratory dance BEFORE you reload and swing it toward your boyfriend."

Molly skipped happily toward Dominic and he felt his youngest's momentary panic turn to adoration instantly. By the time Jagg collected the rest of the weapons, the couple was sneaking off into the woods for a hurried rendezvous.

"She has incredible aim," Jagger stated, slinging the bag of bows and knives onto his shoulder. "Dom better not piss her off. She could probably take him out with a pencil and a slingshot."

Kaius fell into step alongside Jagg, angling his head to ensure he could read his lips. "I need you in the com room in ten. Fallon Derry is ready to deal."

****

Kaius was grim as Nichol turned off the computer monitor, pulled out his phone, and fired off a quick text to the rest of the hauntmates while Jagger stood and began pacing the floor.

"Were you able to save the footage?" Kai asked

Nichol, mentally preparing his speech to the others. Nichol nodded tersely and began swiping across the keyboard of his laptop.

The group was silent while the others arrived. Mickey and Audra were first, the flashing in their eyes cluing him in to the fact they were in the midst of another argument, the constant contact they maintained as they sat letting him know it was nothing of concern.

Louis trailed behind Boy, their scents indicating they were working in the bloodslave quarters earlier in the evening. Though not of Kaius blood, Rhys's fate affected them as strongly as it did his line and to keep them in the dark would be a level of disrespect he wouldn't consider extending.

Bianca strode straight to Jagger, an unidentifiable pink concoction in her hand which she periodically nibbled on while she settled her mate into a chair and adjusted his hood. Dominic and Molly were last to enter, their noisy arrival silenced when they noticed the solemn moods of the others.

Kaius sat back and addressed his growing haunt. "Fallon Derry made contact tonight. He has presented paperwork for my perusal."

Jagger's jaw tensed as Mickey frowned. "What action? Rhys has been there almost five months already. You're talking a finalized release date, right?"

Nichol turned his laptop to the group. "Fallon sent over some video footage to back his claims. Unfortunately, he has a strong case."

Rhys's face appeared on screen, his tattooed arms crossed and fangs extended. "With the death of her master, Lis's ownership has reverted back to me by default as detailed in the contract McConaughey signed.

Therefore, until her punishment is officially carried out and restitution for her actions has been agreed upon by you and myself, her well-being and actions rest in my hands."

The screen flickered slightly as another image appeared, taken from another angle. Lis's lithe form was easily recognized, and Mickey leaned forward in confusion when her voice came over the speaker.

"You know you're being taped. He knows you're taunting him."

"Taunting him. Tempting him," Rhys's flippant reply came from off-screen. "Hard to say which one motivates me."

Several more shots of Lis and Rhys played out silently, one-and-two-second snippets of them conversing until a longer piece began, Rhys's voice low and threatening. "Use this chair. With enough force, it'll break the glass of the shower and provide you with a weapon."

"No way he's colluding with a human," Louis breathed, his eyes wide.

Kaius dropped his head for a moment before refocusing on the final scenes Fallon sent over, the true nail in the coffin. Rhys crouched against the bars of his enclosure and sliding something into Lis's cell. Lis, her hands clasped behind her back as one of the younger Derry vamps entered her space with a large bag in hand. With a practiced movement, the vampire's head was removed, his body disintegrating to sludge atop Lis while her hand gripped a piece of glass.

The video faded to black.

He slid Fallon's paperwork into the center of the table. "Rhys has been sentenced to execution to be carried out within six months of yesterday's date by whatever method the remaining Derry hauntmates deem appropriate."

Nichol's fingers tapped the laptop keys and he pushed the screen back toward the others. "Fallon has also released footage of Lis to the media, identifying her as complicit in her vampire interactions. Basically a cleaned-up version of what we received, eliminating any identifiable clues of her or Rhys's imprisonment. To what end I don't know, but it's out there."

He eased the most intense of emotions swirling through his hauntmates as Mick's eyes flickered with the onslaught. Audra's fingers intertwined with her partner's, pulling him back from the edge.

"This doesn't—" Mickey began, staring at the table. "I mean, this is all on Lis, right? The execution order should name her, not Rhys."

"Apparent collusion aside," Nichol replied with false calm, "Rhys reclaimed the Tender formally in the first clip. Even without the supporting video evidence of conspiracy against the Derry males, reclamation places Lis's actions squarely onto Rhys."

Kaius ran a hand through his hair. "The sentencing documents tie Lis's ending of Derry McConaughey to Rhys and pose circumstantial evidence of Rhys's involvement in Thomas Derry's end. With a third male of their line ended by the same pair…" He trailed off, taking a moment to collect his thoughts and eliminate his growing emotional response.

"This is fucking bullshit," Dominic spat. "Rhys runs a Tender ring, not a fucking assassin one."

Before Kai could acknowledge the statement, Jagger's quiet voice broke through the room. "I'm not so certain we can say that."

****

Jagger could almost feel the holes Kaius's stare was attempting to bore into him.

"What would make Dominic's statement dubious?" Kai gritted out, rising to his feet, and holding his gaze.

Bianca scooted her chair closer to him, her proximity slightly easing the growing tension rippling through his body. The moment he had spoken, he knew he had fucked up.

Simone's positioning in the Stojanovski haunt had been a one-off, as far as he knew. It was also benefitting him and Bianca. The past few months were flush with intel regarding a handful of younger vampires actively seeking out Dovidas's whereabouts, having heard rumors of his link to both the Deepfryer sales and Chen.

He and Bianca were carefully monitoring two of them, ensuring it was little more than a misplaced hero worship. The third, his loyalties to his finances outweighing that to his species as established by Bianca's meticulous research, met his unfortunate end during a hunt on the Stojanovski property.

"Jagger," Kaius growled in warning.

He leaned forward, obscuring his eyes with his hood. "Unless we know the circumstances surrounding Thomas Derry's end, I don't think we can eliminate any possibility," he stated slowly, knowing Kai would sense a blatant falsehood. "Rhys made Lis's trade with Derry McConaughey while he was imprisoned there. I saw the paperwork. He sold Lis for a dollar and a full release from confinement."

Nichol sat up straighter, his hand flicking to draw Jagger's attention. "What were the details regarding future repercussions?"

"There were none."

Kaius, his eyes still watching him warily, sat back down. "So what are you implying? Rhys sent Lis to end McConaughey? Why would she take decades to do it?"

He shrugged and pushed his hood off his head. "I don't know. I never figured Lis for a violent one, but McConaughey, that video…maybe Rhys saw something in her we didn't."

The hauntmates sat in silence, staring at the sentencing proclamation until Mickey spoke up, his voice cracking slightly. "So will you sign it?"

Kai didn't bother lifting his gaze from the paper. "Rhys already did. My signature is a mere formality. The sentence stands."

CHAPTER SIXTEEN

Rhys stared at the ceiling, scratching at his arm slowly. Though it took the better part of the morning, Lis finally cried herself to sleep and was now tossing restlessly on her bed, the stench of Seamus's blood no longer polluting her own sweet scent.

Amazing how quickly it disappeared once Seamus was decapitated.

His sentencing paperwork sat in a neat pile on the desk of his cell, unmoved since he'd placed it there three nights prior. Lis's was nestled in the top drawer, out of sight. Now it was a waiting game, their execution dates known only to the vampire who drafted the official paperwork.

He glanced over at the sleeping woman as she hiccoughed.

He stood at their shared bars, his forehead resting on the cold metal. Lis had bounced back easily after the first bout and her mood lifted exponentially once she realized both she and Rhys had survived. But as the weeks wore on and she recognized the starvation cycle had merely restarted, she became listless, resigned. Although he lost control over his mind earlier during the second round, he had been prepared. He'd strategically placed the largest glass shards throughout his cell to ensure Lis had access to them when he himself would be unable to help her.

And she'd used them. A lot of them.

By the time the nurse began the blood transfusions again, he had managed to remove all but one piece from his body.

Lis definitely improved her aim during their second battle.

But now, with the third cycle revving up, she was at her limit. When her green eyes flickered open this time, it was hopelessness, not elation, overwhelming her.

"I can't do it again," she whimpered, her knees drawn to her chest as she rocked on her bed. "I can't, Rhys. Please don't let them make me do it again. Fix it. Please."

He resumed his intense assessment of the ceiling. He had fixed it, all right. Although a morality coach would probably find excessive fault in his logic, he had put a definitive end to the starvation-battle cycle for both Lis and himself.

He threw down the gauntlet, and Fallon responded accordingly.

Making optimal use of the limited dead video space in the cells, he had armed Lis and coached her through gestures and rudimentary charades to avoid audio detection. But not everything could remain out of view of the cameras. Try as he might, even his entrance into the dead zones gave away more than he wanted.

But he'd used the brief time his mind was fully cognizant to ensure they were released from the game Fallon enjoyed so greatly.

The anticipation had definitely outweighed the event.

Lis's desperation drove the glass so quickly, so cleanly through Seamus's throat. Her green eyes were completely devoid of emotion while she methodically, and messily, completed the task. It took less than twenty-seven seconds from start to finish.

Somewhat anticlimactic, from his point of view.

Within twenty-four hours, Fallon had entered the quarters with the execution documents in hand and his remaining hauntmates trailing behind, far from Rhys's reach.

Her sentence was presented first, read aloud prior to its submission to him for approval and a signature.

Without glancing toward her, he had signed off on the execution and extended his hand to receive the papers for his own.

Fucking Lis.

****

Rhys sprawled across the sofa, patiently waiting while his newest acquisition practiced her eyeliner skills in the magnifying mirror. Her hand had become significantly steadier throughout the evening, but her left lid was still resembling that of a cheap drunken party clown.

"Tilt your chin up slightly," he suggested, arching his head back to get a better view. "And remember to lift the brow to avoid creases."

Resettling, he made a point of ignoring the closed door leading to Lis's empty room.

She was busy. He was busy.

All fucking good.

"Better?" the trainee asked, kneeling before him.

He assessed the workmanship critically, cursing himself for selecting a woman best enhanced through charcoal liner. So few could pull it off properly. "Good enough for tonight," he muttered, reaching over to wipe a small smudge from her cheek. "I'm out for the rest of the evening. Be a good girl and work on your up-dos."

Leaving the woman locked in the training rooms, he grabbed the stack of mail from the table and wandered toward his own suite, running a finger along the paintings adorning the walls.

The new trainee would definitely be dusting soon.

He toed off his boots and socks and flopped onto his couch, flipping through his letters one by one until a sharp knock echoed through the room. With a huff of annoyance, he flung his door open.

And was leveled with a precisely placed fist.

Snarling, he booted his attacker into the hall and prepared himself for a fight until a scent caught his attention. He stepped back, lowering his fists as Mikhail rose to his full height.

He always forgot how fucking tall Mickey was when he wasn't slouching.

Mick pushed past him and stormed over to his sofa, dropping onto it with a glare. "You're an asshole," he growled, running a hand through his long blond hair. "Fuck, Rhys. A little warning would have been nice."

He crossed his arms over his chest and rubbed his healing jaw. "I set it up last week. How much more warning did you need?"

"You didn't tell me she—" Mick turned his glare to the floor. "I thought Lis was with Nichol last week."

"She was. Feeding introductory course," he replied. "I figured the sharpness of his fangs would be a less painful introduction than those snaggles you call teeth. And his control is impeccable. Now where's Lis?"

Mickey leaned over his knees, the area rug immensely interesting. "Sleeping in my bed," he grumbled. "I should probably get back there. I don't know the protocol for this. Fuck, Rhys. You should have told me she was, uh, untouched."

"Untouched?" he repeated, lifting a brow at the propriety of the term. "She likes you and made the request herself. I told you to take it easy and go slow."

Dropping his head to his knees, Mick groaned. "Big fucking difference between 'take it easy' and 'she's a virgin, don't be a dick'. I feel like such a creep," he said, his voice muffled. "How the hell was that even possible? She's been down here with you for, like, eight months."

He pointed to his door. "Return her to her quarters when she wakes. Don't bother letting me know. I'll debrief her at dusk."

Mickey flipped him off as he skulked from the room, his shoulders slouched. Locking the door, he returned to the sofa and resumed his assessment of the mail.

Request.

Request.

Laughable low-ball offer.

Nothing distracting enough to keep his mind off the scent Mick had carried in on his skin and hair.

Fucking Lis.

****

Fallon shoved another two blood bags through the bars, the slight discoloration an indication they were hours from spoiling. Rhys maintained his position in the middle of the cell, unwilling to face the UV light the young Derry hauntmates carried into the basement prison at all times now.

"I hope that foul shit isn't my last meal," he said, wrinkling his nose at the aging blood. "If it is, I'll be giving this place a one-star review online."

With a grin, Fallon began unpacking a bag of human

food through Lis's bars. "I assure you, your final meal will be far more appetizing."

"As long as the menu describes her as brunette and Brazilian, I'm game," he replied, sliding his hands into his pockets. "A redhead for dessert would be nice."

Fallon chuckled, rising from his crouched position and appraising Lis. "What's the matter, Lis?" he posited, false concern etched on his face. "I brought all your favorites."

He adjusted his stance slightly. "No need to speak to her directly," he stated, drawing Fallon's attention away from the woman curled on her bed. "Any communication between you and the female goes through me until I'm no longer available."

"Come now," Fallon scoffed. "We aren't going to spend the foreseeable future adhering to formalities, are we?"

"As long as my sentence is tied to my ownership of the Tender, I would say we most definitely are."

The Derry vamps exchanged an amused look before exiting the room, leaving him and Lis alone again. He occupied himself with the cell bars, rapping them from top to bottom with his knuckles in search of a flaw.

"Release me," she muttered from her bed, her voice muffled by her blanket. "Denounce. Absolve. Whatever you call it. Separate yourself from me."

"Now why would I do that, honey?" he grumbled, his attention on a sloppy weld in the far right corner of his enclosure. "I really hope McConaughey didn't pay full price for this. Sure, it's functional, but some of the handiwork looks like Mickey was set loose in here with a blow torch."

"Rhys."

"Lis?"

"Sign off on me."

He let go of the rough weld, its strength as strong as the rest of them, and continued to ignore her as he picked up the bagged blood and gave it a quick sniff.

Eaten worse.

"RHYS."

Straddling his chair, he used his fang to slice the fresher bag open. "First off, the paperwork for a formal release of duties is a real bitch to complete. The notifications, faxing, phone calls… it's more work than I care to do outside the confines of Egyptian cotton sheets." He guzzled the first bag and sliced into the second. "Next, I already have a Former Tender driving me insane back at the haunt. And a failed Tender. And a psychologist. My quota for women who don't have to listen to anything I say is pretty much filled. This is probably the most peace I've had in almost two years." He balled the bags up and shot them through his bars into the hall. "And third, discussion over. Shut up, baby."

"I'm going to die with your death on my conscience," she whispered.

"Yeah, well, I've had to live with your life on mine. We're even."

CHAPTER SEVENTEEN

"You're burning him!" Lis cried out, struggling against the grip the young Derry vamp had on her. "Fallon! Stop this!"

Despite the tiny bead of smoke rising from the blackened hole under his ribs, Rhys remained immobile. His hands were tucked in his back pockets as though he was waiting for the bus and not slowly cooking.

Fallon continued to hold two lights on Rhys as she was dragged out of her cell and into the hall. "He'll be fine," Fallon Derry chuckled. "A good meal and he'll be good as new. Liam, open the lock and get her in there. Those boxes, too."

While Liam fumbled with the cell door, the younger vamp adjusted his position and shoved her into Rhys's cell. She pitched forward, narrowly missing a hard fall onto the cement when Rhys's arm caught her.

"Moth… fuck," he ground out, righting her before retreating back to his position.

The cell door clanked closed and she looked over at Rhys, his face now bearing a charred streak across his jaw.

"You kids have fun," Fallon called out while he set the UV lights down on the floor, their beams crossing the ground to Rhys's bare feet. When the Derry hauntmates stomped up the stairs, she scrambled to block the light, laying herself across the cement to block the rays.

"Well, this is an interesting turn of events," he

stated, stepping clear of the lights' paths when Fallon Derry was out of hearing range.

"Why the hell didn't you move out of the way sooner?" she demanded, pushing herself up once she was sure his feet wouldn't be hit again.

He grinned, his fangs extended from the pain he was fighting against. "Because it fucks with his head when I don't." He rolled his shoulders, the hole under his ribs opening slightly more as he did. She looked away while he poked at his wound. "Aw, come on, Lis. You've seen nastier shit than this. I know you spent a good amount of time in Nichol's room. That had to toughen you up, sweetheart."

"Could you please just put your shirt back on," she pleaded. "You know I don't like violence and gore."

When he didn't respond for a stretch, she glanced over at him. His eyes were locked on her, brows raised with exaggerated incredulousness. Choosing to ignore the obvious, she set to work opening the boxes Liam had shoved into the cell. "Food," she reported as she rifled through the first box. She jimmied the second open. "A lot of food."

He appeared at her side, his black singlet on to hide his burns. He knelt down and flicked another lid, frowning as he reached in. "Detergent. Clothes. Fan-fucking-tastic. Looks like we're roomies until the guillotine falls. I get the bed."

She sat down on the cold floor, hunching over her knees. She knew he was keeping his tone light for her benefit, keeping the stress and strain knotting his brow from entering his words. In the few unguarded minutes she observed him over the past few days, his features had shown the heaviness of their situation. His navy eyes lost the roguish glint she had come to view as inherent to Rhys. His shoulders would slump while he ran his hands over the bars for the thousandth time. His lips, always bordering on a smirk, were drawn tight across his fangs.

And then, as though suddenly remembering himself, the Rhys she knew would return.

She peeked over at him as he rose to his feet and hesitated a moment before he straightened to his full height. He fixed his gaze on her old cell and began scratching at his tattoos while he scanned the contents of her abandoned room.

"I think," he said slowly, "this is Fallon's final game."

Patting the box lids as she rose, she joined him in his perusal of her enclosure. "But it takes longer for a vampire to starve out than the five months he has left to carry out your sentence. If he doesn't adhere to the sentencing timeline, doesn't that nullify the contract?"

He pursed his lips, nodding slowly. "Then I guess he wants me to eat you before he carries out my execution. I am a little hungry. I mean, you're no Brazilian model, but I suppose beggars can't be choosers."

She calmly pushed the barbell in her tongue between her teeth and rolled it along her lips. The slight shudder in Rhys's shoulders when he caught sight of the metal was payback enough.

He ran a hand through his hair, pushing the stray strands back. "Why?" he sighed, his expression resigned. "Before my head rolls, I want to know what made you think shoving a chunk of steel through your face was even remotely acceptable."

****

"Stop being so damn stubborn and wash your hair before the water goes cold," Rhys grumbled, adjusting his grip on the blanket.

"You're dragging it on the floor again," Lis chastised. "Lift it higher and don't look."

With a low growl, he obeyed. "You've got nothing I haven't seen before," he muttered, the cuffs of his cargos dampening with droplets. "You're being ridiculous."

The scent of shampoo finally filled the air. "Well, you haven't seen mine and we're going to keep it that way."

"I ha—" He paused. "What the fuck, Lis? How haven't I?"

When she began singing an old Bob Dylan song, he knew he was being ignored.

"Add that to the list of things we need to address before I eat you," he called over the hum of the shower. "And I don't think you're singing the right words."

Her voice grew louder and he smirked, rolling his eyes when the water turned off and she began calling out orders.

"I'm grabbing the towel, so take three steps to the left. Your left," she instructed. "And don't drop your arms. I want the blanket to dry out before bed."

He shuffled sideways awkwardly, maintaining the comforter shield while she toweled off and dressed.

It had become a nightly routine over the past two weeks. Lis would shower first while he ensured the cell's cameras were blocked. Then she would sit on the bed with her back to him, huffing at his lack of modesty and chiding him for enjoying her discomfort.

He did.

It was a small amusement.

It was also payback for her using most of the hot water. Every. Damn. Night.

Tonight was no different. With her brush in hand, she took up position on the bed and he stripped down, already knowing the water would be tepid at best.

"Do you think he'll come down?" she called over her shoulder.

"Doubt it," he replied, scrubbing the dried blood from his biceps. "All that thumping around above us, and I haven't picked up a single movement toward the basement stairs in eleven nights. Was the place this busy under old McConaughey?"

"Always," she answered, turning toward him before her cheeks reddened and she quickly faced the bars again. "There was always someone coming and going. Lots of parties. Lots of humans on site. It was a little overwhelming sometimes."

He grabbed the towel she had placed on the chair to dry.

It was definitely not dry.

Doing what he could with the damp towel, he pulled on his cargos and tossed his shirt into the sink to be washed. "All right," he said, walking over to her and crossing his arms over his chest. "Is tonight the night?"

****

Lis placed her brush on the bed and smoothed out the sheet.

There was laundry to do.

She stood carefully, avoiding any contact with Rhys while he stood and watched her walk into the bricked bathroom to wash their clothes in the tiny sink.

A little soap.

Water.

Scrub.

Rinse.

The normalcy of the act was calming.

She carefully placed the wet clothes through the bars, hanging them over the supporting beam and squeezing the last of the heavy droplets from the fabric. Once she was satisfied with her task, she turned back to him.

"Not tonight."

He stalked toward her, his gait slightly more predatory than it had been a mere two weeks prior. "And what's the rationale this evening, angel?"

"The last of the bread will grow moldy if I don't eat it, and that's wasteful."

His brow rose infinitesimally. "Of course."

Resuming his evening assessment of the cell bars, he honored her wishes and dropped the subject.

The subject.

She paced the small expanse of the enclosure, her bare feet padding quietly on the cement. Every night for two weeks, he had asked her. And every night, she refused with a pathetic excuse.

But the time for choice was running out, and they both knew it.

"You know I'll be gentle," he said quietly, staring at his clasped hands and ignoring her while she knelt at his feet. "You won't notice a thing until the final seconds."

She fought the trembling of her lower lip and looked away.

"Lis," he pushed, "Taking me out first isn't an option, and you know it. I've watched a lot of humans die

126

of starvation over the centuries. It isn't a death I would wish upon any Tender. Even if she is responsible for my own execution."

When her eyes flew to his, he smirked at her.

"Fucking Tenders," he said, tossing his hands up in mock surrender. "I always knew they'd be the death of me. I'd hoped I'd be fucked to death, but this method has its own merits."

Drawing a deep breath, she shook her head. "I'm just…I'm not ready."

"You know it's coming," he stated softly.

"I do. But not tonight. Please, Rhys?"

When his navy eyes narrowed in contemplation, she knew she'd been granted a brief reprieve.

"Fine," he finally grumbled. "You have a few weeks to decide. But once I feel I'm losing control, the decision is taken from your hands. Understand?"

With a nod, she dropped her head to his lap and closed her eyes while he ran his fingers through her hair, muttering about the unnatural color choice and the dark roots beginning to grow out.

She smoothed her hair down and joined him at the bars. His jaw was tense, the muscles flexing and relaxing rhythmically as he methodically ran his hands over the welds.

"You're hungry," she stated, watching his lips tighten over his fangs when she stood beside him.

"I'm fine, princess," he muttered. "Be a good girl and set out your meals for tonight."

Lifting her wrist to his fangs, she grazed her skin across one sharp point. His eyes ovaled and he turned his head away with a low snarl. "We aren't postponing the inevitable," he ground out, pushing off the bars and walking away.

She followed him, her anger boiling up. "What happens if you find an out?" she demanded, swatting at his shoulder. "You'll be too damn weak to exploit it!"

He dropped his head a fraction, then rolled his shoulders out and straightened. "There is no fucking 'out'," he responded calmly, gesturing slowly around the cell. "This is your tomb, Lis. And mine. The sooner you accept it, the sooner this is over. And frankly, Lis, I'm finally ready for it to be done."

CHAPTER EIGHTEEN

"Babe, it's not that big a deal," Mickey argued, placing a steadying hand on Audra's thigh. "They've made their decisions. You have no reason to feel guilty for how they end up."

Audra slammed her hands down on the table in frustration, her cat eyes glaring at the vampires surrounding her. The Bloodslave Release Program was stalled out, the remaining humans unreceptive to the promise of life outside the haunt basement. Audra took the setback more personally than either he or Nichol had anticipated, her repeated visits to the bloodslave quarters quickly becoming a bone of contention between them.

"This has nothing to do with guilt," she ground out. "You can't institutionalize people, create a society of learned helplessness, and then call their decisions an exercise in free will."

He sat back, knowing there would be no winning when she broke out her degree and started smacking them in the face with it.

Nichol, however, hadn't learned the lesson.

"You're approaching this from a human perspective," Nichol rationalized. "If you look at it from the point-of-view of the cattle downstairs, this place provides a safe and stress-free environment."

Wrong move, Nichol.

Audra rose to her feet and leaned across the table, her pencil skirt lifting across the backs of her thighs as she did so. And he figured fixating on that view was safer than participating in the shitstorm Nichol had set off.

As she drew in a deep breath, he watched Nichol's hands clench on his chair.

"Kaius," Nichol called out, buying himself a temporary reprieve from Audra's opening arguments. "Any news?"

Kai strode into the com room, a quick nod of acknowledgement to Audra. As she breathed out slowly and sat back down, Mick momentarily lamented to loss of one of his favorite sights.

"The others are on their way up from the sparring room," he said, taking a seat beside Nichol and passing his phone over to his eldest. "There's a red circle on one of the apps. I find it distracting."

While Nichol's thumb flicked across the screen of the phone, Mick sat back and closed his eyes. He opened his mind up, barreling past his hauntmates and aiming directly for Rhys.

Alive.

It was the best any of them could hope for as the clock ticked through the days and weeks.

The rest of the haunt piled into the room slowly. Dominic and Molly reeked of the woods, likely from one of her shooting practices inevitably leading to a romp on the forest.

He suspected Dominic was turned on by Molly's lethalness. It was cute.

Louis and Jagger trailed Bianca as she rushed to Audra's side. The two women whispered furiously about the BRP setbacks and Nichol's needlessly derogative comment which obviously indicated the Kaius males required intensive training in empathy'.

Mickey grinned at Nichol, who had placed Kai's phone down and was now staring daggers at Audra, his best friend and greatest pain in the ass.

Boy was last to slip into the room, wisely giving him and Audra wide berth.

Good.

Audra broke off her conversation with Bianca momentarily and the women waved at the mute vamp.

Fuck you, Boy. Fuck you, fuck you, fuck you.

Kaius rapped his knuckles on the table quickly, bringing the room's attention his way and pulling Mick from his jealous internal chant. "Rhys lives," he reported. "Fallon Derry has been silent since the execution was signed off, but Mikhail can confirm Rhys has yet to be ended."

He nodded, looking down at Audra's hand as she squeezed his knee reassuringly. "I can't get much more than the hum of existence, but he continues to exist, so…" He trailed off, unsure how to finish his thought.

The silence in the com room grew awkwardly long. With four months remaining on the death warrant, the hauntmates had grown more anxious with every passing week, every potential option to reverse the decision meeting a dead end.

Knowing Rhys would be ended was one thing.

Not knowing when was another.

Nichol broke the quiet with a grunt, tossing a stack of papers toward Jagger and Bianca. "Anyways," he opened, refocusing the group's attention, "this should keep you two busy for a few months. Your contacts can follow leads, plant the stories online, and leak the intel. Make sure your tech guys utilize the social media bot systems I forwarded. They should cover all the most popular platforms."

Jagg scanned the papers, shaking his head. "You're a genius," he muttered, passing the pile to Bianca. "There's enough here to tie up the court system for months. Years, for some of these guys."

Mick leaned over and read over the top page in Bianca's hand, ignoring the others while they delved into an argument about acceptable stereo sound levels in the former Tender training suites.

Nichol truly was a genius.

Bianca and Jagger had chosen to take a decidedly less violent approach to fighting the growing anti-vampire movement. With Nichol's assistance, the pair was feeding their increasingly vast network enough intel and leads to place the heaviest hitters from each state into the hands of human law enforcement for everything ranging from parking tickets to embezzlement. The goal was to tie the most adamant and influential supporters up in the courts, to delegitimize them through social media, and to plant the seeds of doubt in their followers.

Most were legit. And those that weren't had been carefully manipulated online by a vampire with a lot of computer time and a hate-on for humans.

Bianca caught his eye and smirked, pointing at a few creatively spun crimes attributed to a woman in Florida.

Nichol truly was a genius. An evil one.

When the discussion turned to a petty argument over acceptable daytime noise levels, he sat back and monitored his hauntmates, pulling the streams of worry over Rhys off of them in small doses. While the others chose sides and voices raised, he glanced over at Kaius, noting the heaviness in the haunt leader's eyes.

"Can we just agree to keep the television and stereo

at 65 decibels maximum during evening hours, 35 decibels from sunrise to sunset?" Kaius finally interjected into the argument, bringing the group's sound level down. "Nichol, if you could print a few signs we can place around the quarters to serve as reminders, we can move on with our night. Agreed?"

He leaned back and drained the small amounts of annoyance hanging in the air, missing the intensely energizing barrage of Rhys.

****

Lis's rhythmic breathing pounded in Rhys's head, a constant reminder of both her presence and her proximity. With nothing else to draw his attention in the pitch blackness of the prison, the steady tempo beat against his every thought.

His every warped, twisted thought.

Overwhelming as it had become during the past few hours, Lis's scent and quiet movements were keeping his internal darkness at bay.

Too bad she wouldn't be able to do a damn thing about the external darkness when she woke up.

Swinging his arm out slowly to judge his distance from the cell bars, he moved forward cautiously, stopping once his forearms could drape across the steel beam.

He had, at best, four more solid days of cognition ahead of him. After that, both his mental and physical control would begin to slip intermittently, leaving Lis caged with a hungry, unpredictable animal.

More so.

Before the lights had gone out in the hours prior, he had been preparing to square off against her, to refute her ridiculous excuses and end her quickly. The time for procrastination was over, and he knew if he didn't do it humanely now, he would do it brutally later.

"Rhys?"

He turned toward her voice, her confusion and panic evident in both her tone and heart rate. His own helplessness raged inside him. Without even the remotest sliver of light to draw from, his enhanced eyesight was useless in the pitch blackness.

"Over here, sweetheart," he called, walking slowly back toward the bed. "It would appear Fallon didn't pay the power bill." He slowed as her scent became stronger. "Scoot against the bars so I don't sit down and crush you."

He waited for the rustling of the blankets to stop before he sat, his hand feeling around for her. Once he located her thigh, he followed a path over the curve of her hip, across her shoulder, and down her arm to her hand. "You okay?"

She intertwined her fingers with his, something she had often done during her time in the Kaius haunt when faced with something new. "I don't like this," she whispered. "It's so…I don't like the dark."

"Join the club, angel," he snorted. "The lights went out a few hours ago. I've been listening for rats or cockroaches, but I think we're in the clear on those."

With a quick squeeze of his hand, she sat up. "What do we do now?"

Feed.

"Shower. Argue over the towel. You eat. I stand in the middle of the room looking dangerously tempting, even if you can't see me, and you fight your overpowering desire to jump me. Same as we've been doing," he replied, standing to guide her to her feet. "The bonus is I won't have to hold the blanket while you rinse off and get the cuffs of my pants damp."

She tugged her arm back slightly. "Why would Fallon turn the lights off?"

"It's disorienting as fuck," he replied, pulling her up. "Your former master's brat seems to enjoy mind games."

Escorting her carefully toward the bathroom, he kept one hand out until his fingers made contact with the rough brick. He eased her toward the door, blocking the grating exterior with his body and keeping a firm grip on her arm. "Move slow, feel around to familiarize yourself with distances. Got it?"

She hummed in acknowledgement and walked tentatively through the doorway. Once she was in, he began making his way around the cell, counting steps, and locating the few items that could trip them up.

Boxes.

The chair.

The desk.

While he moved everything tight against the cell bars in a row, he stretched his senses and listened past the water splashing in the sink, past Lis's heartbeat, and into the main floor of the haunt.

Complete silence.

"Lis?" he called out, making his way back over to her. "When was the last time you remember hearing any noise from upstairs?

The bathroom door creaked open. He held his arm out for her, waiting until she had her hands wrapped securely around his forearm before leading her toward the shower head outside the bricked bathroom.

"I don't know," she muttered. "Five? Maybe six days?"

Guiding her hand to the tap when she began feeling her way around, he backed away from her. "Toss your clothes toward my voice," he instructed. "Count them off so I know how many things I should be catching. I'm going to be pissed if I trip over those ridiculous bloomers you call underwear."

"They're called 'boy shorts' and they're comfortable," she groused.

"They're called boxers and they belong on Mikhail's ass, not yours," he fired back. "So how long do Fallon and the others usually take off for? A week? Two?"

She went silent, the rustling of her clothing halting. "The haunt has never been empty," she said quietly. "Ever."

Fan-fucking-tastic.

"New owner, new rules," he said, the casualness of his voice belying the knot forming in his gut. "Maybe Fallon will bring us back a souvenir. Now start counting."

CHAPTER NINETEEN

Rhys locked his knees around Lis to steady her as he repositioned himself, pushing his back flusher with the wall. She tensed momentarily, pausing her stream of thought before relaxing back against him.

"So every time we fought, I'd add another," she continued. "I think Derry found it amusing, a game of sorts. We'd argue, he'd disappear for a few nights, and when he'd come home he'd be anxious to hunt for my new piercing." She sighed, rolling her head back and forth as she settled lower against his chest. "I've taken most of them out over the past year. Once Der became connected with that waitress on the boulevard, there was nothing I could do to pique his interest. And keeping them was just, I don't know, unnecessary."

There was no sadness in her voice when she spoke of her master's connection to another woman. It was a primal need much like imprinting, out of the vampire's control as much as it was the human's.

He brought his hands to her ears, tracing his fingers over them and her face as he spoke. "You had seven in the left, six in the right. Two on the left brow. One nose stud. One on the lip. Aside from the abomination in your mouth, did I miss any?"

He could feel her cheeks lift as she smiled. "Only other one remaining is the belly ring."

"And why have you kept only the tongue ring and the belly ring?" he inquired, tapping her stomach until his hand made contact with a small hoop.

"The belly ring was the first, the tongue was the last. And I like them," she murmured.

"I don't."

"And lucky for you, you don't have to look at them," she replied haughtily, decisively removing his hand from her belly ring but holding her position tucked tight against him.

They sat in silence, the unspoken question hanging in the air as their second night in complete darkness drew to an end. He kept his ears alert for any signs of life above them, listening in vain for the heavy footfalls of the Derry males, the scampering of their human companions, the low rumble of approaching vehicles.

Nothing.

Lis's heart rate began to slow and her breathing deepened.

It was just too damn late to ask her now. Tomorrow night. Tomorrow night would be the night.

"Hey," he whispered, sitting her up so he could disentangle himself from her before she fell into a deep sleep. "Why'd you do it? And why didn't you call me for help?"

It had preyed on his mind for months.

The how, he knew. The why...

"Derry had drawn up a contract," she said softly. "Passing my ownership over to Fallon so he could pursue his connected woman without guilt or responsibility." She laughed humorlessly. "It was all very proper, his explanation." Her voice changed into a decent imitation of McConaughey. "Lis, girl, the time has come for us to part ways. For you to shape Fallon as you did me. To prepare him for the time he meets his own connection.

You did good, Lis." She cleared her throat. "And I snapped. He was hunched over the paperwork, pointing out my responsibilities and Fallon's rights. He was just so damn pleased he was wrapping up the 'little issue of the Tender', he didn't see it coming. But he didn't sign the paperwork either."

His jaw tensed as he sat straighter. "He had no legal right to change ownership without my permission," he growled. "From our last conversation prior to his ending, you had me believing McConaughey was interested in negotiating your return to the Kaius haunt."

She rolled onto her side, bumping him as she drew her knees to her chest. "How was I supposed to know he couldn't transfer ownership? It's not like Der ever gave me a copy of the sales agreement."

"But I—" He hesitated. "I went over the contract with you, didn't I?"

"No, you didn't. You disappeared for a week, then walked into my room, packed my bag, and put me on a bus to L.A."

****

Despite the blackness of his surroundings, Rhys's internal clock remained steady.

2 p.m.

He paced the same path over and over, his bare feet padding lightly to avoid waking Lis as she slept fitfully on the bed.

Put her on a fucking bus.

Put her on a bus, he had. He could recall every step he took that evening as he entered the Kaius haunt and strode through the Tender quarters in search of her.

The incomplete balance sheets were strewn across her bed as Lis sat cross-legged, hunched over a

139

calculator while she gnawed on the end of her pencil. His arrival at her door was met with a look of excitement and she scrambled to her feet, her happiness morphing into concern when she took in his tense expression.

"All right, baby," he said, walking past her without a greeting and flinging her closet doors open. "I'm going to need you to shower and grab eight outfits with matching shoes and appropriate lingerie." He tossed several dresses onto her bed. "Your hair should be dry by the time you finish packing. Keep the makeup light and clean."

He turned to exit, refusing to look toward his flustered trainee.

"Where've you been?" she called out. "And where am I going?"

He paused in the doorway, his jaw flexing as he forced himself to remain calm. "Your sale has been finalized. You leave in two hours."

Striding out of the training quarters, he made his way into the com room to inform Nichol he was back on site.

"Jagger's looking for you," Nichol barked from the floor, rolls of wire at his feet. "Watch your step. I'll flay you if you disconnect any of these."

"Did he say why?" he inquired, backing away from the tangled mess. "I'll be heading out again in a couple hours, but I'll be back before dawn."

Nichol rose to his feet gingerly and crossed his arms. "He probably wants to know where the hell you disappeared to this week. And where the hell you're going now."

Ignoring Nichol's probing into his whereabouts, he gave a quick nod and headed down to the weapons room.

He walked heavily through the halls as he approached Jagger's work room. Although it had been almost two years, he still struggled with Jagg's deafness and the dangers it posed in their existence. He hesitated in the doorway, a jolt of unease passing over him when his younger brother made no move to acknowledge his presence. Jagger's back was to him, his hands carefully buffing the blade of a longsword.

Completely engulfed, completely unaware.

"Boots still on?" Jagg suddenly called over his shoulder. "What's the occasion?"

He grinned and strode across the room, kneeling alongside him. "I wanted to get all dolled up for you. You like?"

With the precision of a master, Jagger brought the tip of the longsword down within a hair's breadth of Rhys's booted foot. "You look stunning, babycakes," he retorted, the exaggerated batting of his eyelashes drawing a snort from him. "You just get back?"

"Yeah. Heading out again in a few hours. I'll be home by dawn, so you can tell Mick he won't need to check on the Tenders at nightfall."

Jagger lifted the sword and stood, placing it carefully into its sheath. "I'll come with you tonight," he stated, grabbing a rag to clean off his hands. "You can explain where you've been the past week."

"Nothing to explain," he said smoothly. "I was in a sales negotiation and will be delivering the Tender immediately."

Jagg's ice eyes narrowed. "Which one? Nichol didn't mention any deposits into the Tender account during tonight's meet-up."

Deposit. Fuck.

"The sale tightens up our allies on the West Coast," he lied. *"I'll be back soon. If it makes you feel better, I promise to come tuck you in when I return. Maybe read you a story."*

Jagger's fist landed on his newest tattoo, sending a burst of fire through his arm. "Smartass. Who'd you trade for this alliance? I assume it's the McConaughey haunt?"

Ensuring he kept his face angled toward his brother while he began making his way from the room, he nodded. "It's a good deal. Opens our ears at the port. I'll check in when I get back."

Ignoring the other question, he made his way back to the Tender training rooms to find Lis sitting quietly on her bed. Her suitcase sat by the door, her room carefully ordered.

"C'mon, honey," he nudged, hefting the bag, and holding his hand out to her. "Let's see how you look."

She drew in a shaky breath and stood, turning slowly for his perusal.

He catalogued the image, isolating every snapshot in his mind as her blue skirt swayed across her calves. "Hand me a brush," he instructed, keeping his eyes averted from hers. She shuffled to the bathroom and returned, extending her hand toward him.

Circling behind her, he began to run the brush through her dark hair. "I'm going to shift the part from the left to the center. Personal preference. I suspect your new master will favor it as well," he explained as he gently ran his pinky finger through her hair. "Better. Let's go, baby."

Better.

It hadn't looked better. It looked right. With the long

skirt flowing around her legs and the snug black tank top clinging to her body, Lis looked exactly as he had imagined she would look with proper nutrition and a secure roof over her head. It was the vision he had conjured up the night he had met her and watched her walk through the dirty parking lot in search of money.

"Lis?" he called out quietly in the darkness.

"Hmmm?"

"This—" He hesitated, uncertain he wanted an answer to the question he desperately wanted to ask.

Nope. No fucking way.

"Just checking on you, sweetheart," he muttered as he resumed pacing the floor. "Go back to sleep. You look horrific with bags under your eyes."

CHAPTER TWENTY

Lis stared into the blackness, her head turned toward the sound of Rhys's low voice.

"You've been lying to me," he said quietly. "There's one, maybe two days of food left, not a week's worth."

She remained silent, refusing to respond.

"Lis," he growled, "I'm not going to stand here and watch you starve to death on that bed."

"You can't watch anything in the darkness," she snarked, crossing her arms defiantly.

The padding of his bare feet drew nearer and she felt his hands as they searched out her thighs and he knelt before her. "It's time, sweetheart. I'm barely holding on by a thread myself right now. Let's do this under our terms instead of under Fallon's."

She shook her head violently. "No. I can feed you. It'll buy us at least a week, right? And if you link to me, we can extend my time, too. Maybe long enough for someone to find us."

He squeezed her knees gently. "So continue to stand on the gallows with the nooses around our necks for another seven nights? Maybe ten?"

Pushing uselessly against his hands, she felt her anger rising. "Seven for me. You? Once you drain me, you'll get another three months before the madness fully sets in again, won't you? Your noose isn't nearly as tight as mine, it is?"

When he fell silent, she pulled her legs onto the bed

and out of his reach. Her stomach grumbled with demand, not sated by the meager meal she had consumed at dusk.

She had a healthy fear of her own death, imminent as it was. But it was knowing Rhys would be left behind keeping her awake long into the day. He would be locked in the cell with her body for months before the insanity of hunger overtook him once fully, forced to live out his final days in a cage with a corpse.

The thought brought the vivid image into the forefront of her mind. She could envision him pacing the floor rabidly, his navy eyes ovaled beyond recognition and strong back hunched as he reverted to a hungry, feral animal. The self-assured smirk, the cocky swagger, the liquid purr of his voice when he turned on his charm to get his way. All of it would be gone, replaced by a snarling, incognizant beast.

"Rhys, please," she whimpered. "Why? Why are you just giving in?"

A humorless laugh echoed in the quarters. "Fucking Lis," he sighed, his cargos rustling as he rose to his feet and began to move away from her. The rhythmic padding of his walk resumed. The pacing was a constant since the power was cut. "I'm done, angel. I'm done and I'm ready."

The steady sound of his footsteps was augmented by the scratching of his arms.

"In over seven centuries, I've spent more than four of them in confinement," he stated without emotion. "I'm done. I'm done with the scent of mildew clinging to the few stale meals I get. Done with the concrete walls reverberating every sound through my ears over and over. Done with the bars, done with the chains, done with

the whippings, done with the flayings. I'm done, Lis."
He paused, stilling his movements. "We're going to die
on our own fucking terms. Our way. Because I'm sure as
fuck not giving Fallon, or any other ball-less vampire,
the opportunity to put me down like a rabid fucking
dog."

****

Fucking Lis.

The clamor of the metal desk as it collapsed under
his fist was nothing compared to the gulping sobs of the
woman on the bed.

Rhys stood in the middle of the room, his arms
crossed and jaw set as Lis's cries were interrupted only
by her unintelligible mutterings.

Once Lis had started, he immediately felt something
he was highly unaccustomed to feeling.

Guilt.

Regret.

Another dose of guilt.

Maybe a pinch more to really highlight his complete
failure to protect his Tenders.

He had a vague recollection of one of his brothers in
a similar situation, and he had a momentary flash of
delayed empathy for Nichol listening to Audra sob after
she saw Jagger confined and tortured in a human jail cell.

"Lis," he called over her sobs. "Baby. Lis. Hey."

He walked slowly over to her and knelt beside the
bed. The scent of her blood had developed a sour tinge,
easing the pull to drain the meal in his reach. Some
vampires craved whatever hormone it was coursing
through the veins of despondent humans, but he wasn't
one of them. He found both the odor and the taste off-
putting.

"Fine," he murmured, tentatively grasping for her fingers and ignoring the knot in his gut at the prospect of linking to a woman. "We'll do it your way. For now. But when I decide it's over, it's over. Got it?"

The cries turned into shuddered breaths almost instantly. He patiently held position, waiting for her to collect herself.

"You sure?" she finally asked, her fingers wrapping around his.

"Yeah, I'm sure," he huffed. "What's another few weeks added to a death wish anyways, right? Besides, if the link is too much, I'll just drain you in your sleep."

The mattress rustled as she slid off it and onto his lap. Her thin arms wrapped around his neck as her head dropped to his shoulder. "I don't want you to die alone," she stammered out, her breathing still ragged from her tears. "I just want the chance to make that not happen, okay?"

They sat on the floor in silence, his mind flipping through plausible scenarios to ease her thoughts, and her clinging to him like a frightened spider monkey.

The thought of dying alone held no weight for him. He had accepted it as a foregone conclusion for himself by the end of his first century and entered every imprisonment since then with a calm recognition of the probability. The knowledge made him more impetuous, not less. Realizing when he finally went down it would be his fate and his alone, he had taken risks and made deals many others would never have considered.

As expendable as the Tenders.

His arms tightened a fraction around her as he pushed the idea to the back of his mind. He had bigger things to worry about now.

He had to link to her without freaking out.

"All right," he said, breaking the silence and focusing his thoughts. "Let's get this show on the road."

****

Kaius sat on the sofa as Mickey methodically circled the perimeter of the common room.

"I can pull Rhys entirely onto myself until the deed is done," he offered quietly while he funneled Mick's increasing concern and frustration. "There's no reason for you to share the burden."

Mickey froze on the spot, his hands shoved deep into his pockets. "I can deal. I can," he insisted. "I don't want…I need to know when it happens. I need to, I don't know, be there. I just need a few minutes to unload right now, Kai."

Sitting back, he nodded and continued to monitor his empathic child.

The open timeline for Rhys's execution weighed heavily across the haunt, but no greater than on Mickey who was subjected to the distant echoes of Rhys's changing moods. A dark resignation had taken hold several nights earlier, suggesting to both of them the time was drawing near.

Mick had not rested since.

Neither had he, but he held that information close to his chest.

Though it remained unspoken, neither he nor Mick was willing to allow Rhys to meet his end alone, to have his existence wiped from the earth with little more than a formal notice delivered in the mail.

"You realize it could be painful," he warned. "I've been told the death of a bloodline member is greatest for the sire, but given the strength of your empathic skills, there may be a ripple effect of both Rhys's end and my own…discomfort."

Mickey ran a hand through his hair and rolled his shoulders. "I'm fine with the fallout. Audra's already been told to get Nichol or Jagger if the hit's too much for me." He looked over, blue eyes flickering with traces of Rhys as a wave of regret pulsed over them. "I don't remember his other imprisonments feeling like this."

"You need to feed," Nichol insisted, placing an unconscious man across Kaius's legs.

He looked down at the human, noting he had been washed clean and his overcoat sleeve rolled for quick access. "I will shortly," he replied, closing his eyes, and gritting his teeth as another burst of pain ripped through his head and traveled down his limbs.

Nichol squatted at his side, his hazel eyes monitoring his reactions to the punishment Rhys was receiving hundreds of miles away. "How is he?"

"Furious," he snarled. "Furious and determined."

He opened one eye to see Nichol grin. "Good. Once they release him, we'll lay low for a few years, then take out their entire haunt."

The pain dulled to a throb, providing him with a few moments to clear his thoughts. "There's only two left." He flashed his fangs at his eldest. "It will be an easy slaughter."

Nichol sat back on his haunches. "Two? I thought Rhys only took out three of the bloodline."

Pointing toward the small table beside the sofa, he chuckled with a combination of disbelief and pride. "The post boy brought that by last night. Rhys beheaded the fourth and fifth during his transport to the main haunt. Hence the increase in punishment."

Nichol snatched the letter, scanning it quickly. "He could be ended for this."

"He should have been ended two centuries ago." He lifted the man's wrist to his mouth. "But his unbreakable reputation proceeds him. Many are drawn to the challenge but few want to truly succeed in ending a legend."

He drained the rising fear from Mickey.

As with so many of Rhys's imprisonments, the catalyst behind the order had remained a mystery to him and Nichol. When pitted against more vengeful vampires, he had frequently intervened blindly, guessing Rhys's crime based on the severity of the physical repercussions and the amount of money he had to put forth in negotiations.

But Mickey was correct. Rhys had walked into this imprisonment willingly. Knowingly.

Resigned and ready.

CHAPTER TWENTY-ONE

Why is she so fucking calm?

Lis was completely relaxed as she positioned herself between Rhys's legs and leaned back against his chest.

"You've done this a lot," he muttered, pushing his spine further against the wall in a subconscious attempt to extricate himself from the situation. "I wasn't positive Derry maintained a continual link with you."

"Derry was pretty insistent I not age," she replied without a hint of nerves. "I was a little grossed out initially, but it passed. So we exchanged every few months to keep the link strong and ensure I stayed looking the same."

Every few months.

Feigning distraction with the hem of his cargos, he bent forward to adjust the length and to subtly shift her away from him. "So I guess I don't have to walk you through any of this then."

She scooted right back into place. "Nope."

Nope.

Fucking nope.

He brought his wrist to his fang and hesitated. "What are you doing?"

Her movements stopped. "Moving my hair to the side?"

"Why?"

"So you don't get hair in your mouth when you bite down," she said slowly, a tinge of suspicion in her voice.

"Is everything okay?"

"Fine," he grunted. "All right. We're doing this. Now. Be ready." He snapped his fangs once. "Now." He punctured her soft skin, drawing in a single mouthful before he withdrew and sunk into his own arm.

His fangs had barely dislodged from his wrist before he flung it around Lis's head toward her lips. He ground his teeth and squeezed his eyes shut while her fingers wrapped around his arm and drew his bleeding wrist to her mouth.

"Holy fuck!" he gasped involuntarily as she drew the first mouthful in and her existence exploded into the back of his mind. Dropping one leg to the floor, he dug his heel into the cement in a futile attempt to ground himself while her contentment, fear, regret, and anger swirled through his head. The constant burning of his tattoos flared and he fought against the overwhelming desire to sink his fangs back into her throat. He centered his efforts on keeping his arm still, focusing on the fire radiating through his veins and resisting the urge to shred the intricate designs on his skin.

Resisting the urge to drain the woman dry.

Fucking stop.

She continued to pull from his wrist, calmly oblivious to the turmoil ricocheting through his mind and rippling through his muscles.

Fucking stop.

Her own blood was taking on a dangerously irresistible scent, a peculiar mixture of her pleasing B-negative and his own bloodline.

FUCKING STOP.

With his blood in her system, she was already gaining strength. With the physical strength came a surge of exhilaration. He felt his chest rise and fall as he drew in unneeded oxygen, panting through the unexpected high she was transmitting. His eyes snapped open in the darkness and he arched his neck away from the vein screaming to him.

"I can't believe how good I feel!" she exclaimed, her tongue darting across his healing wrist. "I'd forgotten how good feeling good felt!"

He grunted, unable to respond and unwilling to try. She released his hand and he gave in to the burning itch on his bicep, zeroing in on the odd combination of relief and pain while he tore at his skin. Bursts of euphoria slashed through his head, intermingling with a growing concern.

"Rhys?"

He could hear her.

Hear the creaking of the mattress as she turned to face him.

Hear the strong heartbeat.

Hear the blood pumping through her veins.

"Rhys," she called out, her fingers grazing his neck and traveling along his jaw. "One mouthful isn't enough. It's your turn."

****

Fear.

Rhys paused a moment to assess the blast flashing through his mind.

It was intrusive.

Not his.

Lis.

He unhooked his fangs with a snarl, propelling himself backwards against the wall with a thud. The back of his head hit the cement, providing a momentary

153

reprieve from the barrage of concern and fear she was drowning him in.

"Rhys?"

He growled low, a feral warning for her to back the fuck off.

Get it the fuck together.

Her hand found his thigh and he snapped at her, grazing her fingers. He needed a minute. Ten. Or thirty. He needed a whole fuckload of minutes.

"You're scaring me," she whispered in the dark, her weight shifting toward the foot of the bed.

Didn't. Fucking. Notice.

Jumping to his feet, he stumbled clumsily across the cell, stopping only when he crashed into the bars of the enclosure. He hunched over, gripping his knees, and staring into the blackness of the room. Her fear ratcheted with the clamor of his movements, fueling his own turmoil.

"I need you to you calm the hell down," he snarled, his voice graveled as he sunk to his knees. "I really, really need you to just calm the fuck down right now."

So fucking dark.

The pounding of her emotions waned slightly as she began to breathe deeply. He zeroed in on the dull pain coming from the back of his skull while her fresh blood started to heal the damage he did when he bounced it off the concrete. The fright boomeranging in his head weakened. Worry swelled and curiosity seeped in.

"Stay back," he grunted as he caught the sound of her feet dropping to the floor. "All right...angel?"

She stilled immediately.

Closing his eyes, he focused on pushing her existence into the recesses of his mind where he shoved everything he wanted to forget. But unlike his memories, Lis appeared to fight, to press forward. Concentrating entirely on her presence, he barreled her back, knowing even then it would be little more than a temporary reprieve. When she was nothing more than an echo across his consciousness, he rose to his feet.

"Rhys?"

He walked slowly across the cell, carefully reorienting himself. "I'm going to rinse my arms off," he muttered, cringing internally at the weakness of his voice.

"Did you get enough?" she pressed, a flare of worry surging forth before he smashed it back again.

Ignoring her, he felt his way along the brick bathroom walls and turned the sink taps on full blast to drown out her voice and the thumping of her heart. Even without light, he knew his arms were shredded, the skin tightening as it healed under the drying blood. He scrubbed his tattoos methodically, keeping a tight rein on his mind and his core.

That went fucking well.

He ran some ice water through his hair, slicking it back before he tugged at his damp singlet, adjusting the fabric as it clung to his skin uncomfortably.

Fucking stalling.

The longer he hid in the bathroom, the harder her confusion pushed against the thin wall in his head.

And the harder it was to ignore the woman now occupying a room in his mind.

Ready or not, here I come.

Exiting the false security of the brick enclosure, he walked slowly back to her.

Her trepidation fluttered through his head a

millisecond before he heard her scooting away from him.

"Do you remember where I hung my other shirt?" he asked, stopping his approach. "This one will need to be scrubbed tomorrow night."

The slight shudder as she exhaled matched the wave of relief she pushed easily over the wall, before he could bat it back. "The far corner, hanging on the bar," she responded. "Did you get...are you...is everything okay?"

"Fine, sweetheart," he muttered as he began counting steps across the dark cell. "I'm just going to switch shirts and get some rest. You should, too."

****

"Would you just fucking stop?" Rhys grunted, leaning forward on his forearms to avoid Lis's hand. "I'm good. And I'll be a shit-ton better once you fall asleep."

Her fingers grazed his neck again before resting on his shoulder. Again.

"I don't understand why you're being so stubborn about this," she whispered in the blackness. "Just come up here. I feel horrible with you on that hard cement."

Big fucking surprise.

Her guilt had breached the walls of his head repeatedly over the past hour, its strength increasing as she became less tired and more agitated.

And it was that guilt, not the cold cement, keeping him wide awake and cranky.

That guilt, and the strange allure of the scent of their combined blood.

He lolled his head back and growled. "If I come up there, you'll shut up and go to bed, right?"

"Yes, sir."

He stood reluctantly and pushed her across the small mattress.

She had lost more weight since the lights had gone out.

A trickle of contentment inched through him as he reclined back, shoving the pillow toward her, and crossing his arms behind his head. "There. Happy?"

She hummed, snatched the pillow, and curled up at his side.

She shut up for precisely eight minutes, nineteen seconds.

"Rhys?"

He groaned as the contentment warming his mind morphed into curiosity and amusement. "No."

"You kind of freaked out earlier," she pressed on, her voice muffled against his shirt. "Are you..." She paused, her smile lifting her cheeks against his ribcage. "Is the great Rhys Kaius a link-virgin?"

Just fucking drain her already.

CHAPTER TWENTY-TWO

Lis ran her fingers along the collar of his shirt, relishing in the comfort of familiarity Rhys's closeness always brought her.

"Derry panicked the first time, too," she whispered, keenly aware of his discomfort with the topic. "Of course, there was a lot more blood and a lot less clothes involved when he linked to me."

Rhys tensed under her hand. "Were you injured?"

"Nothing major," she replied quietly. "And it was unintentional. He was more rabid than I'd ever seen him up until then, so I was more scared than hurt. It became easier for both of us over the years."

"Yeah, well, at least I know this is temporary," he grumbled.

Adjusting her position to encroach further into his space, she resumed tracing his collar. "Why have you never linked before?"

"Why would I?" he muttered. "It's invasive, irritating, and disorienting."

"Derry said it was reassuring, said he liked knowing when I was happy," she reminisced aloud before falling silent.

HIs hand covered hers, stilling her fingers. "So were you?" he inquired, his voice hesitant.

"Was I what?"

Releasing her hand, he moved a fraction away. "Happy. Were you happy?"

She frowned and sat up. "I've never wanted for anything," she began slowly. "Never had to ask twice. Derry and I traveled the world and met some of the most incredible people, stayed in some of the most luxurious hotels. I've been safe and fed and watched over. Never alone to fend for myself. So I suppose I couldn't really ask for more."

"That doesn't answer the question," he stated, a tinge of annoyance peppering his words. "Were. You. Happy."

"Sure," she replied brusquely. "Eventually, I guess."

"Eventually."

She hunched over her knees, hugging them tight to her chest. "Yeah, eventually. What does it matter now?"

When he didn't respond, her anger began to rise.

"What do you want to hear, Rhys? That you sat me on that bus and sent me off to my happily-ever-after?" she spat, her back going rigid. "That the past forty-eight years have been a living fairytale, a dream come true?"

"We've spoken hundreds of times since you came here, and not once did you indicate you were unhappy," he barked, rising from the bed. "I—holy fuck, Lis, dial back the anger a bit before I get really unpleasant."

"I've been 'dialing back the anger' since the night you put me on that goddamn bus!" she screamed, hurling the pillow toward his voice. "I've spent decades, Rhys, DECADES being paraded around like a prized pony, like some pretty little trinket on Derry's wrist. And after all those years of smiling for the camera and twirling on demand, that bastard had the gall to try and sell me to that despicable creature he called a son. I couldn't even walk away. I have nothing of my own. You got paid. Everything here belonged to Derry. Even me."

She sat back on her haunches, her shoulders shaking as she drew in frantic breaths.

"You should have—"

"What, Rhys?" she interrupted with a sneer. "Called you to come get me? What did you ask me every single time we spoke?" When he didn't respond, her voice grew more bitter. "*Lis, baby, tell me you're well,*" she mimicked. "You never asked. You demanded the answer you wanted to hear."

His bare feet walked closer to her, the familiar sauntering gait apparent even in the darkness.

"One dollar," he stated.

She frowned. "What?"

"I sold you to Derry for one dollar."

****

Rhys shoved his fisted hands deep inside the pockets of his cargos as he prepared himself for the onslaught of Lis's anger.

An anger he damn well deserved.

But the rush of fury didn't come. Neither did the blast of indignation or the wave of hurt.

Nothing.

Not even the steady thumping of her heart wavered.

He slowly freed one hand, reaching toward her and making brief contact with her arm to reassure himself she was still there.

A void.

"Do you remember when Jagger and I took off from the haunt? It was a few weeks before you came to California." He paused, knowing she wouldn't answer. "It was a routine outreach, just touching base with the coastal vamps and gathering any gossip that hadn't made its way across the mountains yet. The McConaughey haunt was last on the list before Jagg and I made our way back through Vegas."

She didn't stir, not a flicker of emotion rippling through his head.

"It was my first mission alongside Jagger since he returned. And I wasn't…I didn't deal with his deafness well," he muttered, running a hand through his hair. "I still don't, I guess. We had a situation last year where he…anyways, I was on edge for most of the venture."

The tiny stream of curiosity trickling into his thoughts relaxed him slightly.

"Our second night here, Thomas Derry began watching Jagger more intently. Like he was looking for something. Jagg's a pretty good lip-reader and he can track movements through vibrations, but it took a lot of practice to get there. It's really fucking impressive to watch now, but a few decades ago, there were still tells if you knew what to watch for. He was good enough to fool humans, but vamps? No fucking way. And Thomas, he was looking for an angle to exploit. He figured it out."

He crossed his arms over his chest and scratched absently at his tattoos.

"Jagg's always been our ghost. Our watcher. Even before he…he has the reputation of being one of the most lethal vamps in our haunt. He's fast, he's meticulous, and he's gone before the head hits the floor. You should see him in action. Really impressive. Probably the best assassin out there."

Her minuscule burst of pride sent a twitch down his neck. "Taking him out would be a prize win for any haunt with a bone to pick. Maybe an even bigger prize than me." He grinned wistfully. "He's such a reclusive bastard, I think his reputation is based more on the unknown than his actual ambushes."

He dropped to one knee and rested his forearms on his thigh. "The week before I put you on the bus, I was here. I took out Thomas McConaughey on the driveway when he arrived home. Unfortunately, I was sloppy, reacting instead of planning. Derry was in the car behind him and pulled up just in time to see his eldest's sludge hit the pavement."

Reaching forward in the dark, he tugged her hand. When she recoiled, he tightened his grip and brought it to his left tricep. He traced her finger slowly over the intricate grey loop. "The cells weren't quite as developed as they are now," he mused. "No beds, no chairs, no desks. Just cement and steel. The upgrades are a nice touch this time."

He continued to skim her finger over the marking, ignoring the small flicker of pity and focusing on the increasing curiosity. "I was in the cell opposite yours. Anyways, in my rush to silence Thomas, I didn't think the logistics through. I had nothing on Thomas, no reason I could provide Derry for the attack without giving up Jagger. On the first night, he took my fangs."

Running a tongue over his teeth, he shook his head slowly. "Jagg's deafness is more my hang-up than his own. He's adapted and evolved. He and Bianca Schumann are a thing now. I told you about her back when you were at the haunt. She... you know, I'm fucking rambling. Bee and Jagg are probably taking over the world while I stammer my ass through this. Fucking bastard doesn't need me babysitting him any more now than he did then. That was my point."

He huffed in frustration. "Holy hell, where was I? First night... second. The second night, Derry tore seven strips off my back and—" He stopped short, unwilling to recollect the night further. "And on the third night, he handed me a proposition I couldn't refuse."

"Me?" she asked, her voice hoarse.

He chuckled drily. "Not by name, sweetheart. He was on my waiting list for a Tender. Had been for several decades. Everything about him checked out, but his wish list was a little more detailed than most, carried a significant price tag, and had proven impossible to fill up until…"

Dropping her hand to her lap, he searched out her face and cupped her chin. "Those damn green eyes of yours," he muttered, picturing them clearly in his head. "Had they been blue or brown, I would have been sentenced to fifty years down here. But you fit the bill. A lovely little green-eyed nymph reminiscent of the lore of his homeland." He released her.

"I should've known who you'd eventually belong to the moment I saw you sashaying across that parking lot. The lack of red hair threw me, but everything else made you an absolute gem of a find. So I signed the deal."

Curiosity gave way to a dark heaviness settling uneasily in his mind. Though her heart beat remained steady, her breath had become deep and labored.

"You bought Jagger time to perfect his skills," he stated quietly as he sat back on his haunches. "I owed him that time, owed him my protection until he no longer needed me. So when I saw the deal, I took it. I was handed one dollar and my freedom in exchange for letting you go."

CHAPTER TWENTY-THREE

Lis pulled her knees to her chest and wrapped her arms tightly around them. Rhys had retreated to the far corner of the cell hours earlier, his presence noticeable only by the periodic scratching of his tattoos.

She came to terms with him decades ago, when the wistful fantasies of her youth were replaced by the mundane realities of adulthood.

But tonight, as the numbing gave way, it stung.

Trying to make out his form in the blackness, she squinted her eyes and held her breath. She knew precisely how he looked, casually leaning against the cell bars with one hand in his back pocket. The other arm would be flexing across his chest while he rubbed the tattoos she noticed had been irritating him since his arrival at the McConaughey haunt. She was pretty certain he was wearing the black tee, the one skimming the waistband of his cargos and riding up whenever he moved.

And she was damn certain he bought those shirts intentionally to show off his perfectly muscled body.

While her amazement over the visual stasis of vampires and their Tenders wore off long ago, she was still taken aback by Rhys's appearance when she saw him after all these years.

The vampire was dangerously beautiful.

The moment she laid eyes on him when he strode onto the bus fifty years ago, she was enthralled. The knowing smirk he wore, the dark, calculating eyes holding a glimmer of amusement, the self-assured swagger…her youthful naiveté latched on to the worldly confidence he exuded.

And by the time he had revealed what he was, she was already head-over-heels in puppy love.

Rhys didn't flinch when her bare foot made contact with his stomach. Launching herself across the room, she scrambled away from the creature sprawled on the sofa. His canines were on full display while she tugged fruitlessly on the locked door knob before throwing her shoulder against the small glass pane.

"Steel enforced and shatter-proof, honey," his voice came from behind her. "All you're going to do is damage that flawless skin of yours."

She spun on her heel, flattening herself to the wall and scanning the room frantically.

"I haven't moved," he drawled, stretching his arms across the back of the couch. "Stay over there if it makes you feel better. I'll talk, you listen. And if after I'm done my spiel you have any questions, I'll answer. Okay, baby?"

Baby.

He always used that term when he wanted her compliant.

It always worked.

Gingerly lowering her feet to the floor, she stood and began walking slowly across the cell. She kept her arms forward, fanning them out to orient herself. When her fingers grazed the cold steel of the bars, she used them to guide herself toward him.

"Three more steps," he said quietly as she approached.

She halted and drew in a deep, wavering breath. "I loved you."

"I know."

Dropping her head, she collected her thoughts. "I'm not finished." She paused, waiting for him to comment, to make some smart-ass retort. When he didn't, she straightened her spine. "I loved you. Blindly. I would have done anything for you." She hesitated. "I DID do anything for you. Everything you asked, every correction you made, every flippant endearment, I clung to. I warped them to fit the image of you—of us—I had created. You were a god to me."

"Bab—"

"NO!" she hissed, digging her finger into his chest. "When you made me walk the training room night after night in those damn heels, I loved you. When you sent me to your brothers, I loved you. Even when you sold me off to a stranger, dumping me in a bus station in the middle of the night, I loved you. And I hated myself for it."

He wisely stayed silent.

"It took years for me to look back at my time at your haunt without the gullible, silly romantic notions I had when I was young. To really see things for what they were." With a humorless laugh, she shook her head. "And do you know what the most warped thing about the realizations I came to was? I didn't hate you for it. I should have. I should now. But I finally understood. It was a business, and I was a commodity. A box on the shelf. And you never told me I was anything more than that. It was me who believed I was more. That WE were more. That we could be more."

She took a step back as a weighted emptiness

resettled in her. "I came to terms with all of it years ago, Rhys. It took a long time, but one night I was able to call you with an update and my stomach didn't knot up. After that, you were nothing more than a business associate on the other end of the phone line."

He was completely motionless. No rustle of clothing, no adjusting of his stance. She took another step backwards to increase the distance between them. "But what you're doing now is bullshit. I'm not here to alleviate your conscience, to be your confessional. You don't get to 'make it better' this late in the game. I'll continue to do my job only because I don't want to die in this cell, and I'll do anything to extend my time as long as I can. But we're business associates, not partners. I know now we never were. Your death wish is yours alone, and your atonements will die when you do."

****

Rhys strode over to the bed, pulling his shirt off. "That wet towel isn't going to do a damn thing for you," he said, tossing his tee in Lis's direction. "Wrap your hair in this and stay under the blanket."

"Yes, Rhys."

Retreating back to his corner, he listened as the chattering of her teeth finally stopped.

He hadn't spoken to her in hours, not since she silenced him with both her words and the complete nothingness of her emotions.

But the shower was now running only cold water, and a sick Tender was even more unpleasant than an angry one.

Though not nearly as unpleasant as an empty one.

He could pinpoint the moment he knew her girlish crush had morphed. It was one of the hazards of his

167

work, and the main reason he was quick to integrate his trainees into the rest of the haunt.

He had stalled with her. It was a mistake he never made again.

He looked over Nichol's shoulder, checking on the pretty nymph sitting on the grass, her attention wholly consumed by the intricate floral wreath she was creating.

"If she's a flight risk, she shouldn't be out here," Nichol muttered, examining his blade in the moonlight. "She's been granted too much freedom. If you won't link her to Boy, she should be inside."

Spinning his own knife in his hand, he repositioned himself in the makeshift sparring ring and ignored Nichol's pointed comment on his refusal to link Boy to her. "Lis needs to be outside," he said, glancing over at her again. "It's rejuvenating for her. Keeping her locked in the training quarters would be senselessly cruel. She won't run."

"If you're so certain, there's no need to continuously monitor her," Nichol retorted. "It's throwing your concentration and affecting your response time. Blades up."

Turning his attention to their training, he and Nichol traded taunts and hits until Nic had enough, pinning him to the ground and embedding his knife into the earth beside his head.

"Focus on anticipation," Nichol groused, rising of him and offering a hand. "You're all attack, little defense. I've been telling you this for centuries. Get it through that hard-ass head."

He stood, passing his weapon over. "Tell Jagger this thing is shit. The steel warps under the slightest pressure." He waited until his brother began his trek back into the haunt before looking over at Lis.

Who was no longer there.

"Goddamnit," he muttered, storming over to the abandoned collection of stems and buds. He scented the air, cursing again when the wind muddied her path. "Fucking Lis."

His booted feet stomped heavily over the terrain as he scoured the lands. Her aversion to insects would keep her far from the densely treed acres, leaving him with the flattened grounds surrounding the topside of the haunt.

"Lis?" he called, hoping none of his brethren were in the area to witness his losing of a trainee. "Where are you, angel?"

His eyes caught a movement across the field. She skipped toward him, her wreath in one hand and a bushel of hollyhocks in the other.

"Look what I found!" she squealed in excitement, her feet skidding to a halt when she drew close enough to see him clearly, to see the blood from his sparring injuries still fresh and marking most of his exposed skin. "Oh my God. What did he do to you?"

He schooled his face, glaring at her sternly to hide his relief. "You weren't given permission to roam the grounds," he growled.

She paled, her green eyes staring at the healing lacerations on his temples. "I'm sorry, Rhys."

Pulling the flowers into his arms, he turned and walked toward the haunt, her shuffled footsteps falling into step behind him. "If I can't trust you to obey the rules out here, we can't do this anymore," he lectured as they entered the garage. "You've been granted a freedom most trainees don't get until the start of their second year. Don't make me regret this."

He led her down the halls, nodding at Mick as they passed. Mickey's mouth opened, snapping shut when he took in his harsh expression and her hung head.

They entered the training rooms in silence. Lis placed her wreath on the table while he rifled through the cupboards for a vase. "The exit to the haunt will be locked again," he stated while he filled it with water. "Do I need to lock these doors as well again?"

He turned to her, crossing his arms in expectation as her gaze fixated on his injuries again. "I need to hear you say it, honey," he prodded.

With an infinitesimal shake of her head, she took a step forward, her hand reaching up before she remembered her place. "You don't need to lock the doors," she whispered.

Leaving his trainee to her thoughts, he made his way down the halls to his room. He pulled his boots off, flicked the lock of his door, and tossed his muddy footwear into the corner. The shower was steaming hot as he stepped in, the water turning pink as dried blood was washed from his face and hair.

Nichol was right. He had been too soft on her, too indulgent.

But the thought of linking her to Boy—to anyone— wasn't on the table. He didn't give a rat's ass if his own process dictated it, Lis wouldn't be monitored by anyone except him.

Wrapping a towel around his hips, he walked into his bedroom and froze, listening to the rustling of fabric and scenting an unmistakable floral scent coming from the hall. He crossed the room, opening his door slowly.

"Should you be here?" he asked, gripping the top of

the door frame, and cocking a brow.

Lis toyed with the hem of her nightdress as her gaze lifted to his healed temples. He held still while her hand rose to his face, her fingers running along his brow while the worry lining her features disappeared. "You're okay," she breathed out, her arms wrapping around his waist as she gripped him tightly.

He held position, his fingers digging into the wooden door frame. "Back to bed, baby," he instructed when she reluctantly released him.

Something shifted in her eyes as she backed up, a wave of relief crossed with something he didn't want to acknowledge. "I just had to know you were okay," she whispered, her hands clasping in front of her chest.

He closed his door, crossing his arms as he leaned against it and waited for the sound of her retreating footsteps. When an hour passed, and her breathing slowed outside his room, he cracked the door and looked down at the woman curled against the frame. Pushing the door tight, he flicked off all but one light and flopped onto his bed, reaching for the phone on his nightstand.

"Mick," he greeted flatly when the line picked up. "Do you have any plans for tomorrow night?"

CHAPTER TWENTY-FOUR

Kaius sat back, his chair rocking back dangerously. "That, Molly, is a Reichstag fire."

His hauntmates sat in silence around the com room table, their eyes locked on Nichol's monitor.

The St. Louis news crews covering the mayhem had retreated into the upper offices of the surrounding downtown buildings, their aerial perspectives providing viewers with a good sense of the chaos filling the streets. Despite the dim footage lit only by the streetlights, the Kaius haunt was able to make out the dozens and dozens of Deviants crawling up from the sewers and launching themselves toward the retreating crowds.

Turnings gone wrong, Deviants were always put down immediately. Their id-driven impulses combined with vampire strength was too dangerous to allow to exist.

Only the most twisted of vamps would intentionally create one.

Or dozens.

Kaspars Dovidas and the ancient vamp Chen fit that twisted bill.

"I thought Deviants were supposed to be mindless," Audra stated, her cat eyes narrowing as she took in the carnage. "This is a hive mentality. A concerted group effort." She pointed to the streams of jolting movements stretching through the streets from the news helicopter filming angle. "They're working together to fan out, to cover as much ground as possible."

Nichol nodded, his gaze never leaving the screen. "Dovidas has probably scouted the area thoroughly and provided a base plan. With male Deviants, the attack would be less coordinated. But females…it'll take weeks, maybe months, for the vamp division to eliminate every one of them."

Pushing his hood off, Jagger leaned onto the table. "Once footage from the ground hits social media, our species is fucked," he growled. "People will start identifying the Deviants, connecting them to the missing women across the south. There's no recovering from this."

Kaius clenched his jaw, trying to keep count of the number of Deviants making their ways through the streets of the Missouri city. Fifty-three. Fifty-eight. "Anyone know the likelihood of Deviants turning more Deviants?"

"They shouldn't have the patience for it," Louis replied, his voice awed by the visuals filling the monitor. "But all I know is what I've heard about males. Females…what the hell was Dovidas thinking? This isn't an attack. This is a fucking scourge. A plague."

The hauntmates grumbled in agreement.

"So what are we going to do about it?" Bianca inquired, placing a hand on Jagg's knee. "If we leave within the hour, we can be on site in two nights' time."

"No fucking way," Nichol snorted. "Special ops will be on the ground before dawn tonight. If we head into the fray, we become targets. Right now, anything with fangs and a shitty attitude is going to be SOS."

Molly frowned. "SOS?"

"Shoot on sight," Nichol replied, cocking his thumb

and forefinger in her direction, and rolling his eyes when Dominic let loose a low snarl.

Kaius spun a pen between his fingers, looking away from the computer screen. "Nichol's correct," he said slowly, his mind whipping through different scenarios and the potential outcomes of each. "Bianca, you and Jagger can feed attack information to the military through your network. If they approach these female Deviants as they do vampires, the death toll will rise significantly. Recommend a city-wide lockdown and day patrols. We can't be guaranteed these ones are solely night-walkers until sunrise. And even then, in their numbers, the oldest may have a higher tolerance than the newest turnings. If you don't receive a response in an hour, forward the information to the news networks. The quicker this is contained, the better."

Jagger rose, extending his hand for Bianca. "The sooner the Deviants are taken out, the less likely they are to be captured and probed," he stated. "We'll name them as a rogue haunt, one we're eager to have taken out. I'll be sending out a quick message to our supporters as well, informing them of our advice to stay away and stay inside. If anyone has anything else to add regarding the Deviants, text me or Bee."

"Make sure the messages are fucking encrypted," Nichol grumbled. "Better yet, route the messages through me and I'll send them out through the main server. I'm not completely trusting the security of the laptops right now."

As the pair exited the room, Molly pulled her legs up under herself and squinted at the screen. "Could we have sound?" she asked.

With a huff of impatience, Nichol turned the volume

up and the frantic voice of the reporter filled the room.

"Officials are now putting the estimated number of creatures at seventy. Reports from citizens who have fled the area are placing the casualty numbers at thirty and rising," the woman stated, her speech rapidly increasing in speed. "We have been told the military is mobilizing and will be arriving on site to assist local law enforcement. As of now, only two of the creatures have been killed."

Mickey ran a hand through his hair and glanced over at him. "I don't think they've connected the Deviants to vampires yet."

"It's only a matter of time," he replied, easing the tension Mick was funneling from the rest of their brethren.

"Then that's where we need to focus," Audra interjected. "If some of these things are taken down in broad daylight, the connection between vampires and Deviants will be muddled temporarily. We need to prepare a spin placing us in a good light before a definitive link is established."

He noted Boy's subtle nod of agreement.

Mick noticed it as well, his blue eyes narrowing and his middle finger lifting quietly behind his seat and out of Audra's line of sight.

"A social media campaign would be most effective," Nichol muttered, sliding his chair across the floor, and pulling his phone off his desk. "We need to prepare for the possibility Dovidas will openly take responsibility. And for the possibility he'll place responsibility on us."

"Fuuuuuuuuuck," Louis groaned, slouching in his seat. "I think I'm going to take a pass on this. I'm heading to Canada for a few months."

"No, you aren't," Mick snarked, booting Louis's chair. "You're going on YouTube and telling the world what a peace-loving, amicable bastard you are, and you're doing it with a smile."

Kaius caught the quick grin forming on Audra's face before she schooled her expression into one of disapproval. "It's not a bad idea," she said as she elbowed Mick gently. "Though Louis isn't spokesman material."

Kai pushed back from the table and stood while Molly leaned into Dominic, murmuring in his ear about his photogenic qualities. "Nichol, you and Mick will continue to monitor the news reports. Louis, Dominic, and Molly, you three will scan the various social media formats for ground footage and anything identifying Dovidas or Chen. We're looking for visuals, mentions, and anything linking the Deviants to vampires. Audra, I would like you to begin putting together a media defense plan. Boy, begin preparing the vehicles in case we require a speedy exit from here."

He strode out of the room, his phone buzzing unanswered in his back pocket. As he neared his bunker, Mickey caught up to him. "I told you I didn't need you to pull Rhys off me," he stated, following him into the bunk.

Tossing his phone onto the desk, he walked over to his closet and pulled out a large duffle bag. "I haven't. There's been a shift in his projection," he responded, opening his dresser drawers, and methodically pulling items out. "I initially thought the intense emotions he was channeling a few nights ago signaled his release. And then the suddenness of the void—" He paused. "Can you still identify his line?"

Mick nodded, his gaze dropping to the bag. "It's there. But it's completely dry."

"If the stream is there, Rhys is as well," he explained, returning to his closet to pull a pair of boots off the shelf. "When he is ended, the line will disappear completely."

He was keenly aware of Mickey tracking him through the room as he reached into the bathroom, pulling a few items from the counter, and tossing them on top of his socks. "Rhys learned long ago how to manipulate his deepest of emotions, how to hide them below his stream," he continued. "Perhaps the emptiness we're receiving now is what he's covered successfully over the centuries. Or perhaps it's what he aims to project." He smirked at Mickey. "Your mate would have had her work cut out for her if Rhys had willingly lain on her sofa."

Mick looked back at the bag. "She would've loved the opportunity," he muttered distractedly. "Where…when are you out of here?"

Zipping the duffle, he hefted the bag onto the floor and sat on his bed. "I'll be leaving at dusk tomorrow," he responded. "I'll be making the announcement when we reconvene in a few hours."

With a nod, Mickey walked from the bunker, his boots echoing down the hall.

He stared at his buzzing phone, willing it to go silent. He could ignore the call for another hour at most, but his leaving was inevitable. Delaying the news was merely a well-rehearsed exercise in futility before he walked out of his haunt again.

Nichol would avert his gaze, his hazel eyes flashing

with deep-seated, deserved resentment.

Jagger would nod solemnly in acceptance before he, too, looked away. Only this time, he wouldn't exchange a knowing look with Rhys as he did so.

Dominic would grumble his protest before he slouched down in his chair and stared at the table.

Mickey would confront him with bitter demands for answers that never came. Then his anger would morph into a frustrated dejection, transforming into a hardened resolve throughout the upcoming week as he accepted the burden of the haunt's emotions and took control.

Boy would give no indication he even heard the announcement, save for the slight tensing in his jaw.

Rhys's festering anger, projected loudly with his hostile snark, would no longer draw the attention of the others, would no longer rally the rest of the hauntmates in defense of Kaius.

He leaned back against the sofa and closed his eyes.

He had been prepared for Rhys's end during most of his second-eldest's first few centuries. The imprisonments, the near-misses, the unapologetic smirk Rhys wore whether he donned silks or chains. He readied himself for the moment Rhys was no longer.

But as time passed, and Rhys sauntered on, he became complacent.

Alessandro Callini greeted Kaius as he walked the stairs into the grand hall.

"Your child will be released shortly," the haunt leader stated, motioning him toward the sitting room. "I have several women of varying tastes assembled for your pleasure."

With a nod, he entered the room and surreptitiously scanned the area for danger. "Rhys will be travel-

ready?" he inquired, summoning a curvaceous brunette to his side as he sat.

Callini chuckled, flanked by two blonde women as he took his own seat. "He is being fed as we speak. While I cannot guarantee he will be a pleasant travel companion, he is capable of movement."

He indulged in his meal quickly, unwilling to pass up the opportunity to reach peak strength before Rhys was released.

"Ah, there he is," Callini called out, rising to his feet. "A quick signature, and he's all yours, Kaius Khthonios."

Fighting the urge to assess Rhys in front of his host, he scrawled his name across the release order. "I hope our alliance has not been irreparably soured," he stated as he bowed and retreated toward his child. "We are well-matched and well-placed."

Rolling the paper into his hands, Callini tucked the scroll into his coat pocket. "Over the past decade, your child has lived up to his reputation," he responded with a fangy grin. "He is unbreakable. And I am honored to maintain our affiliation. Providing, of course, he keeps his distance from my connected mate."

Kaius muttered his assurances swiftly, eager to remove Rhys from the haunt. He kept his eyes straight ahead as he walked through the grounds, monitoring Rhys's proximity through the heavy footfalls behind him.

Once the pair reached the road, hidden from view by the surrounding trees, he turned toward Rhys. "Nichol is up the road, minding the horses and carriage."

Rhys's dark eyes gazed down the narrow path as he nodded and began to walk silently. He followed, carefully assessing the slight limp in Rhys's gait, the peculiar stretching of his arms, and the nearly imperceptible flinch accompanying the sounds of the night.

As Nichol came into view, Rhys slowed.

"Get in," Nichol barked, his relief over seeing his brother overshadowed by his impatience to leave the inhospitable territory.

Kaius folded his long form into the carriage, holding the door open.

"I'm walking."

Nichol scoffed, elbowing Rhys as he passed him to join Kai. "Get in, princess. It's a long way home."

He stared at his youngest for a moment before pulling the door shut. "Lead the horses, Rhys."

A decade in a stone tomb, broken up by feedings every two months. Most vamps would have fallen into their feral core with little hope of recovery, driven mad by the isolation and confinement.

But it was Rhys. And Rhys always survived.

CHAPTER TWENTY-FIVE

"Fucking FUCK!" Rhys snarled as his eyes snapped open to stare into the blackness of the cell. He gripped the bars behind his head, hoisting himself to his feet and stretching his long arms up over his head. When Lis's breathing changed, he stilled and waited for her to resettle.

A shift of the mattress.

A rustling of the blanket as she rolled over.

Blissful quiet.

Keeping his steps light, he paced the enclosure while Lis slept. Over the past few days, he noticed her presence in his mind was strongest when she was asleep, her reserved emptiness giving way to a myriad of other emotions.

Fear.

Hurt.

Anger.

But as negative as her unguarded emotions were, they were immensely preferable to the numbing void filtering through his head during her waking hours, augmenting his own hollowness. Until she rose, he could focus on her misery, using it to center himself in the pitch dark of the cell, to remain grounded in the present. It was keeping his core at bay, keeping his mind clear of the agitation the blackness of the room brought.

The sudden change in her heart rate stilled his feet.

"Rise and shine, angel," he greeted, ignoring the

twinge of relief his cellmate's waking gave him every evening.

She was sleeping more now. Longer.

Without a word, she moved across the floor toward the brick washroom.

Since the night she had unleashed on him, she hadn't spoken to him outside of formal Tender responses to his suggestions. His feeble attempts to initiate conversation were met with silence as she filled her time walking the perimeter of the cell and taking small bites of the scant food left.

He waited patiently, straightening the blanket, and adjusting the weakened metal frame of the bed. When she finally emerged, he sat and called to her.

"We need another exchange," he stated, alerting her to his location. She froze in place. "Your meals aren't going to keep you going much longer. If we supplement you frequently enough, we can stave off the worst of the starvation effects for a few more weeks."

She drew in a deep breath. "Yes, Rhys."

He glowered into the darkness. He fucking despised that phrase now.

"Get over here, sweetheart," he called out, forcing his voice to remain unaffected by her standard response. As she drew closer, he reached out to guide her to his side. The tension in her body when she sat was unnerving, a complete turn from their first exchange. He leaned forward, resting his elbows on his knees. "We can hold off for another night or two if you prefer," he muttered.

When she remained at his side, he straightened his back. "All right. Let's get the angle figured out before I open a vein and bleed all over the bed," he growled, her bitter compliance piquing his ire.

She stood wordlessly and walked in front of him. Nudging his knees apart slightly, she wedged herself between them, her hand gripped his forearm, and she lifted it over his head. "This will work," she said flatly, releasing his arm and standing motionless again.

"Fan-fucking-tastic," he replied, using his fang to inelegantly shred his wrist open. "Enjoy."

Remorse.

He hesitated a moment before lifting his bleeding arm to her. A cool trail of liquid trickled down his forearm before the heat of her mouth latched on to the laceration. Digging his free hand into the mattress, he pushed past his ingrained aversion to blood-letting and focused on the steadily increasing contentment she projected. He closed his eyes and wrapped himself in the emotion as she drank, leaning forward to rest his head against her dangerously concave stomach.

"I fucking hate the dark," he muttered absently, strangely calmed by the waves of serenity lapping through his mind from the space she occupied. But when her muscles tightened, he pulled back. "Fuck," he mumbled, flexing his arm to alleviate its weight in her hand. "Sorry."

An incomprehensible blizzard of emotion suddenly rose in his head, exploding like fireworks against his own thoughts. "Goddamnit, Lis," he grunted as his free hand punctured the mattress. Bracing himself for the continued onslaught, he grit his teeth and zeroed his attention on the searing fire traveling the veins of his biceps.

Then, as quickly as it rose, the storm receded.

The rhythmic pulse of contentment resumed,

erasing all evidence of the assault Lis inadvertently unleashed. Her small hand gingerly sought out the back of his head and brought him back to her stomach.

****

Lis reluctantly pulled away from Rhys's healed wrist, hesitating before she guided it to her waist.

His grip tightened infinitesimally. "Are you sure you got enough?" he asked, his voice muffled by the fabric of her shirt.

"I'm sure."

Logically, she knew the wisest move now would be to step back first, to put as much distance between herself and Rhys Kaius as she could in their cramped enclosure. She needed to retain the delicate balance of power she established nights earlier. Her diminishing hope of escape required her full attention, with every thought revolving around conserving her energy and maintaining her resolve. The only part of Rhys welcome in that sphere was his rejuvenating blood.

But she remained, absently stroking his hair, and staring ahead into the nothingness as the minutes ticked by.

She didn't care much for the dark, either.

She picked up on his aversion to darkness during her first months in the Kaius haunt. Dim lights and candles were a constant in the Tender training rooms. At first, she chalked it up to a comfort level for her, a simple way of ensuring she could move easily through her new living quarters regardless of his presence. But as time passed and her range of movement expanded, she began to notice the faint light escaping under Rhys's bedroom door. Day and night, the light stayed on.

The thought entertained her at first. Mental images

of the hulking, swarthy vampire sleeping beside a nightlight brought more than one smile to her face over the initial months.

But the more she learned about him, the less humorous his dislike of darkness became.

She watched him watch Jagger, his casual saunter taking on a predatory gait and the glint of amusement flickering in his dark eyes morphing into a hardened wariness. He would stalk Jagg through the haunt's grounds, staying hidden in the shadows while the hooded vampire trained in the fields, his muscles tensing whenever Jagg became injured.

She listened, enthralled, when the other vamps traded wild tales of Rhys's escapades from times and places she would never fully grasp. Images of the nightlight were replaced with visions of him removing the heads of vampires who threatened his hauntmates and walking unflinchingly into unfriendly territory with nothing but a blade and his cockiness.

And she observed him as he sparred fearlessly with his brothers, unconcerned with the deep lacerations marring his body and turning her stomach, sending spikes of panic through her with every slash. Her reaction to the training battles was always tempered with the roll of his eyes and a smirk to ease her distress and calm her frazzled nerves.

If Rhys Kaius disliked the dark, there was a damn good reason.

She tightened her hold on his head a fraction. "Thank you," she whispered, her voice still sounding loud in the cement cell.

He tensed under her hands. "Just keeping my own meal fresh," he muttered, pulling away slowly.

Her hands dropped immediately. "Of course. But thank you anyways, Rhys." With her heart pounding in her ears, she took a step back.

"Goddamnit Lis," he groaned, holding her in place and resting his forehead back on her stomach. "Just shut up, all right? If you shut up, I'll shut up, and we can just share silence without fucking it up." He nudged her arms up gently. "Now, as you were."

****

"Rhys?"

He shook his head against her, lightly tapping Lis's hip bone as he did. "You lasted six minutes," he grumbled. "Let's try and beat that record."

When her fingers gripped his hair and tugged his head back, he knew there would be no return to the brief serenity he'd found.

C'est la vie.

"Fine," he said, lightly swatting her hands away and leaning back on his elbows. "What would you like, sweetheart?"

She knelt before him and lay her head on his knee, intertwining her fingers with his. The waves of contentment were shifting, the heaviness slowly returning.

"Up," he ordered. "Your weak little human body is overwhelmed by the powerful stallion blood you ingested. You need a nap."

With an inelegant snort, she crawled over him, her knee dangerously close to causing some real damage to his lower region.

As she made herself comfortable, he sunk to the cement floor, keeping one hand available on the bed.

Just in case.

She dropped off quickly. Too quickly. With the amount of blood she took in, her energy should have spiked for hours.

Feeling under the blanket, he made contact with her hand. Even with his own tepid body temperature, her fingers were cold to the touch.

Three weeks.

He wrapped his hand around hers and leaned back in a futile attempt to make himself comfortable.

****

"Lis," Rhys hissed as he felt around the floor for his boots. "Baby, I'm going to need you to get up. Now."

The rumbling of vehicle engines filtering into the cell lessened slightly while he spoke.

As she sat up, her speech frighteningly unintelligible, he dropped his laces for a moment and reached back on the bed to place a staying hand on her leg. "We have company, angel."

With his boots secure, he rose from the floor and skulked closer to the exit, focusing on the timbre of the voices as they moved through the haunt with heavy steps.

"Rhys?"

Coherent.

"Here," he whispered, making his way back to her. "I'm going to need you to stay silent, okay honey?"

"Who is it?"

Military.

"Don't know, sweetheart. Now shush."

He tracked the movements as the footsteps fanned out from the main hall of the haunt, narrowing his attention to the group approaching the basement door.

Nine.

"Lis," he said slowly. "I want you to stand up and

get into the bathroom."

"But what if—"

"Now," he growled, listening as the footsteps began to descend the stairs.

She scrambled past him, her bare feet padding swiftly across the floor.

"All right, baby," he said, walking to the middle of the room. "Cover your eyes, and don't come out unless I call the order."

CHAPTER TWENTY-SIX

Lis's soft voice whispered from behind the brick barrier. "What's happening?"

Rhys's head dropped to his chest momentarily. "Probably waiting on a lock pick," he hissed as he returned his attention to the muffled discussions on the other side of the steel door.

"Maybe it's Fallon."

"It's 2 p.m," he muttered. "Remember when we practiced shutting up? We're going to try that again." He readied his stance as he caught the tinny sound of a cheap pick. "Stay out of sight, baby."

A sudden hum of electricity and blinding light temporarily incapacitated him as the heavy steel door swung open. He forced his eyes to remain trained on the entrance while his vision adapted, and the murky figures became clear.

"Put your hands up where we can see them!" one of the men leading the group shouted, his face partially concealed behind the glass of his helmet and his weapon locked on the cell.

Cocking a brow, he unhooked his thumbs from his cargos and extended his arms out. The militia spread throughout the cramped pathway, scanning the empty cells for movement. One by one, they booted the doors of the three unlocked cells, assessing the tiny, bricked bathroom of each before all attention zeroed in on him.

"Keep those hands open. How many of you are in

there?" the leader demanded while motioning his group to spread out.

"There's only ever one of me," he responded with a fangy grin. "I do, however, have a rather bland meal cowering in the washroom."

With a barked order from the commander, half the men dropped their rifles to their sides and withdrew flashlights.

"You got any weapons in there?" the leader asked, peering through the scope of his gun, and scanning the cell.

He smirked and glanced down at his crotch. "Nothing dangerous to you."

A stream of UV light slashed across his chest and face and the commander lowered his rifle. "OFF!" he yelled back toward the others. "Tell your partner to come out."

He remained immobile against the searing welts on his jaw and hidden under his shirt. "My *cellmate* will come out once you and I are formally introduced," he drawled, rolling his shoulders, and stretching his neck. The movement set off another flash of light across his stomach.

"OFF!" the leader snarled, taking a step closer to the cell bars. "Andrew Heisner, VEA. If you walk forward slowly and allow a pat-down, you can lower your arms while we sort a few things out."

He sauntered to the bars, locking his arms behind his head as two officers reached into the cell hesitantly and began to check him over. He locked his gaze on Heisner. "Vampire Enforcement Agency? Cute jackets. Tell your boys they don't have to be so timid. I've been down here a while and could use a little rough handling."

When the taller of the men snatched his hands away briefly, he grinned.

Heisner didn't look impressed.

"He's clean," the shorter man called out, backing away from the enclosure quickly.

"You can drop 'em," Heisner said to him, pulling a notepad from his jacket. "We received a call about a vampire holding a woman hostage against her will at this address. I assume you're Rhys Kaius?"

He gave a slow nod. "As you can tell, Andy, the woman isn't the only one being held."

The commander frowned, his thin lips drawing tight. "I'm going to need to see the woman in question before we address that," he stated. "Send her out and we can go from there."

Crossing his arms over his chest, he took a step away from the bars. "Well, Andy, I'd like to reach an agreement before I introduce you to my dinner."

Ignoring the disgusted muttering coming from his group, Heisner assumed the same stance as Rhys. "Like what?"

He tilted his head and scanned the group. Bulked up men, most of them close to his height and armed to the teeth with rifles, handguns, and UV lights. Their stillness and stances indicated heavy military training.

Sending in the big guns now.

He checked in on Lis's breathing and heart rate.

Labored. Steady.

She was broadcasting a constant stream of anticipation and worry, the emotions strong enough to be noticeable but continuous enough to be ignored at will.

Plan A.

"I assume I'll be taken in at dusk. You probably

already know I'm unregistered and obviously unmarked. Which means you have no data on what kind of prisoner I'll make. With that on the table, we're left with two choices," he mused aloud. "I can go easy, or I can make this a really long fucking day for all of you."

Heisner lifted a hand to his men, staying their movements.

"Thanks, Andy." He flashed a grin at the officers. "I want a guaranteed meal before I'm released from here. I don't fucking care if it's a boulevard call girl or Officer Stewart over there." He paused to wink at the man, running his tongue over his fang when Officer Stewart sputtered a few choice words. "I'll even sink as low as a few blood bags, if it's the best you can do. You have five hours until dusk to get me fed before I become disagreeable."

Heisner pocketed his notepad and yanked a phone from his back pocket. "I'll put in a request for a few bags now. Send out your companion."

He clucked his tongue. "My *meal* stays put—and unharmed—until you provide a replacement."

The commander glanced at the bricked room. "I'm going to need confirmation the woman is alive before I submit an order."

"Female," Rhys called out, ignoring Lis's quick spike of annoyance amidst her pulsing apprehension. "Tell the officers you're doing fine."

He kept his eyes on the men as they went still.

"I'm doing just fine, *sir*," she called through the wall, her voice strong even if her pulse wasn't.

Heisner's brows furrowed. "I'm going to need visual confirmation."

He stared the man down.

No out.

His mind blasted through various scenarios. His only bargaining chips were the promised safety of the unseen woman, and his promise of cooperation.

In other words, he had nothing.

He had nothing, and the strength of Lis's heartbeats was wavering.

"Female," he said, walking backwards toward the brick enclosure, "I want you to come out and say hello to the officer."

He tracked the opening door in his peripheral and maintained an unaffected expression when he caught sight of her appearance for the first time since the lights had gone out. Her cheeks had hollowed, giving her face a gaunt, unhealthy frailty. Her clothes hung on her frame, accenting her jutting hipbones and the scrawniness of her arms. Even her hair, with its godforsaken unnatural hue, hung limply down her back and highlighted her angular cheekbones.

She needed out, stat.

She exited the bathroom, her hands extended as she turned slowly for Heisner's visual assessment. The officers began exchanging looks, their weapons held tight.

"Ma'am," Heisner called over, his thumb moving rapidly over his phone screen, "I'm going to need you to walk this way nice and slow."

His arm shot out, halting her progression. "If she had a weapon, she would have turned it on me by now, Andy."

Ignoring him, Heisner continued to address her. "Officer Heisner," the man corrected as he patting his rifle subconsciously. His group picked up on the subtle sign, their own weapons of choice zeroing in on the pair. "Ms. Lis Bruckner. There are three outstanding warrants for your arrest, Ms. Bruckner: Association with vampires, collusion with vampires, and aiding and abetting the vampire agenda."

Fuck.

Transfixed by the gun barrels pointed in her direction, Lis froze in place.

"Rhys?" she whispered, eyes turning to him for guidance.

He kept his gaze fixed on the lead officer. "I didn't give you permission to speak," he snarled, refusing to look her way as he went in for one final push. "Heisner. Two bags, and you get your quarry unharmed."

The leader's finger hovered over the trigger of his gun. "Negotiation time's over," the man retorted. "Ms. Bruckner's facing federal prosecution for treason to the species. You'd be doing her a favor if you ate her."

Lis's breath caught in her throat. He could feel his fangs extending past his lower lip as he stared down Heisner. His plan of getting her released from the cell as a victim of the big bad vamp evaporated.

Treason to the species.

"Walk this way, Ms. Bruckner," the officer barked. "Hands where I can see 'em."

Her feet remained rooted on the spot as she frantically scanned the room for an escape she damn well knew didn't exist. The spike in her pulse was approaching dangerous levels for her weakened system, the imperceptible stutters of her heartbeat setting his own nerves on edge.

Plan. Fucking. B.

As her distressed eyes met his, all hell broke loose

in the small cell.

****

"Release the woman!" Heisner hollered, his voice merely adding another layer to the din in the cement room while the officers scattered their positions to gain better aim with their lights.

Rhys tightened his hold, his fangs strategically puncturing Lis's throat while he shielded her from the cocked rifles at his back. He brought his wrist up to his mouth to reopen the wound before he pushed it back against her lips to give her a final burst of strength.

"When I let go, run to them," he whispered. "I want full-on Drama Queen complete with begging for help, baby."

He caught sight of a small waft of smoke and pulled back, releasing her unceremoniously while he dropped to his knees. Instead of tearing past him like he instructed, her feet remained in place, her screams piercing the air and his eardrums as she stared in horror at his smoking back.

Heisner began shouting commands to her, echoed by the other men.

"Lis," he hissed through the commotion. When she tore her gaze off his injuries, he rolled his eyes and winked. He feigned a half-hearted lunge in her direction, sending her scrambling toward the unlocked cell door.

The number of UV lights increased as she exited the cell, holding him stationary until the lock was reattached. He made a few grandiose attempts to charge the bars, taking the brunt of each hit in his unburnt shoulder while Heisner continued to bark commands into the room.

"Stay back!" the leader shouted, the barrel of his rifle wedged into the cell. "Get Bruckner out of here and to the station. Yes, you fucking cuff her! And call ahead for a medic."

Three officers escorted Lis through the heavy steel door, her hands secured at her back and a dozen puncture holes dotting her neck.

Once the door shut, he ended his futile assault on the cell bars and stood motionless in the middle of his enclosure, unflinching against the barrage of lights searing holes into his skin and singeing his clothes.

"OFF!" Heisner ordered, lowering his own weapon.

They stared each other down for several minutes while the officer's radio buzzed intermittently with updates from the patrol car carrying Lis away from the haunt.

"I offered to go easy," he finally stated, crossing his arms over his damaged chest. "Should've taken me up on that."

Heisner snorted. "We'll do round two at dusk," he grumbled, his breathing still heavy from the activity.

"Get a few bags down here, and I might let you live through round two," he suggested, grinning as the remaining men exchanged hushed awe at the extent of the burns covering his body. He smirked. "The young Cali vamps aren't keeping you in shape, are they, boys?" Turning his attention back to Heisner, he straightened his spine and cocked a brow.

"You need to get me from here," he pointed toward the steel door, "through there, up the stairs, down the hall, out the door, across the walkway, into the van, and then do it all in reverse once we arrive at the cop shop." He rolled out his shoulders, further opening one of the scorched wounds on his pecs and letting the blood trickle. "What's it going to be, Andy? I can go easy, or I can go hard. And right now, I'm feeling a mite disagreeable."

CHAPTER TWENTY-SEVEN

"Head down and keep walking," Heisner grunted at Rhys as they exited the back of the police van.

Ignoring the orders, he glanced around the sidewalk at the throng of reporters pushing toward them. Cameras clicked frantically and he flashed a fanged smile, straightening his back and striding casually to the open doors. "I could put on a little show," he offered quietly to Heisner, running his tongue along one long tooth when a brave photographer ventured close. "Rear up, struggle a bit. I'll throw in some rabid drooling, too. Makes for good headlines."

Heisner's rifle dug into his hip in response.

"You're never going to advance your career if you refuse to play to the cameras," he cautioned in a hush. "I can make you head of the department in forty seconds flat."

"Just walk," the officer huffed under his breath, his anxiousness to have Rhys contained in the station's holding cells obviously driving his mood.

Taking his time to grin back at an attractive reporter in the crowd, he continued to saunter, his hands cuffed behind his back and a dozen UV lights trained on him, ready to be activated on command.

"So reporters just camp out here and wait for you to bring in the bad guys?" he inquired as the door shut out the mayhem outside.

"Not usually," Heisner replied, distracted by the

instructions being hollered at him from the portly guy manning the front desk. "Ms. Bruckner's arrival earlier probably caught the media's attention."

Feigning disinterest, he followed the man through the hallway, guided by the weapons behind him. He kept his head straight and scanned the halls, doorways, and signs as the group made their way to the basement. Passing through five security checkpoints, he was finally led to the opening of a single barren cell.

"Nah," he pshaw'd, turning back to the exit. "You don't want to keep me in here."

Heisner's hand flexed beside his gun. "Let's go, Mr. Kaius."

Grabbing one of the bars, he snapped it clean off the cell and dropped it, lifting a brow when it clanged on the floor. "This is fine for young ones, but I assure you, you don't want to keep me in here."

Flashlights lit up around him, their beams angled to the floor as Heisner pulled out his radio. "Backup in holding D," he barked, his eyes locked on Rhys. When confirmation came through, he scanned Rhys's arms. "When the hell did you bust outta those cuffs?"

With a smirk, he placed his hands behind his back again. "When I was tired of the game, around the time we took the second left turn on the way here," he responded cheerfully. "This area reeks of whiskey piss and ass. Where are the actual vamp cells?"

Heisner stepped to the side as his backup arrived. "We're going to need to clear out one of the units in F," he called over his shoulder. "Double up two of the newest arrivals and we'll deal with them later."

"Good plan, Andy," Rhys concurred, keeping a slow pace while he was led back through the security points and into a separate wing of the station. As he entered the vampire cells, he nodded. "Better. Why the hell didn't you bring me here first?"

Heisner fumbled with the electronic code and moved back to allow his officers to escort a young vamp from the enclosure. "Never had a problem using that holding wing before," he grumbled.

Eyeing the vampire struggling against his guards, he stepped into the cell and pulled the door shut. "You're lucky I'm fed and agreeable then, aren't you?"

Heisner turned away, led his men from the block, and locked the heavy security door behind him.

He rolled his eyes and looked around his new surroundings.

Bed.

Pillow.

Young vamps he could use as messenger pigeons.

"Minimalism at its finest," he muttered, sitting on the hard mattress.

"Are you—"

"Shut the fuck up, kid," he snarled at the young vamp brazen enough to speak. He pulled the bed into the middle of his cell, far from the reach of his cellmates. The room went silent while he stretched out on the bed, the newly turned vampires wisely holding their tongues as he flung his arm over his eyes.

According to Heisner's radio, Lis was being held in a secured medical facility and would be transported back to the station once she was deemed well enough to be detained.

She was currently resting.

And drugged.

He came to this realization while he was downing

his fourth bag of blood an hour before dusk. He'd been hit with a peculiar fog weaving its way through his head, the haze clinging to every corner of his mind and bringing with it an unnatural serenity. It took almost until sunset before he was able to wade through the mist and regain his coherence.

Fucking Lis.

With more effort than expected, he managed to push against the cloud as it wafted through him, shoving it into the back of his head so he could function. Even now, hours after the initial hit, he felt off. It was different from a blood high, more numbing and less euphoric.

He was stoned as fuck.

He lifted his arm off of his head and lazily opened one eye. "Anyone want to fill me in on vamp legislation changes from the past, say, eight months?"

The young vamps in the cell block went still, their gazes averted.

"Let's try this another way," he drawled. "Fucking. Talk."

The wiry kid in the adjacent cell backed away from their shared bars before he spoke. "The registration law pa—"

"Eight months, boy," he interrupted. "Fast-forward through the tattooing and shit. Hit play right around the time the Tender went public about the trade system."

With a nod, the vamp shoved his hands in his pockets. "She went missing. Some news reports were saying she was kidnapped, others saying she hoofed it out of L.A. Things died down a bit after that. I mean, I think every human has a UV flashlight now and a lot of buildings have them mounted around their stores, but if you stay to the alleys and out of sight, it ain't too bad."

He sat up slowly and pulled his burned shirt over his head. "Back to the shadows, then." The young vampires murmured in agreement, most of them wandering into his line of sight. "Are any of you in here recent turnings in the last three months?" Two of the vamps raised their hands. "You being fed enough?"

One of them shook his head as the other frowned and looked away.

"I'll see what I can do," he muttered, scratching at his arm. "So what's the climate now?"

The wiry vampire side-eyed the others. "The L.A. cops were sticking with catch-and-release for a while, but since the Deviant invasion in St. Louis, they've pretty much followed suit with the rest of the country."

He rose to his feet. "You're going to need to give me a few details on that," he growled.

"Female Deviants," a young guy called out from the back. "Dozens of them. They came out of the sewers in downtown St. Louis and went on a total rampage. Last I heard before I was brought in is some are still on the loose."

Fucking. Fuck.

"Death toll?" he demanded, walking to the edge of his cell.

"Eighty-six as of last week," another chimed in. "Though I heard there may be more that haven't been found."

The fog settled over his mind earlier evaporated as he contemplated the ramifications of such an attack. "Any word on who was responsible?"

"Nothing official," the wiry vamp replied. "A lot of rumors in the haunts." He paused, his eyes dropping to Rhys's tattooed arms. "You're Rhys Kaius, right?"

"Who the fuck else would I be?"

"The rumors say it was the vampire you guys tried to take out a while back in Memphis. Kaspars Dovidas," the young vamp continued. "Some are saying he's allied with an ancient, and that's why he had so many Deviants. It was pretty nuts. The videos of the attack, I mean."

He crossed his arms and narrowed his eyes. "What was the fallout to all this?"

The cells went silent again, the jaws of the vamps tensing.

"Deepfryers were legalized two months ago. It's now against federal law for humans to interact with vampires in any way, and any unregistered vamp caught is being held indefinitely," the talkative one finally responded, looking around at the others. "I was brought in four nights ago. I don't think the cops are equipped to house many of us at once, so until the Deepfryers are actually set up, we're getting released."

"Eight nights ago," another grumbled.

"Seven."

"Two."

He fixed his gaze on the bars as he contemplated the new information. "Have any of you seen any vamps released?"

"Yeah," one snorted. "Once they mark you, you're out. I'm next in line. This is my ninth night. I've watched six others leave."

"So you gave up your haunt location?" he inquired.

The vampire smirked. "Most L.A. vamps are newbies like me. Our haunts are condos consisting of ourselves and a big-ass T.V. while our sires live outside the city."

"And a sweet bank balance from back home," a

dark-haired one called from the far cell.

Trust fund vampires.

He narrowed his eyes. "Do you intend to return to your big screen TVs?" Several of the young vamps nodded. "You're fucking morons. When you get out, head home. Wherever that is. This isn't the time for children to be playing outside after dark. Hit the road as soon as you can, watch your back, and stay tight to your haunt. Capisce?"

As they nodded again in deference to his name, the wiry one moved tight to Rhys's cell. "There's no surveillance in here, right? I mean, you old bast…older vampires would know, right?"

Raising one brow, he strode over to their shared bars. "Us old bastards can hear the hum, yes. From my short tour of the facility, video monitoring is limited to specific interrogation rooms, hallways, and exits. With the exception of the ancient camera above the security door," he said, pointing over his shoulder. "It's wired for visuals only, though. So don't enunciate too much and you're fine. What's your name, kid?"

"Angelo Arlo," the vamp responded. "Arlo Wallace is my creator."

He grinned, extending his fangs slightly. "When you see Wallace, tell him Rhys says, 'the West window'. He'll know what I mean."

Angelo's features pursed in brief concentration before he snickered. "That's how you got into the queen consort's room," he chuckled. "Arlo's cursed your name a few times over the past decade. Said if you hadn't been such a tramp, he'd have died a human, nice and peaceful in his bed instead of spending eternity tied to ungrateful vampires and their constant demands for money'. Said the only way into her quarters was through a window too small for any man to squeeze through. Who was he guarding?"

With a smirk, he rolled his shoulders. "Henrietta Maria, consort of Charles I. The west window was only too small for someone to enter if he wasn't determined."

"How'd you end up here?" the dark-haired vampire called from the back, interrupting the brief levity. "I thought the Kaius haunt didn't get caught."

He prowled to the corner of his cell to get a clear look at the young vamp. "We get caught," he replied casually, hooking his thumbs in his burnt cargos. "We're just very fucking good at getting out if we want to."

"Then get yourself out. And us, too," one of the others interjected.

"I don't want to."

CHAPTER TWENTY-EIGHT

All eyes were on Nichol, demanding answers he didn't have.

With his lips drawn tight over his elongated fangs, Jagger leaned forward across the com room table and shoved a stack of papers back toward him. "How the hell is this not included in the write-up?" he demanded, gesturing angrily at Rhys's execution order. "Fallon doesn't get to hand off the punishment to humans. He wants to take down Rhys, he fucking does it himself."

He carefully collected the paperwork and returned it to its neat pile. "Unfortunately, nothing in here specifies Fallon has to be the one to carry out the execution. Therefore, he's within his rights to farm the job out to another." He ran a hand through his hair, annoyed with his own oversight. "Future contracts will include an addendum specifying punishments must be carried out by the individual or haunt making the request, but this—"

"This," Mick snarled, "is bullshit. Fallon should carry the stigma of Rhys's end until he meets his own. Fucking coward."

"Coward or not," he interjected, "the contract doesn't limit or define the execution protocols. And with the method of capture, Fallon will forever be associated but not proven directly responsible for Rhys's cowardly end."

Audra placed a hand on Mickey's thigh. "What does

this mean for Rhys? If the courts don't complete the task within the next three weeks, does the order still stand?"

He shook his head. "Once the clock turns to 12:01 a.m., the order is dead in the water."

Louis shuffled his chair closer to the group and faced Mick. "What are you picking up from him? Anything? He didn't look too bad in those pictures Jagg pulled off the news."

Mickey put his booted feet on the table, dropping them when Audra's expression soured slightly. He glanced over. "I don't know how much I can say."

Nodding tersely, Nichol clenched his teeth and glared at his computer. With Kaius gone again to wherever it was he disappeared to every time he left them, the hauntmates were once again deferring to him on everything from training schedules to the newest sabotaging of the ranking members of the Species Purifiers. Every decision needed to be weighed against the potential outcomes, the magnitude of the impact, and the fallout.

It was the fallout pushing him to hold Mickey's tongue up until now.

"Go ahead," he stated.

Audra's hand sought out Mick's, her manicured fingers gently drawing circles on his as he stared at the table for a stretch.

"There's an undercurrent to Rhys," he began slowly. "Everyone has one. It's the base emotion which basically determines the strength and longevity of the others." He looked to Audra, who gave a quick nod. "Audra's is determination. So every other feeling springs from it. Whether it's happiness, frustration, or anger, they all originate from the base determination. The negatives are short-lived, but strong, and the positives are more stable, more long-lasting."

"What's mine?" Dominic asked, leaning forward.

"I think about it as anticipation. It used to focus more on the bad shit, but that's turned around a lot," Mick said, smirking at Molly. "It makes your hunger intense, your—bow-chicka-bow-wow—more intense but decreases things like surprise and disappointment. You don't get the full hit of those because you're wired to expect them. Make sense? Now Rhys...he somehow managed to mask his undercurrent. Like, really, really hide it. Enough that it took a comment from Kaius to make me look deeper." He leaned forward, resting his elbows on the table. "Think of it this way. The bottom of the river is usually where the base is. For Rhys, it's always been desire. Everything stemming from that has made sense. Quick temper, women, money...I never looked deeper because it fit. But if I dig—which I don't like to do—there's an underground stream."

Nichol, having had several long discussions with Mick about it, briefly debated tuning him out.

It wasn't anything he wanted to hear again.

"I'm fucking rambling," Mick huffed, running a hand through his long hair. "Rhys's undercurrent is emptiness. And it runs parallel with apathy."

Jagger pushed his chair back and stood. "That's bullshit," he spat, dodging Bianca's hand as she tried to calm him. "If we hadn't written him off, and we ALL FUCKING DID, we wouldn't be having this discussion."

Nichol rose from his seat, watching Boy as the tall, mute male moved within take-down distance of Jagg. "I can back up Mick's claims with everything Kaius has shared with me over the centuries."

Jagger froze. "Centuries?"

Motioning for Jagg to sit, he spun his own chair around and straddled it. "It's what made—makes—Rhys the perfect vampire," he stated as Mickey nodded. "Even during his human years, he was reckless, taking risks no one with any sense would take."

He looked to Jagg. "I used to refer to Rhys as a virus. Those who survive him, like his hauntmates, become immune to his indiscriminate attacks. But anyone weaker, anyone he can essentially infect, he does. He exploits, assaults, beats down, hunts, and kills without guilt or question, because he doesn't care if he goes down in the fight."

Louis frowned, crossing his arms in thought. "He would've had ample opportunity to take any of you out. Or me, for that matter."

"I have a theory on that," he replied, grabbing a pen and paper. "In our haunt, Rhys is the original Typhoid Mary. He himself was immune to the plague but carried the disease forward while he worked as a quack doctor during the time of the Black Death." With the flourish of his pen, he drew a passable stick-figure Rhys and a dozen dead stickmen. "For humans, Rhys as a virus was fatal.

This changed," he added two vampires to his artwork, "when Kaius and I came along. He had to adapt to a new species, had to mutate for survival. With his strength and speed, Rhys was able to continue to seek out death and destruction, but in a more direct way. However, the more advanced viruses don't kill their hosts quickly. Our haunt being the host, if you follow."

Adding crude drawings to represent the rest of his brethren, he pushed the drawing toward Louis. "As the host body, we've ensured Virus Rhys could survive long enough to virtually infect others with little reprisal—"

"Aside from how many fucking centuries in cells?" Jagger interrupted, his voice graveled.

"But he survived," he continued, adding to his illustration. "I theorize the only reason Rhys has continued to exist this long is because he functions on that base, primal survival code viruses possess. There's no thought or desire, merely doing and adapting with the environment. Viruses can mutate, but only so quickly. And we, as the host, have cut off his last two means of infection by eliminating the Tender trade and forming official alliances throughout North America. Maybe this—Derry, Fallon—is the inevitable antiviral."

The room remained silent, the eyes of every hauntmate fixated on the drawing he had done.

Sitting back in his chair, he watched the others as they processed what he'd said. It was a theory he had discussed frequently with Kaius, a way of understanding Rhys's actions over the years.

"Bullshit," Jagger muttered, pushing away from the table and standing. "I'll buy that Rhys is done. Done with existing, done with surviving, however you want to say it. But no fucking way has he fought alongside this haunt for nearly eight goddamn centuries just because we're convenient."

Waving his hand to keep Jagg's attention, Nichol sat straighter. "I've obviously misstated my main point," he said, glancing toward Audra. "Like a virus, Rhys survives because he's genetically programmed to survive. He is still capable of loyalty, of anger and happiness and frustration. What he lacks is an anchor to capture those emotions. There's no will. No desire. And never has been."

****

His artistry crumpled in a ball on the floor, Nichol looked over at the only hauntmate remaining in the room. "Know how to work this?" he asked, pushing his laptop toward Boy. When the silent vamp nodded, he turned to his main computer and fired it up. "Keep flipping through the tabs at the top and refreshing the pages. We're looking for any news reports of Rhys's incarceration. The buzz says California is going to be in the first round of Deepfryer dispersals, and I want his whereabouts tracked and accounted for before that shit hits. With any luck, the execution contract will expire before those death machines hit the law courts. It would untie our hands." He paused. "If Rhys wants them untied."

Boy crouched down and began clumsily tapping at the trackpad.

"We're not wrong, are we?" he grumbled, dimming the screen's brightness. "Kai and me? We've kept him going as long as we can. Kaius knows it. I know it. Hell, Rhys knows it." He flicked through a few pages, scanning them quickly for intel. "At some point, isn't it almost crueler to keep him going? To force him to stay around because we think he should?"

Boy remained as silent as ever, focused entirely on his assignment.

"It's fucking selfish," he stated, becoming more resolute vocally, if not mentally. "If Rhys wanted out, there's no way humans could have captured him and held him. He'd be out if he wanted it. Out and feeding on some starlet."

He knew he was rationalizing the situation, forcing

a logical explanation onto himself and the others in an effort to alleviate their collective guilt. He was actively taking the decision for Rhys's death entirely out of their hands and placing it squarely onto Rhys's shoulders.

Demonizing him.

He shrugged off the unpleasant feelings accompanying the thought and ran a hand through his hair, doubling down on his attention to the monotonous articles flashing across his screen.

The laptop dinged loudly.

"Click that," Nichol instructed, pulling his chair alongside Boy. "It's a news alert."

With some fumbling, Boy managed to open the message. They read through the article, Nichol reaching across Boy to scroll through the images on the screen.

"Motherfucker," he barked, booting at the table in anger. "That's fucking Lis, isn't it?"

CHAPTER TWENTY-NINE

"Heisner," Rhys cooed, lifting his arm off of his eyes and raising his head enough to see the tall officer. "I'm feeling a mite peckish. Another, say, seven bags?"

His first three nights in the human jail hadn't been too bad. The guards were suitably skittish around him, the younger vampires were properly awed, and Andy Heisner was most accommodating.

"No can do," Heisner replied, crossing his arms. "You and I need to talk."

He swung his legs over the edge of the bed and rose to his feet slowly.

Fucking Lis and her fucking medications leaving him high as a kite.

"I don't talk," he grinned. "I negotiate."

Heisner crossed his arms and glared. "Well, I'm going to talk, and you can do whatever the hell you want." He took a step toward the bars. "We need to discuss the occupants of the house we brought you in from."

"Shouldn't I have a lawyer?" he asked, blinking purposely. "Shouldn't all of us have lawyers?"

The rest of the vamps grunted in agreement.

"Since you aren't persons under the law, you get squat," Heisner replied. "Even if it was allowed, I can't imagine too many lawyers would be anxious to flush their practices down the drain to defend vamps."

His harsh words were tempered by his matter-of-fact

tone.

Statements of reality.

He could respect that.

"Eight bags, and maybe we can have a quick exchange," he countered, striding to the locked door of his cell. "Here?"

Heisner looked around and frowned. "There's potentially some sensitive info." He trailed off and cleared his throat.

"Well, Andy, you have a few choices then," he said, draping his arms through the bars and smirking when the officer stepped further out of reach. "You can move these guys somewhere else for a bit. Which seems like a lot of work and may present minor issues of containment during transportation." Several of the vamps walked casually over to their cell doors and mimicked Rhys's position. "We could talk here, but you won't be getting anything out of me as long as I have an audience. Which makes the concept of discussion a moot point." Widening his stance slightly, he leaned into the door. "Or we could form a gentleman's agreement. You supply eight blood bags, I come with you into whatever private room you deem appropriate, and we have a nice chat."

Glancing at the remaining seven vampires in their cells, the officer huffed and pulled out his radio. "Seven units in the vamp wing."

"Eight, Andy." When Heisner hesitated, he cocked a brow. "Nine, Andy."

Heisner's frown deepened as he evaluated the options. "Let me get those bags down here and I'll be back."

He waited until the man disappeared before he turned to the others. "Divide the meals up. Anyone still good from yesterday's feeding can pass their rations to one of the newbies," he instructed, eying the youngest. "No false heroics. You're all due for marking soon, and you'll need the strength to avoid reacting when that mercury hits your systems. Got it?"

"I'll monitor it," Angelo offered. "You gonna bolt if he opens that door?"

"It's too close to dawn," he replied, leaning against the bars to steady himself as Lis's lethargy pulsed through him. "Where the fuck would I go?" He looked over the remaining unmarked vampires. "Everyone knows who to contact when they get out, right? Whether you have a place to go or not, touch base with Jagger." He narrowed his eyes at the youngest. "If you don't have a safe hideout, Jagg will hook you up."

The vamps nodded, quietly reciting Jagg and Nichol's cell numbers to him.

Almost an hour passed before Heisner returned, six armed guards in tow. "All right," he announced, setting a box of blood bags onto the floor. "I secured eight bags."

The officer used his foot to push the box close to his cell. One by one, Rhys unloaded the box and set them in the corner of his enclosure where Angelo would have access. "I asked for nine, Andy. That's going to cost you when we head topside for a tete-a-tete," he shrugged, winking at the jumpy guards.

"First, I watch you eat. Then we go," Heisner commanded, his hands resting on the UV flashlights on his holster.

Scenting the air subtly, he pulled the oldest blood from the pile and sliced the plastic open with his fang. He stared blankly at the guards while he fed, purposely locking his gaze on their jugulars until they squirmed. When the bag was empty, he held it up for Heisner's inspection.

"You'll walk beside me," the officer stated, unlocking the cell door. "No fast movements, no stopping. One wrong move, we're opening fire."

Smirking, he strode out of his enclosure. "Lead the way, Andy."

The halls were deserted as the group made their way to a small room. He glanced around the space, his attention drawn to a laptop sitting on a small wooden table. Heisner motioned toward a chair, watching him intently as he spun the chair and straddled it.

"The guards'll be waiting outside the door," Heisner said as he sat.

Absently scratching at his arm, he grinned. "I can kill you in one second," he mentioned casually. "I could demonstrate on that guy over there." The guard tensed. "Yeah, you, fuckboy. Stop staring at my arms."

Heisner's hand lifted to his men. "It would be a suicide mission and we both know it," he said as he glanced over his shoulder. "Close the door, guys." His eyes dropped to the tattoos. "Can I ask about those?"

"No."

The officer shifted in his seat, leaning back and crossing his arms. "How did you and Ms. Bruckner end up in that basement?"

"Took a wrong turn at Albuquerque."

Heisner's jaw flexed. "Why did we receive a call to that address?"

"Good Samaritan?" he suggested.

Heisner stood and glared down at him. "If you aren't willing to give anything up—"

"Look, Andy," he interrupted, draping his arms over the back of his chair, "until I know what you know, I'm not filling in any blanks." He tilted his head. "We both know you have nothing to hold over my head. Unlike the other kids in the cells, I'm not waltzing out of here with a stock tattoo and a fine."

Heisner's lips tightened into a thin line. "How old are you?"

"768."

The man's brown eyes widened as he whistled. "That's… holy shit, that's old." He stared at the floor for a few moments, nodding slowly to his internal debate. "I suppose that's plenty of time to make a few enemies," he began, looking back to him. "An anonymous call led us to you and Ms. Bruckner. Our forensics department has linked the voice to another call we received the night after you were brought in. Seems someone is willing to pony up a lot of money to have you held until the county's Deepfryer arrives on site."

He remained motionless, bored.

Heisner tapped at the keys of the laptop. "There won't be a sentencing hearing for you," he continued. "The courts have already classified you as a dangerous offender due to the circumstances surrounding your arrest." The cop looked straight at him. "The presence of a human female pretty much sealed your fate."

Of course. Fucking Lis.

Fucking Lis, who was apparently high as a kite and getting hungry.

"All I'm aiming for is a name," Heisner stated. "Something we can put on the report to legitimize the calls, the donation, and the video footage which arrived in our email system."

"Video footage," he echoed in a low growl. "Show me."

Heisner turned his attention to the laptop, frowning at the screen as he worked. "It's been trickling in every few hours since you were brought in. Ms. Bruckner is featured prominently as well." He paused. "Give me a name."

"Show me the footage."

His hand on the laptop, Heisner held fast. "Look, Rhys, I'm not here to save your ass. It ain't happening. But this is pretty damning for Ms. Bruckner, and if you can add some context to what we've received, there's a chance we can have the Treason to the Species charge dropped. Now, a name."

He felt his fangs lengthening against his will, a combination of his anger and Lis's hunger. "Fallon Derry," he grit out. "My best guess is he'll be making his way toward Ireland eventually."

Heisner pulled out a pen and paper from his pocket and scrawled the intel down as he pushed the laptop toward him. "There's eight videos in all," he muttered.

"Only seven tabs open," he countered, filling the screen with the first footage.

"Yeah, well," Heisner grumbled, "one of them features Ms. Bruckner and isn't necessary for anyone to view. I've managed to eliminate the email, but the video is encrypted on here in the off-chance this Fallon Derry ends up linked to any other missing women."

The officer's back straightened as Rhys's eyes ovaled and focused on the screen. The videos were a compilation of scenes from the McConaughey cells, carefully compiled and edited to provide viewers with the impression he and Lis were a unified couple, a voluntary pairing.

Images of them lying on his bed.

Him holding a blanket to block the camera from Lis while she showered.

His fangs in her wrist.

Her lips on his wrist.

He shoved the laptop back at Heisner. "There are a few missing pieces," he said, forcing his voice to remain calm.

"Fill them in for me," Heisner countered.

He rested his forearms on the table and rolled his shoulders. "Nothing you need to know," he growled.

"Who is Ms. Bruckner to you?"

"A convenient meal with a half-decent rack."

Heisner leaned back and crossed his arms over his stomach. "Let me set the scene for you," he drawled, nonplussed by the flippant response. "Ms. Bruckner has stabilized enough to be transported back into the station for holding. These videos, along with her disappearance after she made a name for herself on television, make Ms. Bruckner out to be a willing accomplice to the vampire agenda. Combine that with this Fallon Derry's financial donation toward the purchase of a Deepfryer, and I think you can see where the problem lies."

When he didn't flinch, Heisner cleared his throat.

"As it stands, Ms. Bruckner is being sentenced alongside you," he stated. "Despite your attempts to separate yourself from her, we have clear evidence of ongoing positive interactions regardless of the circumstance surrounding it." He tapped the laptop screen. "The media's already picked it up and put a rather unsettling spin on everything."

He cocked a brow. "More unsettling than publicly

baking me."

With a sigh, Heisner pushed the computer back at him. "Love triangle. Jilted lover. The 'anonymous donor' has made sure the press has a shortened version of the videos we received here, and they're being shown on every network news program in the country."

"I take it I'm not the sympathetic character in the narrative?" he snorted, digging his fingers into his biceps to alleviate the itch.

"See for yourself," Heisner replied, clicking the play button on the screen.

Fighting a strange heaviness in his arms brought on by Lis's drugged state, he tilted the screen, listening intently to the reporter awhile she waxed poetic about the sordid vampire love triangle 'culminating in Shakespearean tragedy'.

"What the fuck is wrong with people?" he mused aloud, staring at the images of Lis and himself on the screen, their faces outlined with a vibrant pink heart. "This," he stated, gesturing toward the laptop, "is why humans will always be inferior to vampires. This isn't news. It's the speculations of horny fiction writers. And who the fuck decided that was the best still image of me?"

Heisner snorted. "I'm not disagreeing with you. But this is the yarn being spun, and it's being swallowed whole by the public. And that, Rhys, is a problem." He closed the laptop. "You know how Shakespe... of course you do," he muttered, shaking his head. "You probably met the guy. Anyways, long story short? This is the bandwagon, the headline of the year. The pro-vamps are pushing this supposed love story as romantic, fated lovers and all that shit. The anti-vamps are pushing this as proof of how evil and messed up vampires are. Everyone wants the Shakespeare ending, and the courts are going to be pressured to give it to them quick. Which means everyone's going to end up dead. Ms. Bruckner included."

The officer watched him like a hawk, waiting for a reaction. He pursed his lips and leaned back. "As long as that 'everyone' includes Fallon, I'm on Team Deepfryer. Do I get a novelty shirt or something?"

****

Nichol grumbled his agreement while Jagger continued his rant.

"I can't even remember the last night I woke up and there wasn't some new shit-storm brewing," Jagg groaned, staring at the lips of the reporter on his screen. "And I have an infallible memory. What the hell does THAT say about the past two years?"

Nudging Jagger's hand away from the laptop, he closed the browser and sat back. "With the mess in St. Louis cleaned up, one issue is eliminated."

"And three more popped up in its place," Jagg muttered back.

"We aren't getting involved in the human issues," he stated, batting Jagger's arm away when he attempted to reopen the news links. "As far as I'm concerned, the anti-vamps and the pro-vamps can wipe each other off the face of the earth. The fewer extremists there are on both sides, the easier things will be in the long run." He grinned. "Are you and Bianca still getting messages from your FANG groupies?"

Jagger's head dropped to his chest. "When I find out who gave our email to those lunatics, I'm going to de-fang them and shove those fake-nail teeth right up their asses. Bee's wading through hundreds a day. Every time she marks one as spam, another three come up."

He yanked the laptop toward him. "You might get a kick out of this, though," he said, tapping the keys quickly and tilting the screen to Jagg. "I came across it early this morning."

Jagger's ice eyes narrowed as he scanned the page. "What the hell is fan fiction?"

"Click on one and read it."

He had stayed up late into the morning reading the fan sites emerging for Jagger and Rhys. They'd sprung up suddenly, garnering thousands of hits an hour while the news continued to speculate on the relationship between Rhys, Lis, and the mysterious vampire financing a Los Angeles Deepfryer. Although he had initially been hunting for any information of potential danger to the hauntmates, the sites were relatively harmless collections of gossip, grainy video footage, and professions of adoration.

And stories.

Graphic, detailed stories.

"I'm too young to read this," Jagg groaned, shoving the computer away. "Do NOT show this to Bee. She'll read it out loud and I'll never live it down."

"I sent her the links fifty-nine minutes ago," he stated. "Next time I tell you to meet me here in one hour, don't be late."

Jagg booted his chair. "Asshole. Heard any more from Kai?"

He nodded, shuffling his seat away from his hauntmate. "He messaged me earlier. He'll be on site within the next few days. He's keeping to the back roads, so he couldn't guarantee a day."

"Did he say where he was?"

Staring blankly at Jagger, he ignored the stupid question. No one knew where Kaius went. Ever. "Before the others arrive, I want your take on the Lis problem."

Jagg sat up straighter. "There's a lot missing in the leaked footage," he began slowly. "Fallon released what he wanted to put out there. I'm not sure he intended to be portrayed as a jealous ex-boyfriend, but it's gotten the attention he was likely aiming for."

He glared at his younger brother. "Lis," he growled. "Is there anything I need to know to explain why she wasn't dead within minutes of being placed within Rhys's reach?"

"Given the starvation cycle Mickey and Kai were monitoring, I'd bet he was smart enough to maintain her as a food source," Jagger mused. "I didn't see anything in that footage I haven't seen Rhys do in the training rooms hundreds of times. Except the bloodletting. But the longer Lis lived, the longer his meal did. It makes sense."

Nodding, he grunted his agreement.

He'd reached the same conclusion.

Nothing more than the mindless instinct of a survivor.

Pulling up a screen's worth of notes for their nightly meeting, he shoved Rhys into the back of his mind and focused on the things he could control.

****

Thwack.

Lis stumbled as her shoulder made contact with the door frame.

"Sorry," she mumbled, regaining her balance before falling back in step with the armed guard escorting her through the halls of the hospital.

The men surrounding her ignored her, their readied weapons keeping her hazy mind from drifting too far into itself. It had been hours since her last injection, and the effects were finally beginning to wane enough to assure her what she was experiencing was tangible.

She flexed her fingers, rattling the chains of her handcuffs and drawing a glare from the officer in front.

"Check her wrists," the man barked to the others. "I don't need another Houdini," he grumbled under his breath.

She stopped, swaying slightly on her feet while one of the men tugged roughly on the steel.

"All good."

The group continued their procession through the hospital, winding through the narrow halls of the lower levels until they came to a door.

"I want her flanked," the leader commanded, stepping aside to allow the others to pass. "Into the van, doors closed. The fewer pictures, the better." He turned to face her. "Ms. Bruckner, you're going to keep your head down and walk fast."

She nodded in acknowledgement as the door opened and the guards stormed through. Despite the drugs clouding her senses, she could make out several voices calling to her over the barked orders of the commander behind her. She walked as fast as she dared, her eyes trained on the ground until the bumper of a vehicle came into view. Large hands gripped her upper arms and hoisted her into the vehicle, propelling her forward until her knees scraped along the metal floor.

"Get her up!" the voice of the commander yelled while the heavy boots of the guards thumped into the van and the doors slammed shut.

Within moments, she was lifted to a bench.

"You all right?" the officer asked, the van lurching while it began moving through the streets.

She nodded, keeping her head down and eyes on all of the boots on the floor.

"It's a short trip," the man continued. "Once we arrive, we'll get you booked in and settled. Your doctor has pretty strict dietary orders for you, so we want to make sure we're sticking to those."

Another nod.

"You might not remember me. Andy Heisner. I was one of the officers who released you and Mr. Rhys Kaius."

At the sound of his name, she lifted her eyes but remained silent.

Heisner gave her a tight smile, his thin lips stretching across his sun-damaged skin. "The doc said you'll be more alert by tomorrow once those meds are out of your system. But you let me know if you need anything, okay?"

The van went quiet, save for the shuffling of the men lining the benches. She leaned back against the hard wall and closed her eyes, focusing on balancing the movement of the vehicle with the swishing in her brain while hazy recollections from the past days and nights flashed across her mind.

A blur of lab coats.

The raised voices of doctors and guards.

The cocooning warmth in her veins when the injections hit.

The blissfully interchangeable minutes and hours.

"Here!" a voice boomed beside her. "Are we

flanking her entrance?"

Heisner rose to his feet and into her line of sight. "Yup. Make it fast. The photographers have been like vultures out there since we brought in the old guy." He steadied her as she stood. "Same as last time. Head down and don't respond to anyone but me until we're in."

The frenzied shouts of the reporters caught her off-guard when she gracelessly descended from the van.

"Ms. Bruckner! Over here!"

"Where have you been these past months?"

"Can you tell us anything about your relationship with Rhys Kaius? Is he your boyfriend?"

Her head shot to the side, her brows furrowing at the peculiar line of questioning.

"Go," Heisner hissed into her ear. "We're almost in."

The slamming of the metal doors simultaneously shut out the racket of the streets and sent a chill down her spine. The guards hustled her forward down a barren hall and into a sparse room.

"Someone will be in shortly to book you," Heisner said, motioning toward a chair. "Once that's done, I'll be by to get you settled. I need to check on something quick."

****

Rhys lifted his arm off his eyes and peered at the officer. "What would you like me to do with this information?" When Heisner leaned against the cell unit door and shoved his hands in his pockets, he reluctantly sat up and straddled his cot. "Unless you're sending her in here for a quick meal, I'm not sure why you felt the need to come down here."

A look of disgust crossed the officer's face before

he shook his head. "Just figured I'd keep you informed," he said slowly, walking toward his bars. "Ms. Bruckner and I will be meeting tomorrow to discuss a few things. Anything I should know beforehand?"

He glanced to the ceiling, feigning contemplation. "Nope."

He waited until the man stomped out of the room, then resumed his position on the uncomfortable bed.

Of course he fucking knew Lis was in the building. Her proximity was the reason he was barely functioning. His limbs felt heavy, his muscles relaxed to the point of uselessness. His thoughts were murky and scattered, fragments of ideas flitting by without context or reason.

It was fucking annoying.

Recognizing the eldest vampire in the room was a bit surly, the others kept to themselves, keeping their eyes on him for any sign of aggression.

Aggression.

In his current state, he could hardly walk, let alone attack.

But even if he could attack, why the fuck would he?

****

The heavy clunking of metal tore Lis from her sleep, sending a flurry of adrenaline through her as she scanned her small cell. Heisner's hard expression softened slightly, and he stopped in his tracks.

"Sorry," he muttered, glancing back at the accompanying guards. "That door always shuts fast." He grabbed a paper bag from one of the men and brought it to her. "I'm going to need to watch you finish this," he said, setting the bag down on the cot. "Doctor's orders and all."

She moved slowly, not wanting to draw attention

from the armed security. "Thank you," she mumbled, examining the iron-heavy meal. "What happens after this?"

Heisner shifted his weight awkwardly. "You and I are going to have a little discussion."

Lifting her gaze to the man, she pursed her lips. "I think I need a lawyer before we talk," she stated, trying not to obviously marvel at the clarity of her own speech and vision.

"That'll be part of the discussion," Heisner replied, shoving his hands in his pockets, and looking away.

She polished off her meal quickly as the guards stared at her intently and Heisner studied the floor. With every passing minute, she felt more normal, more controlled. More her.

Heisner led her out of the tiny room. "We've secured the shower room for you," he stated, sending half of the guards through the doorway before motioning for her to follow. "We'll be waiting outside when you're done."

It wasn't until the lukewarm water was rinsing the shampoo from her hair that her memory flashed a voice through her head.

Can you tell us anything about your relationship with Rhys Kaius?

Her hands stilled in her hair.

Rhys Kaius.

The reporter called him by name.

Which meant the world knew who he was.

She finished her shower in a hurry, anxious to know what turn of events had brought the Kaius name into the human media.

And what it meant for Rhys.

Heisner was pacing the hall when she emerged, his phone tight to his ear and his brows knotted. With a few muttered words, he slammed the phone into his pocket and approached her. "Let's go."

Within minutes, she and Heisner were back in the room she'd been brought to the night before for booking. She sat, adjusting the ill-fitting orange jumper.

"There's no lawyer," Heisner began, opening a laptop. "We're in uncharted territory here. The charges against you range from Accomplice to the Vampire Agenda to Treason to the Species. The legalities surrounding these charges are different than those of your standard B&E and murder ones."

He cleared his throat, refusing to make eye contact. "The Vampire Criminal Code is based on the concept of guilty until proven innocent. Which means there'll be no lawyer, no trial. Sentencing is already in the works and will be handed down within a week or two."

She stared at the table as the words sank in.

"You and Rhys are a national test case," Heisner stated, pulling out his buzzing phone and placing it face down beside the computer. "With the media attention the story has garnered, every move we make is being reported whether we like it or not." He rested his elbows on the table, his head dropping a fraction as he rubbed his blond buzzcut. "I've been appointed the lead on this shit-storm. Vamp experts with the feds are issuing the orders, and I'll be the one ensuring they're followed."

Shifting her gaze to the vibrating phone, she shrunk into herself. "That's them?"

"Yeah," he sighed. "Look, kid, this is going to end badly. Your only hope is to gain mass sympathy in the public. Maybe enough to have the inevitable death sentence pulled back to life imprisonment."

Kid.

She tilted her head, assessing the officer. "What are my chances of that?"

"If I was a betting man, I'd say none. Your history as a vamp companion, your disappearance, your reappearance alongside a vampire… you've got a big ol' scarlet letter on your back." Heisner finally looked her in the eye. "It's basically a waiting game now, Ms. Bruckner."

"And where will I be waiting?"

****

Angelo remained close to Rhys's bars, watching as the only other remaining vampire was escorted from his cell and through the heavy steel door.

"Wonder if they actually get released," Angelo mused aloud. "Or do they hold them until dawn and push 'em into the sun?"

He stretched his arms up, gripping the top bars of his cell. "I'm sure you'll find out soon."

The cell block had been drained quickly over the past two nights, leaving him and Angelo alone.

"If you aren't fried on release, I need you to pass on a message to Jagger," he continued, monitoring the movements outside the door. "Tell him I'm all good, and to release the Tender. And tell him he's a small-dicked fuckwad."

Angelo frowned. "I'm not saying that to any Kaius vamp," he said resolutely. "I'm young, not stupid."

With a grin, he pulled his feet off the floor and slowly lowered himself back down. "Think of it as a password. Code-speak. That way Jagg will know the message is from me and you aren't full of shit."

The footsteps outside the door grew louder until the door swung open and six guards came barreling through.

"You," one of them barked to Angelo. "Back to the bars and hands behind you."

Rhys held his position, watching as Angelo hesitated before complying. Within moments, the young vampire was cuffed and being escorted out of the block.

"Small-dicked fuckwad?" Angelo whispered as he passed, his voice too quiet for human ears.

"Yeah," he returned, his lips barely moving. "Baby-fanged, small-dicked fuckwad."

Alone in the block, he absently scratched at his arms and waited while he pushed back against the darkness Lis was radiating through his head.

One hour.

Two.

Four.

Heisner finally strode through the door, his guards in tow.

"Andy," he greeted, flashing his fangs at the men behind him. "Is it my turn for release?"

Heisner stopped just outside his reach. "You're being moved," he said, his eyes focusing on Rhys's arms. "We should get those looked at."

Hooking his bloodied thumbs into his pants, he widened his stance. "Nope."

"Suit yourself," Heisner muttered, continuing to stare at the shredded markings. "Same rules as before. No sudden movements, no stalling." He unlocked the cell as the guards turned their UV lights on and trained the beams on the floor. "This unit's being updated. We have a brand new holding room for you."

The cell door swung open, and Rhys remained in

place.

"Let's go," Heisner ordered.

"What's my incentive?"

The officer's face scrunched in frustration. "How about a shower?"

"And fresh clothes."

Heisner ripped his phone from his pocket. "Fine. Now move."

With a pleasant smile, he sauntered out. "You're a decent guy, Andy."

****

"What the fuck is this?" Rhys growled as the UV lights guided him forward into the crowded room.

"Just get in," Heisner whispered behind him.

He crossed the threshold and scanned the seated men and women lining the back wall, purposely keeping his attention averted from the bright orange jumpsuit in his peripheral. Pens, papers, and recording devices were positioned in laps, several already in use as he stalked to the middle of the room and stared down the most inquisitive of the humans. The door clicked closed, Heisner stepping up to his side.

"Ladies, gentlemen," Heisner began, one eye on his reactions, "I'll open the floor to questions after the examination is complete. Ms. Bruckner, Mr. Kaius, your cooperation in this will make it significantly easier. And shorter."

The guards advanced on him first, armed with chains and lights. Heisner motioned for him to sit, tapping the UV light on his hip in a subtle warning. Assessing the chain strength while the guards drew nearer, he straddled the chair and placed his hands behind him.

"Not all vamps are in to bondage," he remarked while the links were tightened around his chest. When a young guard knelt in front of him to secure a padlock, he ran his tongue over his fang. "Though this pretty boy makes me open to the idea."

He didn't flinch when a UV beam bore into his shoulder blade in response.

But Lis did.

Fucking Lis.

"Stop!" she called out, hurling out of her chair and toward him with her handcuffed hands at her back. He snapped his fangs at her in warning just as her feet tangled in the oversized prison garb and she pitched forward.

Good ol' Andy was quick, catching her before she hit the floor.

He glowered at her while Heisner guided her back to her chair, the echoes of her panic still rattling in his head. Out the corner of his eye, he could see the spectators scribbling notes frantically, their small recording devices held high to capture the moment.

Heisner backed away from Lis and gave him a stern look, his face angled away from the viewers. "Let's get this over with." Andy stared pointedly at him. "I'm going to need this room a little quieter before we can proceed."

The territorial growl emanating from his chest ceased instantly.

CHAPTER THIRTY

"I didn't give you permission to fucking speak," Rhys snarled as Lis began to answer Heisner's opening question.

Her jaw snapped shut immediately.

Heisner hesitated a moment before addressing him instead. "All right, Mr. Kaius. How did you and Lis meet?"

"Mail-order bloodwhore," he replied, locking his gaze on one of the women in the spectator row. "It's a good place to get quantity, if not quality." He dropped his gaze to the woman's thighs, smirking when she shifted and crossed her legs.

"Okay then, why don't you tell us about your time in the basement of Fallon Derry's home."

"Nope."

Heisner turned to Lis. "Ms. Bruckner?"

"She won't be answering any questions," he stated.

"That's not your decision, Mr. Kaius," the officer responded.

He chuckled. "It sure as hell isn't hers." He tilted his head and looked at her with a sneer. "And she knows better than to disobey."

The audience murmured amongst themselves, a hushed shock at his blatant disregard for the woman sitting across from him.

One of the shorter men looked mildly impressed.

Heisner glanced between them. "What's the nature

of your relationship?"

Meeting the eyes of one of the disapproving women, his fangs extended further over his lower lip. "She feeds me three times a week, I make her come three times a night."

Clearing his throat, Heisner took a small step back. "So it's a physical relationship then."

"Very," he purred.

"And how long has this, uh, physical relationship been going on?" the officer asked, keeping his eyes averted from Lis.

"A while," Lis piped up as she caught on to his plan, shrinking back in her chair when he growled. "My apologies, sir."

Good girl.

Heisner opened his mouth to speak again, only to be cut off by Rhys.

"No more questions. For either of us."

Another look of warning came from the officer before he nodded slowly. "I suppose we could move on," he said reluctantly before motioning toward the guards and addressing the audience. "Please remain on alert and make no sudden movements. The following has been pre-approved for study by the federal Vampire division."

The first UV beam to bore into Rhys was trained on the tattoos on his left arm. Within moments, a second began heating the skin on his right bicep. He remained motionless, zeroing in on the burning sensation to keep his focus. Seconds ticked by and the scent of burnt flesh filled the room.

"Please, stop," Lis whimpered in the quiet, breaking his concentration and snapping his attention her way.

"What did I tell you about talking?" he snarled,

baring his elongated fangs at her.

"Turn 'em off," Heisner grunted, holding a hand up to halt the beams. He looked over at the spectators. "Good enough?"

A murmur of agreement rose from the back wall, with the exception of one man. "Has a reversal been pre-approved?"

Heisner's jaw tensed as he nodded. "You," he said, pointing to the largest guard, "secure Ms. Bruckner."

Rhys ignored the wounds on his arms, ignored the blackened holes and the numbing pain accompanying the beginnings of the slow healing process. Lis's fear and worry pulsed in his head, distracting him from his efforts to remain nonchalant and suppress the low growl building in his chest as the burly guard wrapped around her and angled her chin toward the ceiling.

Heisner dug into his pockets, pulling out a lighter. He flicked it a few times before the flame held steady. Stepping to the side to allow the onlookers a good view, he brought the flame tight to Lis's cheek while she struggled against the guard's grip.

"Hold real still," Heisner whispered soft enough for only Lis, the guard, and Rhys to hear.

Her fear barreled through his head, punctuated with spikes of pain as the lighter inched closer to her skin.

Don't fucking move.

Don't fucking move.

Over and over, he recited the mantra, willing it to reach her while it tempered his own rage. Heisner was watching him intently after every shift of the flame, examining him for any reaction to her situation.

Don't fucking move.

The salty scent of tears wafted over to him, her panic

rising the longer Heisner continued.

Don't fucking move.

Her tears were overpowered by the stench of burnt hair as stray strands became singed by the small fire.

Don't. Fucking. Move.

Heisner's hand began to shake almost imperceptibly, the tremors increasing the predictable scope of the lighter flame. The observers were silent, their eyes on Rhys while he remained motionless and unaffected in his chains.

"I think that's enough," Heisner stated loudly, snapping the lighter closed and shoving it deep into his pockets. "Let her go."

The large guard eased his grip on Lis, setting her back in her chair and stepping away as she drew deep, trembling breaths.

"I'll be escorting the accused to their cells and I'll return for questions after. All right?" Heisner said, waving the guards over. "Get him unchained."

With a quick flexing of his arms, Rhys broke himself free of the bindings and rose to his feet.

****

Lis stared at the tiny cement room, recoiling from the dark space on instinct.

"I'm going to need you to go in," Andy Heisner said softly behind her while he turned on the lights. "It's a new unit. Toilet and sink over there. Shower's up there and comes on at 8pm every night for ten minutes. Bed's brand new."

"It's lovely," she replied, her voice hollow as she stepped inside.

"Isn't it?" Rhys muttered behind her, his bare feet padding into his own unit across the narrow hall as he called out to the dozen guards blocking his escape. "You can turn off the flashlights now, asshats."

She moved gingerly across the tiny floor, touching the hard metal of the sink.

"Heisner," Rhys's voice echoed in the quiet. "Put this in there."

The officer appeared beside her, an extra blanket in hand. "I'll be back before dawn with your meal and whatever I can scrounge for toiletries," he said, his brown eyes apologetic as he backed out of the cell and closed the door. Rhys's door slammed shut, the lock thudding into place as the heavy footfalls of the guards disappeared down the hall and out of the wing.

Touching her cheek, she leaned against the wall and stared at the tiny slot in the door. "It's like a tomb," she whispered to herself, running her fingers along the rough cement.

"This is luxury compared to a tomb, sweetheart," Rhys's deep voice rumbled through the cells.

She fell silent, pulling gently at the remaining burnt strands of hair.

"Turn off your light for a moment," he instructed, his voice more graveled than it had been in the interrogation room.

Without thought, she obeyed.

"We're good," he finally muttered in the dark. "I can't hear any extra currents running in here, so there's no surveillance in this unit. Turn your light back on."

The single bulb came back to life.

"How's that cheek feeling?"

"Fine," she lied, staring absently at the perfectly aligned slot in her door.

He went quiet, except for the pacing of his bare feet

on the cement.

Time passed as her legs went numb and her body began to feel weighted. "I'm sorry," she finally said into the silence. "I should've let you end this back when you could. Or I should have taken you out with that glass. I just didn't think…I didn't know this is how we'd end up."

"Apologizing for the human frailty of hope makes as much sense as apologizing for your height or your shoe size," he called over to her. "If you feel the need to make apologies, start with making one for that goddamn metal contraption in your tongue and we'll go from there."

"Never," she sighed, pushing off the wall and sitting on her bed. "How are the arms healing up?"

"Slow," he answered. "You shouldn't have reacted. I was fine."

"You weren't fine," she shot back, bouncing lightly on the mattress to test the firmness. "You were smoking. They had no right—"

"No, angel, WE have no rights," he growled, his voice growing louder. "Those self-righteous crayon-eaters in there were watching for your reactions. For mine. They're trying to build an iron-clad case against you to solidify that fucking treason charge. And you handed them everything they were fucking drooling for."

She froze, her knuckles turning white as she dug her fingers into the bed.

"You made yourself out to look like a lovestruck groupie," he seethed, his anger palpable. "Heisner wasn't going to light me up in that room. He needs me for the grand unveiling of the Deepfryer. If you'd held off for another few seconds, he wouldn't have been pushed to pull out the motherfucking lighter. GODDAMN IT, LIS."

The sound of his bare foot hitting the cement caused her to jump.

"I'm sor—"

"I don't want to hear your fucking sorries," he roared, the echo of flesh on metal punctuating his words. "Whatever rules you think apply here DON'T FUCKING APPLY. Don't you get it? You're going in to that Deepfryer with me." As she choked back a sob, his voice lowered. "How many bakings have you seen, sweetcheeks? Ever watch a human in one of those things? Seen how th—"

"STOP!" she screamed, slamming her hands onto the bed.

He went silent instantly, her gulped breaths the only sound in the unit.

If only.

If only she hadn't killed Derry in a rage.

If only she hadn't gone to the media for vengeance.

If only she'd followed Rhys's logical lead back in the McConaughey cells.

If only she'd asked Rhys for help.

"It's done," he muttered quietly. "You wallowing in guilt for the next however long is only going to sour my mood. Does your bed move?"

Her brows furrowed at the question. "Yes?"

"Pull it in front of the door," he instructed.

Gripping the metal frame, she dragged the small bed over.

"Look through the hole."

Lifting the metal flap, she bent down and peered through the small opening. His long fingers were draping over his own slot. He wiggled them briefly.

"Lie down and rest," he ordered, the usual authority in his voice replaced with a foreign weariness. "I'll wake you when Heisner returns. Got it, baby?"

CHAPTER THIRTY-ONE

Rhys stood with his back to the door of his cell, his hand wedged through the narrow slot.

Again.

Fucking Lis.

Heisner had come and gone hours ago, providing Lis with a hefty collection of food and toiletries, and carefully threading two bags of blood through the small opening in Rhys's door.

The man spoke little and moved quickly.

Now, with the sun high, she was finally out cold, and he was left with two empty blood bags at his feet and two unhealed holes in his arms.

Unhealed holes burning like a bitch.

Easing his fingers out of the metal flap, he lowered it silently to avoid waking her.

Again.

He was in desperate need of fresh blood. The lacerations were bone-deep and required something stronger, something more potent than two pints of stale blood from a contaminated cooler. His fangs had yet to retreat back to their normal length, a result of his hunger, his injuries, and the memories of Lis's face when the lighter seared her flawless skin.

He eased himself onto the small bed slowly and flung a damaged arm over his eyes.

"Rhys?" she called out, a hint of panic in both her voice and her presence in his head.

"Here," he muttered, thumping his feet to the ground, and walking back to the door. He pushed his hand back through the slot. "Back to sleep, angel."

Her exhaustion and disorientation were only amplifying his own weariness.

"Could you talk to me until I fall asleep?" she asked hesitantly.

Groaning, he wiggled his fingers and lolled his head back. "Once upon a time there was a Tender who went against everything I taught her and mutilated her body with horrendous metal spikes."

"I know this one," she whispered, the smallest hint of amusement rippling through him as she spoke. "Tell me about your tattoos."

He stilled. "Maybe tomorrow," he finally replied. "How about I tell you about Catherine the Great's sex room? Kai graciously left me to my own devices in Russia while he was sizing up Mickey."

"He was always so good to me," she sighed, her bed creaking as she shifted. "I miss Mick."

"I bet you do," he grumbled before catching himself and switching gears. "So Cath—"

"The tattoos," she interrupted. "The long, loopy one on your right arm. When did you do it?"

Looking down at the grey marking on his skin, his eyes trailed the intricate design as it disappeared into the open wound and reappeared on the other side. "Nichol," he said, smirking as he thought back. "He's on an abstinence kick right now, but back in the 1400's, he was like a dog in heat." Her unladylike snort of laughter echoed in the cement chamber. "Goddamn it, I thought we broke that habit," he ribbed. "So Kaius took us to meet an ancient in Spain. He was one of those old turnings done to preserve the man and the intellect. The guy must have been on death's door when he was brought over, because he was one decrepit, nasty-looking vamp."

"Does that happen a lot?" she asked. "Creating vampires for posterity, I guess?"

"Posterity," he chuckled. "Not often. The opportunity rarely presents itself. Most geniuses are on the cusp of insanity and run too high a risk, and most older humans don't gain the strength quick enough to survive more than a century." He paused, debating how much to reveal about Nichol.

Doesn't matter much at this point.

Leaning his weight against the door, he continued. "This vamp had a personal harem of over fifty women for himself and his hauntmates. The only rule he had was to leave this one redhead alone. All the others were fair game. We were there for two weeks when the ancient, a guy named Vanito, rips the door off of our sleeping quarters and goes ballistic. Seems the Kaius scent was all over his favored woman."

"What did he do to Nicky?" she called out.

He frowned. "Aren't you supposed to be getting more tired? Kai tried to talk the guy down. Nichol sat on the bed and began explicitly reviewing every liaison he could recall since our arrival to prove he hadn't soiled the preferred woman. By the seventh or eighth, Vanito was foaming at the mouth and Kaius's head was dropping. So, rather than punish us all with forty more of the mental images Nichol was conjuring, I claimed the offense."

She was quiet for a moment. "But did Nicky do it?"

"Yeah," he said slowly. "Nichol had a bit of a

problem with blood highs back then. In the rare times ancients offered theirs up, he indulged. Vanito and his hauntmates were weirdly generous with their blood, so I don't think Nichol even realized who he was fucking.

With the scent of Vanito and his hauntmates all over the place, neither Kai nor I picked up on it. But we'd also gone our separate ways that evening, so neither of us noticed anything off." Frowning, he traced the unburnt lines of the tattoo. "Given my history of taking what wasn't mine, Kaius bought my admission without question."

"Did Nicky ever figure out you took the blame for him? What did Vanito do to you?"

He could hear her moving around on her bed, the blankets rustling as she did. "Lie down," he ordered before continuing, ignoring her inquiry about Nichol. "The punishment was seventeen years in the pit. Lots of bugs. Lots of rodents. But aside from that, I was pretty much left alone, so it wasn't bad."

The creaking of metal drew his attention and he knelt down to look through the slot. Lis's green eyes met his.

"So every time you were imprisoned…" She trailed off, her eyes disappearing as her small hand wedged through the hole. "Did they feed you?"

"Standard starvation cycle," he answered, rising back to his feet.

Verbally, she went silent again.

In his head was a different story.

"But I made it out," he continued, lightening his tone. "Made it out and snuck back in a few years later to sample the redhead I did time for."

"You have GOT to be kidding me!" she gasped.

"Lie down and close your eyes," he demanded. "Most sexually unsatisfying ninety minutes of my existence, but on the vengeance front? So fucking worth it," he concluded. "Story time's over."

He stood at the door while she finally went quiet in his mind again.

Stood at the door and stared hard at the floor.

"They're just so pretty!" Lis cooed, swatting his hand away as he tried to stop her from tracing the patterns for the millionth time. "This is the one you did when we met, isn't it?"

He rose from the sofa, prying the small hands from his arms as he did. "Whether you like it or not, we're finishing this budgeting lesson. Kaius is expecting you in an hour."

Eyes narrowing, she sank to her knees and hunched over the book on the coffee table. He paced the floor while her pencil flew across the paper, the scratching of the lead periodically interrupted by an annoyed huff.

"There," she said with finality. "Both balances match. Double line. Done. Can we go for a drive now?"

He scanned the assignment quickly and checked the time. "A quick one," he relented. "Shoes on."

She led him through the haunt and up the stairs to the garage, her floral skirt swaying across her calves as she skipped happily to the stolen convertible. "Never, ever get rid of this," she commanded as she sat. "Someday I'm going to drive this."

He revved the engine and tore onto the driveway, kicking dust and stones up behind him.

She arched her neck and looked back. "Nichol's gonna kill you."

Grinning, he hit the highway.

It had become a weekly amusement for them since her arrival, these short trips through the highways and side roads outside Denver. Initially, he used it as an incentive for Lis to complete her lessons. She needed the artificial sense of freedom the trips provided, and it was a risk he was willing to take for her compliance.

And her happiness.

The wind ripped over the car as she pushed a button and the soft-top folded back, her arm reaching out into the open air.

"One of these nights, you're going to lose that," he warned, slowing slightly in the darkness to ensure he didn't miss a wayward tree branch along the tight roadway.

She leaned back in her seat, smiled, and closed her eyes while her arm arced and wove against the wind. He held a steady speed, unwilling to pull her from the trance she'd put herself in. Some nights, she chatted nonstop about whatever flitted through her mind, and other nights she sat quietly, breathing in deeply and settling into a content lull.

When he slowed the convertible to turn back, her eyes opened.

"Already?" she asked, looking out into the black trees.

"You have a place to be," he replied, stepping on the gas harder than intended. "And we need to brush that mop of hair out before you go."

She tapped the button reluctantly and dropped her head to his shoulder.

As she did every time the convertible turned back to the haunt.

"This one," she said quietly, running her thumb

across a small grey loop. "The dips into the center are so close, they almost look like one thick line."

His arm tensed involuntarily. "Almost home," he muttered, pulling off the highway and on to the road leading to the haunt.

She sat up and smoothed her hair down as they pulled into the garage. "I'm not going to be late, am I?"

"Nope. Right on time. Just how Kaius likes it."

Jumping out of the car, she flashed a smile at him and waved. "I'll check in after he dismisses me," she called over her shoulder, her feet flying down the stairs.

He sat in the running car for a few minutes before he reached down to the radio and cranked the music, blocking all thoughts of his haunt leader's fangs burying into her soft skin. Pulling out of the garage, he doubled back onto the highway and took off toward the Rockies.

Keeping his hand in the metal opening, he eased himself to the floor, leaned back, and closed his eyes. There were few sounds as satisfying as the sound of metal hitting rock. Had the moon been full that night, he'd have had an even better view of the convertible as it careened off the road and bounced off every protruding stone on that mountain.

Lis's breathing changed for a moment, then resumed its steady rhythm.

She was exhausted.

So was he.

****

Lis peered through the tiny opening. "Rhys?" she whispered softly.

His hand remained motionless.

She tiptoed across her small cell and brushed her teeth as quietly as she could.

Which, with the echo in the chamber, was most definitely not quiet.

"Rhys?" she called again softly.

Silence.

Sitting back on her bed, she hugged her knees to her chest and waited for him to wake.

CHAPTER THIRTY-TWO

Lis sat on her bed, her freshly washed hair dampening her back through the orange jumpsuit.

"How are your arms tonight?" she asked as she placed her laundry into the paper bag.

"Fine," Rhys growled back, the pacing of his feet coming to a halt.

Bullshit.

He had remained motionless all day, unresponsive while she called out to him louder and louder. His hand stayed wedged in the metal slot, his fingers slowly paling as the hours passed. When the showers turned on, he finally woke in a sour, sullen mood.

"If you need more blood to heal, I'm sure Mr. Heisner—"

"Leave it, Lis," he snarled, the rhythmic sound of his bare feet on the cement resuming.

She pushed the flap of her own slot open and peered through. "Could you look at me for a moment?" she asked. "Please?"

He hesitated a moment before his fingers appeared and pushed the flap open.

The navy of his eyes was completely gone, his irises little more than black slits. The cover slammed shut and the pacing resumed.

Outside of her time in the McConaughey haunt cells, she had little experience with injured vampires. Derry and his hauntmates were vamps who flew under the radar of vampire politics, who stayed close to home and maintained a lifestyle conducive to a continual supply of blood and few risks. Derry McConaughey himself, while older and stronger, had little desire to hunt and even less desire to fight. A self-admitted lover of luxury, he did everything in his power to maintain his easy lifestyle.

Even the few times she'd seen Rhys injured during her training time at the Kaius haunt were softened by the amount of available fresh blood from the bloodslave quarters and his own flippant reactions to the wounds he received during sparring.

But now, he needed more than the bagged blood Heisner was carting into the unit.

She kept her fingers reaching through the slot and waited for Heisner to arrive for his dusk visit. Her stomach was beginning to make itself known, grumbling in demand.

When Rhys stilled again, she stood and pulled her bed away from the door in preparation. Heisner's arrival was loud, his booted feet stomping through the hall and his muttered curses accompanying the shuffling of another paper bag.

"Rise and shine," he announced, knocking lightly on her door before he began fiddling with the lock. "I managed to wheel some fresh fruit and a cucumber along with…I don't really know what the meat is. Looks like pork, smells like turkey."

Heisner entered her room and gave her a tight smile. "I see the shower works in here," he said conversationally. "There were some plumbing issues in another wing. I was wondering if it affected this area, too." He trailed off as a low growl began to echo through the cells.

She looked through her bag, pulling the banana from the pile and carefully opening it. "Did you bring Rhys's meal?"

"Sure did," he replied, glancing at the closed door. "I'll get it to him as soon as I can sign off on your meal. Bon appétit."

Eating quickly, she became increasingly bothered by the growling sound emanating from Rhys. She finished off the mystery meat and added the container to the bag holding her laundry. "I'm running low on clean underwear," she mentioned, handing Heisner the bag.

"I'll get on that by dawn," he replied, rising to his feet. "Sentencing is being officially handed down tonight. I'll be by later with your next meal and an update."

As he moved to close her door, she stepped forward. "He needs more than two bags," she whispered, knowing Rhys would hear her regardless of how quietly she spoke. "He needs fresh blood."

"Leave it, Lis," Rhys barked.

Heisner frowned. "I can't do that without an assessment of his condition," he said. "More bags, I mean. There's a limit on vampire feedings, and two a night is already the max amount allotted."

The door closed, the lock clicking into place. She peeked through the slot and watched as Heisner lifted Rhys's and eased the first bag through.

"It's not enough," she pushed, ignoring Rhys's order.

"LIS!" he snarled, startling Heisner.

The officer shoved the second bag through, keeping his hands as far from the opening as he could. "I'll see what I can do," he muttered, backing away from the cell door, and picking up her laundry.

When the door to the solitary unit slammed shut, Rhys's growling intensified.

"You need to learn when to shut the fuck up," he hissed. "And I don't want that asshole in your cell any longer than necessary."

Emboldened by the amount of concrete and metal between them, she shoved her bed against the door and slammed her hand against it over and over. "You need to learn that when you're weakened, I am too," she seethed. "So maybe YOU need to shut the fuck up. We don't know if those bastards are going to put us through more of those little tests, and if they do, and you're in this state, you're a danger to me."

The growl's intensity lessened.

"You know damn well I have more control than that," he finally said as the sound of tearing plastic filtered into her room.

She refused to respond.

A second blood bag was ripped open.

****

"We're going to need you to back away from the door and put your hands on your head," Heisner instructed, looking through the slot. "I'm going to open this door. One wrong move—"

"And you'll give me a tan," Rhys finished for him, backing up to the far wall. He lifted his arms slowly, the damaged muscles of his biceps making it more of an effort than he let on.

The boots of several guards shuffled in the hall while they positioned themselves. Heisner cracked the door open, motioning for one of his men to hold it. "This here's Dr. Winestar," he said as a tall man in a black suit came up behind him. "Turns out there aren't any vamp specialists, so this is the best I could do." He glanced back at the doctor. "He's doing me a favor here, Rhys. So play nice."

He looked past the men toward Lis's door. Her green eyes were visible through the narrow opening.

Dr. Winestar walked in front of Heisner. "Andy said your arms are giving you some trouble," he said. "Lower them and I'll take a look."

"Check his shoulder blades, too," Lis called over.

Fixing a dead glare in her direction, he dropped his arms to his side.

The doctor leaned forward, unable to hide the fascination from his face. "Clean through to the bone," he muttered, bringing his hand up to the wound.

"Look, don't touch," he snarled.

The doctor snatched his hand back immediately and Lis and Heisner began protesting.

"He can't check you over if you're being an ass," Heisner barked while Lis chastised him for being difficult.

Gritting his teeth, he widened his stance. "Fine," he growled.

Dr. Winestar dropped to one knee and pulled a small light from his pocket. "Just a regular flashlight," he stated before he turned it on. "I need to see inside there."

Humming and muttering, the doctor carefully looked at both arms. "Shirt off," he finally ordered, rising to his feet.

He pulled the singlet off and turned, exposing the healing burn across his shoulder blade.

"All these are from the same night?" the doctor asked.

"Yeah," Heisner responded, his voice slightly remorseful.

Dr. Winestar backed away and looked at Rhys. "Those markings on your arms, those are mercury-based?"

He nodded and pulled his shirt back on.

"How long have you had them?"

"Some of them are centuries old," Lis interjected. When he growled in warning, she met his eyes defiantly. "They've been bothering him for as long as I've known him."

Heisner joined in, a hint of concern on his face. "Since his arrival on site, Mr. Kaius has often scratched those spots until they bled."

The doctor nodded slowly. "The burn hole on your back is almost completely healed," he said. "But from what I can see, some of the mercury from your markings is now coating the bone, and those spots show no sign of repair. This looks like a localized blood poisoning." He turned to Heisner. "That's going to be something your department will want to monitor. The mercury used to mark the vampires coming through here appears to be a toxin."

Walking over to the sink to wash his hands, Dr. Winestar continued. "I'm no expert on vampires, but I suspect if we clean out the wounds and provide enough blood to promote healing, those holes will close up."

"He needs fresh blood," Lis said from her cell. "The bagged doesn't work."

Dr. Winestar looked to him. "Blood poisoning in humans is fatal if left untreated. Your physiology is obviously more capable of combatting the most adverse effects, but I suspect those markings are a continuous source of pain."

Refusing to acknowledge the doctor, he brought his hands back up behind his head and stood motionless.

The doctor left the cell, followed by Heisner. As the door closed and locked, the two men continued to discuss his condition. "I'm going to send over some syringes and sulfur powder. Those wounds will need to be cleaned out with diluted sulfur, then rinsed. It will probably cause significant discomfort until the bone and raw edges are cleaned, but it should work." There was a long pause. "Is that the woman from the news?"

"That's her all right," Heisner replied.

"She's probably in the best position to know how to treat injured vampires," Dr. Winestar stated. "I know securing a live blood donor will be impossible, but it's likely the only way to ensure the wounds heal before more of that mercury leaks out and makes its way deeper in his system. Injected subcutaneously, the toxic effects appear to have remained localized to their zones, but if it makes its way further into his body, the chance of the adverse effects increasing is significant."

Lis's voice rang through the cells while Rhys stared at his closed door. "I'll feed him. He needs it, Mr. Heisner. Please."

The men ignored her, their footsteps and those of the guards drifting down the hall until they disappeared out of the unit.

"Lis," he growled, "I'm going to need you to cover your ears for a few moments. Got it, angel?"

Without waiting for a response, he began driving his fist into the cement wall, bloodying his knuckles, chipping the bones, and channeling the agony of his burns into something he could control.

****

"Mr. Kaius?"

"He's resting," Lis said softly, pulling her hand out of the slot and looking through it at the officer.

He knelt down to meet her eyes. "The sentencing panel came back with their orders. Death by Deepfryer in eight nights. You and Rhys."

She drew a deep breath. "I figured as much."

Heisner glanced over his shoulder. "Dr. Winestar sent the supplies over. I put in a request to the federal vamp division for treatment, but it was denied immediately."

"So you're just going to let him live out his final days in this state," she whispered bitterly, flashing back to the sound of Rhys's fist making contact with the concrete wall over and over until his bloodied fingers eased through the metal slot and he went silent.

Heisner dropped his head for a moment. "I should," he opened. "I could lose my job for going against the feds. I have a mortgage. A dog. Girlfriend, too."

"How quaint," she replied, her voice hollow.

"Yeah. Not as exciting as your life's been, I'm sure, but it works for me." He gave a tight smile. "I want your assurances you know how to handle him."

She frowned. "What do you mean?"

"I'll be off shift in two hours. If I was to make my way down here with the sulfur and syringes, and if I was to open your door and open Rhys's, and if I was to turn my head while you went in there, can you guarantee me I wouldn't be pulling your dead body out of that cell?"

"Yes," she breathed, her shoulders dropping with relief. "Yes, I can."

"The doctor warned the sulfur could be painful,"

Heisner cautioned. "From what I've witnessed, Rhys has a high tolerance, but he's injured. And hungry."

"Then give me a UV light," she insisted. "Rhys will want the precaution."

With a nod, Heisner rose to his feet. "I'll be back later. You can always change your mind."

CHAPTER THIRTY-THREE

Lis's soft voice filtered into Rhys's head, interjected by the low timbre of Heisner's.

"I'm waiting in here."

"That'll make this a lot harder," she whispered. "He doesn't need an audience. Just give me the flashlight and go be seen in your office."

Heisner grunted in annoyance. "How long do you need?"

"Two hours."

"You get one."

He rose to his feet, using the wall to maintain his balance. "What the fuck's going on?" he demanded, bending to peer through the narrow opening.

Lis's door was wide open, a UV flashlight in one of her hands and a small plastic bag in the other. She met his eyes and smiled. "I'm coming over to play."

"Like fuck you are," he snarled, placing his hands on the door. "Heisner, she isn't coming in here."

"You try telling Ms. Bruckner that," the officer replied, standing beside Lis as she approached his door. "Against the back wall, hands where I can see 'em."

"I'll drain her dry," he threatened, refusing to move despite the lock being popped.

"No, you won't," she sighed, motioning for Heisner to open the door. "Now step aside and let me in, Rhys. Please."

After a moment's thought, he slammed his hands on

the metal door and backed up against the wall. "Heisner," he muttered as she entered his cell, "she reeks of cheap soap and chemicals."

The officer's brows rose and he tightened his grip on his UV light.

Lis crossed her arms. "You reek of dried blood and bitterness. Andy, you can go."

Heisner remained in place for a minute, looking between them. "If this goes bad—"

"It'll be fine," she reassured him, emptying the contents of the plastic bag onto the small sink ledge.

Backing out of the cell, Heisner closed the door and slowly clicked the lock into place. "One hour," he called to them as he walked down the hall and through the heavy door securing the wing. "I'll adjust the timer on the shower so you can rinse that shit out."

He eyed the collection of syringes, vials, and cups. "What's that for?"

"We're going to fix you up," she replied, lifting a small paper for examination. "If I'm going to be down here with you for the next eight nights, you need to be more pleasant and less snarly."

"What happens in eight nights?" he asked, looking over her shoulder to read the neatly written instructions.

She arced her head back and gave him a tight smile. "You and I are going to be Deepfryer buddies."

She worked silently over the sink, carefully mixing the yellow powder with water and pulling it into the syringe. When she was done, she eyed his arms. "I'm not sure how to do this," she muttered, tilting her head for a better look. "If I stand on the bed and you hold your arms to the side, I can angle the mixture directly in there." She looked up at him. "We need to do this before it clumps up. It's not dissolving at all. How long can you hold your arms out?"

"Eighteen hours," he replied drily. "Longer when I'm uninjured."

"Show-off," she grinned, flinching slightly when water suddenly burst from the shower head. "That'll make rinsing this out so much easier."

He watched her as she climbed onto his bed and balanced near the edge. She shook the syringes a little, examining the mixture before she called him over. "The doctor said this would hurt," she said softly. "Are you ready?"

Hurt.

"Yeah, I'm ready," he grumbled, turning his back to her, and backing up until his calves hit the mattress. He raised one arm, gritting his teeth with the strain of the movement.

A strange flash of cold radiated through his bicep a second before the searing pain started. He clenched his fist and growled, staring at the floor while the sulfur mixture seeped into his wound.

He could feel her hand stroking the back of his neck as his muscles tensed in a desperate effort to hold his position.

"The sulfur is supposed to be bonding to the mercury," she said quietly. "The directions said it may take a few tries before the bone is cleaned off enough to start healing."

The effort to remain motionless, to resist the overpowering need to feed and lash out, kept him silent. Her hand moved across his forehead, brushing the stray strands from his eyes.

"Let's get that rinsed."

Taking his untreated arm, she attempted to tug him toward the shower.

"Wait," he growled low, his chest heaving involuntarily as his gaze fixated on her hand touching him. "Let go."

When she didn't release his arm instantly, he snapped his fangs at her. "Now."

He walked to the shower under his own power, angling the spray into the burning wound. The pain began to decrease as the sulfur and mercury washed away.

Manageable.

Without looking at her, he returned to the bed and extended his arm again.

"Are you ready?" she asked, her voice trembling.

"Yup."

The second syringe of sulfur emptied into his arm.

****

Lis pushed Rhys's damp hair from his brow, ignoring the hungry look in his eyes as the water rinsed the toxin from his body. "Once more and I think this side will be done," she said quietly.

From her angle, the visible bone had begun to whiten as the mercury was pulled out and eliminated. If it hadn't been for the obvious agony he was experiencing, the procedure would be fascinating. The mercury bonded to the sulfur, creating small yellow beads which circled the drain and disappeared.

But Rhys was in pain and was trying his damnedest to hide it.

His lower lip was scored by his fangs, tiny droplets of blood forming before the splash of the shower water turned the red drops into pink trails running down his chin and throat.

His muscles twitched incessantly.

His eyes were blackened and dull.

"Rhys?" she called to him, gently nudging him back to the bed for the final treatment on the first arm.

"One bite," he purred, reaching across the shower stream to stroke her cheek. "One bite and we continue."

She took a step back out of his reach, refilled the syringe, and climbed back on the bed. "We can't run the risk of you healing over any remaining loose mercury."

He stalked toward her, his ovaled eyes locked on her neck. "One bite, and I'll do anything you say," he growled, a smirk on his face when she subconsciously brought her hand to her throat. When she didn't respond, he stepped tight to her, lifted his arm, and bowed his head against her. "It really fucking hurts."

The split-second she hesitated with the syringe was long enough for him to notice.

"Angel," he murmured, dropping his head to her chest, "one bite and I can keep going."

She narrowed her eyes and pushed the solution into his wound, stumbling back when his spine arched, and his head flew back with a curse. His arm remained locked in place, giving the sulfur mixture time to work as the foulest word combinations she ever heard poured from his mouth.

She approached him carefully, keeping one eye on his fangs and another on the whitening bone of his injury. "Done this one," she announced, keeping out of his reach as he turned toward the shower and dragged his feet across the floor.

The yellow beads swirled at his feet while the water did its work. She busied herself with filling the syringes again and shaking the remaining solution in the cup.

"Lis?"

She glanced over at Rhys, dropping the syringes on the ledge as he sank to his knees and fell forward onto his hands.

Panting.

She was at his side in an instant, her hands spanning his broad back as it expanded and contracted under her touch.

"I can't... fucking... do this," he snarled.

"You're half done," she insisted, laying her head on him to feel the strangely human movements of his chest. "One more arm and this is done. Over."

"Once more and I'll drain you dry," he rasped. "What the hell were you thinking?"

She clung to him tighter, glancing at the UV light sitting on the bed. "Let's get you against the wall over there," she said softly, lifting off him and pointing at the dry patch behind the shower spray. "Sit there and wait a minute."

Her heart clenched as he forced himself to his feet and straightened his back. The tension in his body while he walked the few steps made his once graceful gait lumbering and awkward. When he reached the wall, he slid down the rough cement, his head bowed.

She snatched up the syringes, remaining powder, and UV light, and approached him carefully. "We're going to try this a different way," she whispered, squatting down to his level. She took the untreated arm gingerly and crossed it over his chest. "Hold it there."

He obeyed, his dark head tucked into the crook of his elbow.

Arranging her arsenal at his hips, she nudged his

bent knees down slightly and straddled him.

"Don't do this," he growled.

She leaned across him and grabbed the flashlight. "If you bite me without permission, I'll zap you." Picking up the powdered sulfur, she settled into his lap and examined his wound as the splash of the shower dampened her back. "I'm going to pour straight sulfur in, then you're going to lean forward and get the spray on it to rinse it."

"Get. Off."

His voice was muffled under his arm, his shoulders twitching.

"Hold on," she whispered, ignoring his command.

The moment the yellow powder hit the hole in his arm, tiny beads began to form.

And the snarl tearing through him nearly sent her running for the door.

She gripped his arm in a futile effort to steady him should he move. His fingers dug into his own shoulder, drawing blood as his knuckles whitened. She watched the powder pull the mercury from his body and form into marble-sized pellets.

"Okay, honey," she hushed, "I need you to stretch this arm out into the water."

His fingers unhooked from his shoulder, exposing deep divots in his skin. He kept his head down as he reached past her.

Eight inches shy of the spray.

With a deep breath, she lifted her weight from his lap and sat on her knees beside him. "You're going to need to move forward about a foot," she instructed. When he didn't comply immediately, she ran a hand through his hair. "You need to do this, Rhys."

His body heaved forward slowly, his heels digging into the cement and pulling his large form across the floor until the spray of the shower aligned with his untreated arm. His other one lifted in her direction, making contact with her hand, and gripping it.

Globules of yellowed mercury dropped to the floor and down the drain. When the water began to run clear again, she climbed back on his lap.

"Two more," she said, blocking the spray from his wound as she eased his arm back across his chest. She guided his other hand to her thigh. "When it hurts, squeeze."

A mirthless laugh came from under Rhys's arm. "If I squeeze, that scrawny toothpick will snap." His deep voice was tight, scratchy.

"I'm tougher than I look," she replied, aligning the syringe with the wound. "Round two."

She braced herself for the pain of his fingers digging through the rough fabric of her jumpsuit. His shoulder was bleeding again as his nails dug in, but the hand on her leg merely tensed slightly with the initial blast of liquid.

"Rinse," she ordered, leaning back to allow him enough room to move. He extended his arm into the water, leaning forward to rest his head on her chest and wrapping his other arm tight around her waist.

"Last one, then you can eat."

With those words, Rhys's hips shifted slightly underneath hers. She bent her head down to his ear. "I thought you were in agony."

"Can't fight instinctual responses to a woman on my lap."

CHAPTER THIRTY-FOUR

So. Fucking. Warm.

Rhys nuzzled against the soft skin of the female on his lap, keeping his aching fangs as far from her jugular as he could without losing the heat her body radiated.

"I think we got the last of it."

Lis.

He reared back, loosening his grip on her instantly and dropping his soaked arm to the cement. Yanked from the warmth of her proximity, the blistering pain in his biceps barreled back into his consciousness.

A slim wrist appeared in his line of sight, the bright orange cuff of her jumpsuit pushed to her elbow.

"Go on," she urged, frowning when he lay back on the concrete as far from her offering as he could get in his current state. Shifting her weight slightly, she followed suit.

"Tell Heisner to bring a few extra bags," he muttered.

Her green eyes narrowed. "At the rate those tattoos are seeping, we'll be going through this again tomorrow night if you don't eat. Now what's the hold up?"

His gaze flicked to the gaping neckline of the ill-fitting jumper. "I could drain you."

"Blah, blah, blah," she murmured, bringing her wrist to her own mouth, and pausing. "If I open a vein, it'll be painful and messy. If you do it, it'll be neat and painless. Your call."

He parted his lips in response, glaring daggers at her while she bent forward and lowered her wrist to him.

Easing his fangs into the pale skin, he tightened his hold on her hip when the pinch of the bite hit. When the first taste of her fresh blood hit his tongue, a low growl filled the room.

Holy. Fuck.

Unhooking his fangs, he glanced up at her. "The light," he rasped.

She lifted it from the floor and held it tight as he sunk back into her vein, tuned out the familiar look in her eyes, and focused on the heat she provided.

****

Such a slow eater.

Lis smiled as the random thought passed through her head. She opened one eye and watched the movement of his Adam's apple every time he swallowed.

She had expected an aggressive attack, braced herself for the deep piercing of his long fangs and the sharp pain accompanying a bite of desperation. She was prepared for a fast feeding, one draining more pints than she could safely give.

But this, this was almost leisurely.

Restrained.

Her head lay on his shoulder, her wet hair draping down his back. She eased her free arm along his, trailing along his forearm until she reached his hand. His fingers intertwined with hers, giving her a light squeeze. Every few minutes, he would dig his heels into the cement and adjust his hips, steadying her with one hand until she regained her balance, his thumb absently tracing circles on her hipbone.

Closing her eyes again, she allowed herself to fall

into blissful contentment.

"That's enough," he whispered, his fangs pulling out of her wrist. "You okay?"

She hummed and nodded. "You?"

His tongue traced the punctures in her skin before he lowered her arm to his chest. "Better," he replied, draping his arm over her back. He turned his head and looked down at her, the reappearance of his navy irises a welcomed sight. "Heisner will be back soon. Make sure he brings you some dry clothes."

Her gaze fell to his mouth, to the still elongated fangs.

"Lis—"

Her lips were on his before she could think, before she could rationalize the overwhelming impulse. Her hand traveled to his jawline as a low growl rumbled through his chest and his arms tightened around her. She ran her tongue over one fang, then the other, letting the steel ball drag across the smooth enamel and sending a tremor through his body. He ground his hips against her core languidly while she trailed her lips across his jaw and flicked her tongue against his earlobe before returning to the lips and fangs she'd been craving for decades.

****

More.

Spikes of lust ricocheted through his mind, amping up his instinctive post-feeding desire and driving his free hand toward the zipper of Lis's jumper. He could feel the outline of her ribs as he traveled from her hip and along the side of a breast he was pretty fucking determined to see. Her tongue, with that goddamn silver ball, trailed down his fangs again, sending an involuntary jolt to his hips.

Fuck. Yes.

Pushing her up, his fingers latched on to the zipper pull while his vision narrowed in on the excruciatingly slow exposure of the body he was hellbent on ravaging. A small hand covered his, urging him on as a warm haze trickled through his head, pouring a shitload of ice water on his lust.

"Playtime's over," he muttered, easing the zipper back up and putting his hands behind his head. "Let's get you away from this shower spray so you're ready when Heisner returns."

He kept his gaze averted while the warmth in his head morphed to confusion, and then hurt.

She rose off him slowly and began collecting the syringes and vials peppering the floor. As she reached for the flashlight, she paused.

Blast me. I fucking deserve it.

Her thumb hesitated on the switch before she tucked it into the crook of her arm and turned her back to him to wait for the heavy footfalls signifying Heisner's arrival.

****

Rhys leaned against his door, silently monitoring Heisner as he ensured Lis ate her doctor-ordered meal.

"I'll see if I can scrounge up two more suits for you. Maybe get a good rotation going."

She paused from whatever she was eating. "Did you bring me any clean underwear?"

"Right here."

The snarl ripping through him was contained immediately, his control returning with the intake of Lis's B-negative.

By the time Heisner left the unit in search of dry

jumpsuits, he was fuming.

"You're freezing," he called over to her. "Why the fuck didn't you push for the shower to be turned on. That asshole did it once, he could do it again."

Silence.

He turned to face the door, locking his attention on it as though he might be able to see through to the woman in the other cell. "And he should be adding iron supplements and orange juice to your meals." He slammed his hands on the door and began pacing the floor. "Goddamnit, Lis. You're still too fucking skinny to stay warm enough down here. Now add in the blood loss, and Heisner should fucking know a jumper and an extra banana won't make a fucking difference."

He could hear her moving around her cell. The rustling of a paper bag. The running water of her sink.

The sound of her brushing her teeth.

He waited for her to finish. And waited. And waited.

"What the hell are you doing over there?" he asked, his brows knotting as she ignored him and continued to scrub her teeth for another two minutes before the water ran and she stopped. With all of his strength focused on healing his injuries, he had little left to block the turmoil she was unleashing in his mind.

"Lis."

No answer.

He glared at the door. "LIS!"

"Calm down," she finally replied, her voice hollow despite the rolling waves of emotion she was transmitting. "I was just getting the bitter taste of you out of my mouth."

Fucking. Ouch.

271

****

Kaius leaned against the garage wall, watching Jagger and Bianca loading supplies and weapons into one of the vehicle hatches. "What's this about?"

Bianca smoothed her hand over Jagg's forearm and nodded his way. With a quick reshuffling of one of the larger bags, Jagger approached him. "Welcome back," he greeted formally, his ice eyes hard.

"What's this about?" he repeated, gesturing to the stockpile of blades and guns.

"Bee and I are heading to L.A."

Bianca came up behind Jagg and held his arm. "Good to see you again, Kai," she smiled warmly. "We've received a message from Rhys." She glanced up at Jagg. "I think Nichol would be the best one to talk to about it."

He frowned. "I'll head to the com room now. No one goes anywhere until I'm filled in. That's not a choice."

As he descended the steps into the main haunt, Jagger's voice filtered down the hall.

"Yeah, like you have any right to give the orders around here anymore."

He froze in place, instantly torn between ignoring the slight and removing Jagg's fangs for the insolence.

"Hey man!" Mickey called out, temporarily saving Jagger. "When did you get in?"

He stepped to the side to allow Mick to pass through the narrow stairwell with the oversized load in his arms. "Ten minutes ago. Where are you headed?"

"Los Angeles," Mickey grinned. "I'm aiming to see Audra in a bikini. Also, we should put in a pool down here, so I have an excuse to watch her walk around in one every night. Just a thought."

He grinned at Mick, pleased to see his second-youngest had pulled out of his low during his absence. "I'll consider it," he said, continuing on his trek to find Nichol and answers.

His eldest was predictably hunched over his computer in the com room, his brow knotted in concentration. He entered the room, giving a quick acknowledgement to Boy who sat at the table, scrolling through news on a laptop.

"Kaius," Nichol greeted without averting his attention from the screen. "Which font do you prefer?"

He pointed out an elegant script. "What's this for?"

"Monogrammed towels," Nichol muttered, making a few more clicks on the keyboard before the printer whirred to life. He snatched the receipt and handed it to Kai. "What do you think?"

Baby-Fanged, Small-Dicked Fuckwad.

"I—" He read the inscription over again. "Who's this for?"

"Jagger," Nichol replied. "We got word from a vamp released out of Los Angeles who was housed with Rhys. He passed on a message." He turned back to his computer and pulled up an email. "'Rhys is all good. Release the Tender. Jagger is a baby-fanged, small-dicked fuckwad'. There's a list of names of some of the other released prisoners. Most have already touched base with Jagg and Bianca. Two young ones have been placed with Wolfgang Vicente at his Vegas haunt." Nichol sat back and looked him straight in the eye, a hint of challenge in his stare. "Boy and I are attempting to coordinate an extraction for Lis."

He pulled up a chair. "You don't feel a rescue effort for a turned Tender who should have met her end at

273

Rhys's hand months ago is a high-risk operation and a waste of resources?"

"No, I don't think fulfilling my brother's final request is a waste of resources," Nichol replied with a snarl.

He stared his eldest son down. When Nichol refused to look away, he rose. "Call the others. Meeting here in ten."

****

Nichol passed the monogrammed towel receipt to Mickey under the table, clenching his teeth to keep a straight face while Mick surreptitiously passed it on to Dominic and Louis. The feigned stoic faces of his hauntmates were comedic in themselves as they tried to hide the source of their amusement from Jagger.

Bianca was completely on-board. She was, after all, the one who demanded Nichol order a matching set in fuchsia to coordinate with their bathroom decor.

Kaius sat at the head of the table, the place usually reserved for the computer monitor during his absences.

"I want summaries of our current situations," Kai announced to the hauntmates, bringing the room to a frigid order. When none of the brethren volunteered to open, Kaius's jaw tensed and he looked to Dominic. "How's the Bloodslave Release Program going?"

Dom glanced at Louis and Molly. "It's on hold. We have a lot with no desire to go. Audra's been working on them, but so far only one more is showing a willingness for resettlement."

Kaius flicked his wrist before addressing Jagger. "How's the arsenal stock?"

"Fine."

"And training?"

"Good."

Mickey glanced around the table. "Deepfryer shipments have landed in every major city with the exception of Denver and a lot of smaller counties expected to receive theirs by the end of next month."

"The situation in St. Louis is under control," Audra piped in, her voice unusually light. "Deviant sightings have dropped to nothing over the past two weeks. Unfortunately, sightings of Dovidas and his accomplice, who we assume is Chen, are also sitting at zero."

Kaius turned to Bianca. "How are the hacking efforts progressing? I saw several of your targets in the headlines over the past weeks."

"We've had eight convictions and currently have seventeen of the higher-ranking anti-vamp organizers under investigation," she replied, placing her hand on Jagger's thigh when his eyes narrowed at his creator. "Our allies are doing most of the work on the investigative front now, so Jagger and I are freed up to pursue other avenues."

Kai leaned forward with interest. "What would these other avenues be?"

"Getting Lis out," Jagger responded, his voice cold. "She and Rhys have been sentenced to the Fryer in seven nights' time. Since tonight's now a bust, that leaves us on a tighter schedule."

"Her extraction hasn't been approved," Kai reminded Jagg harshly, provoking Nichol's ire.

"I approved the request, as designated head of the haunt in your absence," he stated, straightening in his chair.

"And my return negates any orders not yet carried out," Kai responded. "I'll consider arguments tonight in support of the mission, but I see no logical reason to risk the lives of our haunt to release a female who turned very publicly on our kind."

Jagger stood up, storming from the room while he called to him over his shoulder. "I'll be in touch once we hit our first stop."

Mickey was next to leave. "I'll drop that package of old surveillance cameras off in Vegas," he offered, picking up the box Nichol had been itching to clear from his com room. "I want Audra to meet Vincente. That old pervert makes me look like a saint." He waggled his tongue at Audra, ducking when she swatted at his head.

"Get. Back. Here."

His muscles tensed with Kaius's growled order. The haunt leader's eyes were blackening, his fangs lengthening as he rose to his feet. "One of you, get Jagger's ass in here. NOW."

Molly shrank into Dominic as the youngest vamp slowly eased himself between his connected and Kai. Louis fixed his gaze on the table and inched his chair back toward Boy.

"Kaius," he began, eying Mickey as he re-entered the room, "this is between you and me."

Kai's black irises turned to him. "I'll address your inability to set boundaries later," he snarled.

"Low blow, Kai," Mick interjected, setting down the box of equipment. "Nichol's been doing a damn good job in your place over the past few years. Decades, really."

As Kaius launched himself across the table, Audra entered the room, Jagger and Bianca hot on her heels. Mickey was on his back before anyone could react, Kai's hand tight on his throat. "Your insolence proves my case."

"Bullshit," Jagger barked, pushing Bianca behind him. "Backing up our brother isn't fucking insolence." He lowered his voice and glanced behind him. "Sorry for the language."

Nichol rose cautiously, ensuring Kaius had a good view of his hands at all times. "Let him go, Kai. We'll discuss this one-on-one."

Kaius's palpable anger set Nichol on edge, but if push came to shove, he was far more equipped to go toe-to-toe against the haunt leader than his younger brothers. He scanned the room for the most delicate equipment, pricing out replacement costs in his head while Kai rose to his feet. Bracing himself for attack, he widened his stance in time to watch Kaius storm from the room.

****

"She's out cold and doesn't need to be woken," Rhys warned Heisner when the officer entered the solitary unit.

"I'm not here to talk to Ms. Bruckner," Heisner replied.

He tracked the man's approach, listening to the sloshing of the blood bags.

Appetizing.

"So you can tell when she's sleeping?" Heisner asked. "Do you feel it or something?"

"I monitor her heart rate, breathing patterns, and the frequency of her movements 24/7."

"Ah."

The flap lifted and the first bag began to drop through the slot.

"Did you and Ms. Bruckner have a falling out?" Heisner ventured. "I've noticed some tension over the past two nights. It's been a bit frigid in here."

Fucking glacial.

"We're good."

The second bag appeared in the narrow opening. "I've been re-watching the interviews Ms. Bruckner did prior to her disappearance." He paused. "You're one those trainers, aren't you?"

He placed the bagged blood in his sink, ignoring the officer.

"That's gotta be a messed-up job," Heisner mused. "I mean, taking the whole morality issue off of the table, the work itself has to be weird. Spending all those months working so intimately with a woman, knowing she's going to spend the rest of her life with another man—vampire—I'd think some of those attachments would be hard to break."

"You ever lose a colleague?" he asked, leaning against the door. "No different. One moves out, another moves into her place."

"That easy, hey?" Heisner didn't sound convinced. "I lost a partner a few years back. It took me... hell, I don't think I'm over it even now."

"My girls don't die."

"Yeah, well, this one's about to."

He could feel his fangs lengthening at the accusation in the officer's voice. "Lis made a lot of decisions placing her here," he snarled.

Heisner's fingers tapped at his door. "See that's what I found interesting," he said slowly. "Ms. Bruckner's containment is explainable. Yours? Not so much. You've had ample opportunity to escape. The van ride. The first cell block. That little trick you did with the chains was pretty impressive. And it got me thinking."

The officer stopped for a moment. "That girl in there cares for you."

"That girl is almost sixty."

A low whistle pierced his eardrums. "You don't say. Damn. My girl's not even forty and she isn't nearly as—"

"Finish that thought, and I'll suffocate you with your own balls," he growled.

Heisner cleared his throat. "Anyways, that woman cares for you. A lot. And the fact you're even down here now speaks volumes."

"Continued monitoring of placements is part of why I get paid the big money," he countered. "Reading anything more into my actions is both futile and foolish." He paused. "Good morning, Lis."

****

Nichol rocked his chair, balancing precariously on the back legs before dropping forward again.

"I'm not going to apologize for speaking the truth."

Mickey's voice broke his rhythm, sending him forward with a clunk. "I appreciate the sentiment," he muttered, snapping out of his daze, and returning his attention to the wiring blueprint in front of him.

"Do you think Kai will return?" Mick prodded, walking closer to peer over his shoulder.

"If he doesn't, he wouldn't be the first ancient to walk away from his haunt," he replied distractedly, pointing at the screen. "This would be the most logical point to tap into, right?"

"There or over here," Mick suggested, dragging his hand along the screen. "Jagg's prepping the other vehicles tonight. We'll hit the road at dusk."

He clicked on the image and the printer fired up. "Jagger and Bianca can travel alone, but I want Boy alongside Louis, Dom, and Molly. I'll pair up with you and Audra."

"Who's staying back to watch the haunt?" Mick asked, his brow furrowed.

"We'll lock up tight."

****

"It's looking better," Dr. Winestar commented, prodding Rhys's arm as he turned to Heisner. "If we could get one more live feeding into him, I think that will do the trick."

He clenched his teeth while the men discussed his condition, completely shutting him out of the conversation.

Lab rat.

Heisner pulled out his phone and tapped away at it. "I'll see what I can arrange."

The guards followed the men from the unit, their boots clomping gracelessly across the cement.

"You're not feeding me," he called over to Lis from his bed. "Your iron levels haven't replenished enough to sustain another significant loss."

"Of course not, sir."

His fangs snapped down.

Sir.

She hadn't spoken to him in 57 hours.

Of course not, sir.

"Do NOT 'sir' me," he growled through the steel door.

"My mistake," she replied, her voice light. "I thought since you were issuing orders like a trainer, you expected the response of a trainee. SIR."

He slammed the heel of his palm into the door. "You want to play that game? We can play," he snarled. "Try enunciating your words instead of slurring them together like a goddamned drunk. Let's start with that."

"As. You. Wish. Sir," she snarked back. "Want me to repeat it in Spanish?"

He ran a hand through his hair and dropped his forehead to the door. "French, please."

He knew her French wasn't strong enough, even for such a basic sentence.

And she knew he knew it.

"You're such an asshole," she muttered.

"Enunciate and try again," he responded, closing his eyes in frustration.

The pair fell into a hostile silence, neither speaking or moving until Heisner arrived alone.

"Ms. Bruckner?" he called out, the lock of Lis's door clicking open. "As you heard, Dr. Winestar recommends another feeding for Rhys. Obviously, I have no other options, so if you're open to the idea—"

"She's not," he grunted.

"I AM," she spat back. "Give me that light."

"So help me, Lis, I will fucking end you if you step foot in here," he roared, sending Heisner's heart rate through the roof.

"Oooooooh, I might die five days early. Big threat, vampire. Just the thought of missing those final lukewarm showers has me prostrate in despair."

"Andy—"

"There's no united brotherly front when angry, sarcastic women are involved," Heisner stated, unlocking his door. "Back to the wall and hands up, or I'll give her two flashlights."

He backed up, his fangs slicing his lower lip as she strode into his space and met his eyes with narrowed green slits.

"How much time do you need?" Heisner called in, pulling the door closed.

"NONE."

"Thirty minutes," she countered, stalking toward him while Heisner lumbered from the wing. She turned on the UV light, aiming the beam at the ground while extending her wrist. "Eat."

Bluff.

"I'm good."

The light slashed across his chest.

"What the FUCK!" he roared, taking a step toward her. "Give me the light."

"Eat."

Her wrist brushed against his fangs, scoring a thin line in the pale skin. The scent of B-negative assaulted his senses, drawing his already-extended fangs out further.

Fine.

His fangs dove into her wrist without finesse, the punctures far deeper than necessary. The jolt of pain quickened her heart rate, sending the blood through her body faster. He gripped her arm to steady it, unwilling to risk a torn artery despite his spiking temper. Refusing to meet her eyes, he stared at the collarbone still protruding more than it should.

She needs to regain fourteen more pounds.

He was locked on to her breathing and heart rate, listening for any stutters in the steady rhythms, when her free wrist brushed across his forehead and pushed the stray strands of hair out of his eyes, her fingers still wrapped around the UV light.

He tightened his grip on her wrist as he unhooked his fangs, lifting her arm up to help stop the blood flow. "You can put that thing down," he said quietly, glancing at the flashlight.

Kneeling first to place the light at her feet, she wrapped her hand around his arm. "Can I check?" she asked.

"Can I stop you?"

With a small smile, she examined the healing injuries on his arms before she began lifting his shirt to check his latest burn.

"Don't worry about it," he grunted, pushing her hands off of him. "It'll be gone by tomorrow."

When she refused to release the hem of his singlet, he grabbed her wrists. "Don't. Touch. Me."

She stepped back, shaking herself loose from his hold. "You're being ridiculous," she huffed. "You do it then. Let me make sure I didn't do any significant damage."

He ran his tongue over one canine and focused on the musty odor of the cell as he exposed the reddened strip across his stomach.

He ignored the flash of regret passing over her face.

Ignored the slight increase in her heart rate.

Ignored the quick hitching of her breath as she knelt down for a better look.

But he couldn't ignore the soft fingers tracing the path of the burn.

He had the forethought to protect the back of her head with his hand while he shoved her against the door, had the forethought to actively avoid slicing her with his fangs as his lips descended on hers. But that was as far as his mind was willing to stretch.

By the time her surprise echoed through his head, her right hand was already tangled in his hair and her left was making its way under his shirt toward his chest. He tugged on her hair gently, nudging her lips apart with his tongue until she relented, and he felt the smoothness of that godforsaken metal ball. His other hand found the zipper of her jumpsuit and yanked it down without an ounce of artfulness.

"That's the ugliest fucking bra I've ever seen," he grunted, pushing the hideous orange jumper off her shoulders, and sending it to the floor. As she reached back to unhook the atrocity, he took matters into his own hands, ripping it in two and shoving it off her arms. He took a second to memorize the view before he dove back to her lips and guided her hands toward the zipper of his cargos. "We've got eleven minutes."

He ignored the speed she was able to maneuver the hooks and zipper of his pants and focused on the heat of her hand as she grasped him.

"You know this is a one-off, right?" she panted, arching her head back as he trailed his tongue down her neck and hooked his thumbs into the elastic of her underwear. He pushed them past her thighs, gracelessly dodging her knees as she stepped out of the cheap fabric matching the equally offensive bra.

"One-off," he echoed, stepping out of his cargos as he guided her to the bed. The second-rate metal of the bed frame creaked in protest as they fell on to it, instantly yanking her from her haze.

"Maybe we shouldn't—"

"Yes, we fucking should," he groaned, bending his head down to take one perfect nipple into his mouth. She arched into him, and he trailed his lips back up to hers. "Just a one-off," he muttered as her tongue traced his fangs again and he reached between them to guide himself into her.

"I don't think we have enough ti-oh-God, right there."

He shook off the blast of longing ricocheting through him as he pushed inside her and instead focused on the heat and friction her body provided. Circling her sensitive nub with his thumb, he zeroed in on her breathing and adjusted his speed and pressure, smirking when a cursing moan escaped her.

"This means nothing," she gasped, her nails digging into his shoulders as his speed increased.

He clenched his teeth, the combination of tight and wet testing his control. "Nothing."

He sat back on his haunches, pulling her hips along with him and providing him with a view which almost sent him over the edge. With the change of angle, her body began to tighten around him. She drew in a deep breath and held it.

"Breathe," he growled, pulled from the moment until she complied and began panting.

Four minutes.

No way in hell was Heisner going to be allowed to hear her.

He shifted forward again, covering her body with his and burying his head in the crook of her neck as he slammed into her. Her pants morphed into curses, her legs tightening around his hips as he sunk his fangs into her throat and the first tremors of her orgasm began.

It had been a long time since he'd fucked and fed at the same time outside of a meticulously planned and executed training session.

The euphoric disorientation he felt as he released inside her caught him off-guard. All thought disappeared when his body instinctively took over, pulling warm blood into his mouth while he pushed into her addictive wet heat until he was spent.

His mind went into overdrive, her emotions and his bouncing off each other in his head as he jumped off her, snatched his cargos from the floor, and hiked them up roughly.

"Two minutes," he muttered, keeping his gaze everywhere but on the woman sitting up on his bed. He gathered her clothing and set it beside her, taking an inordinate amount of time to pull his singlet back over his head.

Tracking her movements in his peripheral, he retreated to the back of his cell and listened for the telltale sound of Heisner's boots.

"Rhys."

He glanced toward her, looking just past her shoulder.

"It was a one-off," she stated softly as she tucked the UV light under her arm. "Done and forgotten."

Done and forgotten.

That worked just fucking fine for him.

CHAPTER THIRTY-FIVE

Nichol and Mick exchanged a look of amusement while Audra attempted to keep her eyes averted from the intimate scene playing out behind the glass of Wolfgang Vicente's private viewing room.

"What is she going to do with THAT?" Molly gasped, leaning forward and elbowing Bianca in the process. "Oh. OH. Yikes."

Vicente's brows rose at Molly's reaction. He turned to Nichol, his voice low enough to remain unheard by the humans in the room. "I was under the impression these were Rhys-trained Tenders accompanying your hauntmates."

He stifled a grin when Audra subtly shushed Molly before fixing Mick with a stare clearly stating he was NOT to get any ideas. "How have the two young ones we sent your way been adapting?" he asked, changing the subject to avoid too much interest in the women.

"Undisciplined, spoiled, and demanding," Vicente replied. "Much like myself. They will do well here."

As the curtain dropped on the show, the hauntmates rose from their seats and thanked their host.

Nichol hung back as the others made their way out of the room and toward the secluded resting area. "Vicente," he murmured, keeping one eye on his retreating hauntmates, "if Fallon Derry makes his way through here, a call would be greatly appreciated. And well-compensated."

"Before or after I end him and the rest of that sniveling brood?" he chuckled. "It is true then…the rumors of his involvement in Rhys's capture?" When he didn't respond, Vicente nodded slowly and began heading back into the private screening room. "Some may feel Rhys deserves to be taken down, but most of us agree he deserves a better end than falling to a coward like Fallon Derry."

****

Rhys sat on his bed and glared at his door, willing his eyes to burn through the metal and into Heisner's thick skull. Unaware of the death wish being placed on him, the officer continued to chat with Lis while she ate, filling her in on ridiculous celebrity gossip and poorly describing humorous social media posts. In between bites, she would laugh, ask a senseless question, then resume eating while Heisner stumbled through another pointless story.

"She's trained for this," he muttered under his breath. "You aren't that fucking funny."

For the past two nights, he had sat back and listened to the pair. Once he realized Lis was interested in his tales, Heisner became a verbal little bastard, spending twice as long in her cell than he had previously. Her bi-nightly meals were now social events.

And it was fucking annoying.

As she laughed at a particularly long-winded story, he lay back on his bed and flung his arm over his eyes. "I can feel her boredom, asshole."

A sharp pang of annoyance rang through his head from the corner of his mind he had corralled her emotions into.

He may have said it a little louder than intended.

By the time Heisner left for the day, he'd heard enough about which starlet had been caught in bed with which musician, and which B-list actor had been brought into the station and charged with drug possession.

"You don't need to be so rude," she chastised from her cell. "I think it's nice of Andy to spend a little time making me feel normal."

"How the fuck does listening to ramblings about people you don't know make you feel normal?"

She sighed, the sound of her creaking bed bringing flashbacks he was more than happy to quash. "I don't know," she muttered. "It just does. Like shopping used to. And eating fast food. Those little slices of normalcy other women have. Besides, I like hearing about his girlfriend and his cat and the leaking shower in his basement. He's ready to propose but has reservations because he's not sure his salary is enough to support a family. It's sweet."

Rolling his eyes, he flopped back onto his bare mattress. "It's monotonous."

She laughed drily. "Monotony doesn't look so bad from this cell. Have a good night, Rhys."

He monitored her breathing and heart rate as she settled, making a mental note to suggest Heisner add another iron pill to her final evening meals. When she finally fell into a fitful rest, he flung his arm back over his eyes and waited until she awoke.

"Get those filthy feet away from me," he growled, swatting the bare toes wiggling toward him. "The peasant girls I grew up with had less mud caked under their nails. Where were you?"

"The forest!" Lis exclaimed, sitting up in excitement. "Mickey took me tree climbing." She paused

and frowned. "He's a bit of a show-off."

"For fuck's sake. Show me your fingers."

She extended her hands, proudly displaying her shredded manicure.

"You, shower," he ordered, rolling his shoulders out. "I'll be back."

As the faucet turned on, he stalked out of the training quarters and into the haunt.

"MIKHAIL!" he bellowed into the halls. "Get your ass out here."

Mickey rounded the corner, his brows knotted. "What?"

Lowering his voice, he closed in on his youngest brother. "I have a trainee downstairs covered in dirt and scratched to shit."

"Oh, yeah!" Mick laughed. "Nichol asked me to do a camera check on the new surveillance system and I figured Lis was probably up for a night outside. She's a pretty decent climber."

"I'll add it to her sales pitch," he growled, stepping into Mickey's space. "Trainees don't leave these walls without my permission. Got it?"

Mick's good humor disappeared when Rhys's fangs elongated. "It wasn't a big deal. We were on site the whole time, and I stayed under her in case she lost her grip. What the hell's your problem?"

"My problem," he snarled, slamming his brother into the wall, "is I have a bleeding product downstairs, and your stupidity is the cause. Next time she's returned to me with one hair out of place, I'll remove your fangs and shove them up your ass. We clear?"

Rhys ran a hand through his hair and rested his healed arms on his knees.

Bleeding product.

Eleven scratches and a hangnail.

The dirt caking Lis that night probably saved Mick, since it masked the scent of her blood when she waltzed into the training rooms, her face flushed with an excitement and happiness he hadn't caused.

He could still remember the knot forming in his stomach when he examined her damaged hands. His mind scoured every possible outcome her tree-climbing adventure could have had, shoving aside the resentment he felt knowing it was Mickey who brought so much light to her eyes that evening.

Her breathing changed abruptly, her blankets rustling.

"You okay?" he called over, counting her heartbeat in his head.

"Thirsty," she mumbled, her feet padding across the cement. "What time is it?"

"Three."

The sink faucet turned on for a few moments before she made her way back to bed. "I really hate this," she whispered as her bed creaked.

"Me too, angel."

****

Lis lay awake for hours, listening to Rhys while he paced, sat, lay down, and paced again. Every so often she could hear him scratch at his arms before he would stop and resume the restless walking across the tiny room.

"Would you just stay still?" she finally huffed, her voice louder than she intended.

His low laugh rumbled through the cells. "I was wondering how long you could pretend to be sleeping. Impressive."

She rolled onto her side and looked toward her door. "Why are you still up?"

"Why are you?"

"Because I'm counting down the hours and I'm afraid to waste any by sleeping. Even though there's absolutely nothing I can be doing in here," she muttered, her stomach tensing as she verbalized it.

His footsteps grew slightly louder as he approached his door. "You need rest," he said quietly. "There's still a while to go."

"Yeah," she scoffed. "What, fifty hours?"

"Fifty-two."

"You really suck at making me feel better," she sighed, wrapping her blanket tight around herself. "Are you scared?"

He went silent for a moment. "No."

"I am."

"I know," he said and she picked up the sound of him scratching at his tattoos again. "I'm working on that, baby. Now close your eyes and I'll tell you a story about the Wicked Witch of the Haunt, her evil lists, and her complete inability to mind her own fucking business."

CHAPTER THIRTY-SIX

Nichol uncrossed his legs and stretched out on the concrete floor, tossing a withering glare at Louis. "What is it with you and shitty hideouts?" he demanded, shifting his laptop screen for a better view. "My goddamn ass is numb."

Louis grinned, pulled a ball cap over his unnaturally bright red hair, and walked to the door. "Boy and I will be back in a bit. Make yourselves comfortable."

"Be careful out there!" Bianca called after them, pointing an accusing finger at Louis. "Don't you get him in any trouble."

Louis glanced up at the ancient vampire and smirked. "C'mon, kiddo. I'm gonna introduce you to the bright lights and big city."

The door creaked closed, and Bianca turned to Audra. "I think we should send Mick or Jagger with them. Boy isn't used to large cities."

Audra nodded.

Mickey snorted.

Jagger stared off at the wall.

"I need those two to map out the area," Nichol interjected, earning a look of gratefulness from his brothers. "I want a full report of the three blocks surrounding the station. Take those drones over there," he ordered, gesturing toward a meticulously packed box. "They have a two-mile control radius. No. Closer. Am I clear? The video will feed directly to me, so keep your phones on and maybe answer them when I text you."

Flashing false apologetic looks at Audra and Bianca, the vamps grabbed up the equipment and ducked out the door.

He turned his attention back to his computer until he became acutely aware he was under the glare of several women. He looked up slowly, meeting unimpressed eyes. "Dominic," he said slowly, reaching into his back pocket, "I need you to shadow the women." He pulled out a wad of bills and held it out to Audra. "If we're successful tomorrow, Lis will need a temporary wardrobe. And this shit-hole has nothing for food. Stock up, call if you run out of cash."

Bianca cocked a brow at the money. "You're sending us to the mall."

Pulling his knees up, he balanced his laptop in front of him, blocking the accusing stares until the door opened and three pairs of angry footsteps stormed away.

"Thanks a lot, Nichol," Dominic grumbled, shoving his laces into his boots, and sprinting out. "I'm going to hear about this all night."

He smirked and resumed tapping away at his keyboard.

****

"You're late," Rhys commented when Heisner arrived an hour past dusk.

"Got held up in front of the station," the officer grumbled. "Goddamn place is crawling with reporters."

Lis's lock flipped open.

"I brought you a few things," Heisner announced as he entered her cell, the sounds of rustling paper and plastic echoing through the unit. "Have a look."

He stretched his arms up to the door frame and

listened in while she rifled through the bags.

"What's this for?" she asked.

"What's what?" he inquired, his mind producing a plethora of options, none of which he was pleased about.

"Clothes and makeup," she called over. "Andy, where did you get this?"

Heisner cleared his throat, his boots scuffing on the cement. "My girlfriend suggested it," he muttered, his heart rate jumping up. "Jamie said you might want to look nice tomorrow."

"That's really fucking morbid," Rhys stated, clenching his jaw when he caught the hint of jealousy in his voice.

What the fuck.

"It's very SWEET," Lis corrected.

Heisner's heart rate jumped up a little higher. "Yeah, well, she doesn't agree with this execution. Says it's a witch hunt." He laughed nervously. "Who am I to argue, right? Jamie's been following you since your first interview. She's kind of a fan, I guess."

Lis hummed a distracted reply.

"She said if you're not keen on the idea to remember looking good going in there will be a huge fuck-you to the anti-vampers," Heisner continued, his voice tight.

He listened in silence, waiting for her response.

"I'll, uh, leave this stuff here. You can eat in peace tonight and I'll come back in the morning with your next meal," Heisner stammered out when she remained quiet.

The officer left quickly, pulling her door closed harder than usual and moving down the hall swiftly.

"Lis?"

She sighed. "It's stupid, really. A nice gesture, of course, but stupid nonetheless."

He could hear the bags rustling before they were slid across the floor, and she began opening her evening meal.

"It's not a bad idea," he opened. "His girlfriend's motivations are wrong, but the concept is rock solid."

She stopped chewing. "What do you mean?"

"There's going to be a lot of media attention tomorrow. Lots of photos and videos being taken. If we're going to be photographed walking in to this together, I'd prefer you look good. And honey, that orange jumpsuit doesn't look good."

Dead silence.

"You're kidding."

He grinned and rested his forehead on the door. "Half-kidding."

****

"What is that stench?" Rhys roared over the sound of the sink faucet.

Lis snickered and resumed rinsing the dye from her hair. "Jamie was thorough," she called out.

"Jamie doesn't have to endure that reeking chemical for the last hours of her existence," he groused. "I can't believe you're using drug store hair dye. Were you trained by a neanderthal?"

He hadn't let up all night. His snarky commentary over the scent of lotions and dyes and lipstick had been relentless. Relentless and comforting. Whenever the enormity of her situation darkened her mood and thoughts, his remarks had become more crude and more salacious, keeping the atmosphere of the unit from growing too heavy.

"This is ridiculous," he grumbled from his cell. "I'm going to be walking the plank with a dime-store tart.

What dye color did Andy leave you with? You know you can't pull off anything with an orange or purple undertone. If it's brassy, you'd be better served shaving it off."

She snorted gracelessly. "You're such a control freak."

"Yeah, well, last time your appearance was left in your hands, you turned your hair the color of Nichol's phone and mutilated your tongue. I'm justified. Heisner incoming."

She wrapped her only towel around her wet hair, momentarily pleased by the thought it would be stained beyond repair.

"How's it going in here?" Heisner called. "I brought breakfast for both of you."

The metal slot to Rhys's door squeaked as it was opened, the blood bags sloshing as they squeezed through the narrow opening.

"AB-negative," Rhys announced. "That's the truffle of blood types, Andy. Nice work."

The officer shuddered as he opened her lock, knocking before he entered. "Bacon and eggs," he stated, holding out a paper bag from a fast food joint. "Greasy, artery-clogging, and delicious."

He looked around the small cell, seemingly pleased to see the opened hair dye box on the sink counter. "Does everything fit okay? I used the sizing I pulled from the evidence box when Jaime asked."

"All good," she said distractedly, digging into the beautifully runny eggs.

"Eat up," he instructed. "I'll be back in a few minutes. I have a few things for Rhys."

Curious, she listened in while Heisner locked her

door and began to rifle through plastic bags.

"I asked Jamie to scrounge up a few things for you from home," the officer called out to him. "Just in case you'd prefer something that isn't burnt through. I used to be about your size. At least before I moved in with a woman who could cook." The metal slot squealed again. "I tried to pull your boots from evidence, but no luck."

Rhys's low chuckle caught her attention. "How long have you two been together?"

"Nine years."

"I can pull off vintage-chic," he mused aloud. "Thanks, Andy."

Heisner cleared his throat and muttered something close to a verbal acknowledgement as he reentered her cell. He crossed the room and sat uninvited on her bed. "I put a few extra snacks in there." He sighed and leaned forward, resting his elbows on his knees. "Guard presence will increase in about an hour. No one will be allowed in the cells again until 11 pm. Are you catching all this, Rhys?"

"I'm a vampire."

Heisner's brows knotted. "Of course." He refused to meet her eyes. "At eleven, you'll be escorted to the holding area and secured. Rhys will be brought along after. There shouldn't be any spectators, but I can't promise anything."

"Will we be held together?" Rhys called over.

"Separate," the officer replied. "Ms. Bruckner will be moved first every time. Once she's secured in the— unit—you'll be brought in." He finally glanced over to her. "The sentencing will be carried out at 11:55 pm. Any questions?"

Numb, she shook her head.

"Rhys, you'll be under my watch during that time. I'll be coordinating with the lead for Ms. Bruckner," Heisner added.

"Nope." Rhys's voice was solid, brokering no argument. "You're on Lis's case. She knows you, and I don't want some cowboy with a superiority complex and a gun in charge of her safety."

"The Feds believe you'll be better controlled under my watch," Heisner stated slowly.

"Funny."

CHAPTER THIRTY-SEVEN

The charged enthusiasm of the past three nights was gone, replaced by a bitter silence. Nichol ran a hand through his hair and met Jagger's narrowed ice eyes. "Unless we're all in agreement on the attainable priorities of this mission, we abort."

Jagg pushed his hood off of his head with a snarl. "When the hell did one of our own become a debatable commodity?"

"When he issued his own command," Mick interjected quietly, pulling some of the heat off Nichol. "Rhys's priority is yanking Lis, by his own words. Lis's priority is placed under keeping our own hides safe. That puts Rhys in third position."

Louis frowned and crossed his arms, his wiry frame disappearing in his oversized shirt. "I get it, but I don't like it."

"None of us do," Nichol stated, keeping his attention on Jagg and Dominic, the most oppositional of the group. "There's also the issue of Fallon Derry's execution order. As long as that's in play, our hands are tied."

Bianca knelt beside Jagger, placing a calming hand on his shoulder as she addressed him and Mick. "But it's not off the table, right? If the stars align, then Rhys—"

"Will be pulled out whether he likes it or not, yes," he reassured her, his tone lighter than his mood. "Are we in agreement?"

Dominic relented first, Molly sniffling loudly beside

him. "I suppose if we aren't, Rhys's chances drop to zero."

Rising to his feet, Jagg began to pace the small space. "I'm doing this only because he requested it," he growled. "But I want it out there that anything we can do to make his end less painful and less public is done."

He sat back against the wall. "Deal. That brings me to our next order of business." He could feel a tightness in his shoulder blades that often came with tough nights. "Not only will the humans be tuned in to the Deepfryer, vampires across the world will also be watching. I was up all day monitoring the online chatter, and there's a messed-up combination of fascination and disgust circulating among our own kind."

All eyes in the room narrowed.

"I think if it was anyone other than Rhys, the opinions would be less divided. Although none support the method of execution, the execution itself has gone unquestioned. That makes Rhys the sacrificial lamb, the uncontested offering to the human authorities if you will." Jagger growled as Audra huffed in disgust. "Being what it is, we have to toe the line tightly. That means no fuck-ups. No second-guessing. No going off course." He glanced at Dominic and Molly. "No improvising. Everything by the book, everything according to plans A, B, C, and Z. Am I clear?"

The group muttered their acknowledgement.

Meeting the eyes of all eight hauntmates, he rose. "Boots on the ground."

****

It wasn't hard for Lis to feign fear when the guards stormed through the solitary unit and began assessing Rhys through the tiny slot.

For a glorious moment when her eyes first opened that evening, she had forgotten where she was. Now, twenty minutes into the rabid snarling, violent pounding, and howled curses, she was very, very aware she was in a cell waiting for her death sentence to be carried out.

"I want Heisner," Rhys growled, punctuating his demand with the booting of his door.

The lead guard stood with his back to her door, keeping her from peeking at the unfolding events. "Heisner's off until ten. What can we do for you?"

"I. Want. Heisner," he repeated, his voice graveled. "I'm going to drain that lying fucker dry and use his skin for boots."

One of the guards shuddered audibly while the others murmured their disgust.

"If you tell me what the problem is, maybe I can fix it for you," the lead guard stated, his voice not nearly as confident as it was initially.

Rhys chuckled darkly. "I was promised release if I turned on the whore," he growled. "I turned, Heisner didn't return."

The lead went silent for a moment. She held her breath as the man held an internal debate.

"I'll check into it," he finally said.

The heavy stomping of the guards disappeared down the hall and out of the wing.

"Hey, angel," he called over, his voice as calm as ever. "How're you holding up?"

****

Rhys picked up the sound of Heisner's approach long before the man reached the door to the solitary wing.

"Lis, baby," he said quietly, "Are you ready?"

302

She'd remained silent all evening while she moved through her cell preparing for her execution. He monitored the steady beat of her heart and the blanket of numbness breaching her corner of his mind and spreading, waiting for the inevitable panic to set in.

"Heisner's coming and he's not alone," he whispered as the footsteps grew louder. "I'll see you soon."

Nothing.

He took a few steps back from his door and waited until Heisner and his guards were close before he ran at it, slamming his shoulder into the metal. "Open the fucking door, Heisner!" he snarled, beating his fist against the cement wall. "That little bitch lured me in. Now get me the fuck outta here so I can watch her burn."

Heisner's heart rate skyrocketed for a moment and the accompanying officers eased away from his cell. "My hands are tied," the officer replied, his voice calm as he seemed to realize Rhys's angle. "I'll be escorting Ms. Bruckner this evening. Your escorts should arrive within the hour."

Switching hands, he continued to pound on the wall while he listened to Heisner quietly whispering to Lis. He could hear her feet patter along the cold cement alongside the cop's boots, pausing at his door.

"Rhys," Andy hushed, his voice inaudible to the guards in the hall, "if you can, make this quick for her."

Lis's cell door eased closed and the group made their way out of the unit.

Without Lis's pulse to steady his attention, he paced the floor of his cell impatiently. He turned his focus to the corner of his mind where he'd attempted to corral her emotions and allowed them to filter through unabated.

Beneath the chilling numbness lay nothing more than hopelessness.

He began to scratch at his arms, glancing down and frowning at the lightened tattoo lines where Lis had applied the sulfur. Flexing his fingers, he turned on his sink, washed the blood from his knuckles, and waited for the guards.

****

"We need to move," Heisner whispered to Lis, extending his arm toward her.

Guards armed with UV lights and rifles lined the front reception room of the station, extending out the door, down the stairs, and up to the large glass enclosure sitting in the courtyard. Voices of protestors and supporters filtered into the large room, the chants and shouts becoming little more than background noise to the pounding of her heart in her ears.

Heisner nudged her, his eyes regretful. "If you don't walk under your own power, they'll make you," he said quietly.

She looked around as several of the guards stepped toward her. Squaring her shoulders, she placed her hand on Heisner's offered arm and willed her feet to move toward the Deepfryer. As they made their way down the steps, her grip tightened. Parallel to the armed guards ran a second line of officers, their riot shields held high to prevent the deluge of items being thrown from hitting their targets.

Her.

Rhys.

They approached the open door to the Deepfryer and she stopped, releasing Heisner's arm. "I can take it from here," she said. "Thank you."

Eight more steps. Blocking out the chanting, the insults, and the cheers, she lifted the hem of her skirt, walked into the Deepfryer, and waited.

****

"Time," Nichol demanded, his eyes scouring the blueprints for any potential flaws.

"11:43," Audra replied, pacing in front of the small TV. "This is barbaric."

He looked over to the live footage as it closed in on a brunette standing alone in the Deepfryer. "This is humanity," he growled, tearing his eyes off of Lis and texting the others. "Turn the volume down."

Audra complied and continued to prowl the tiny room, her trademark heels sitting in the corner after he had snarled his frustration at the distracting sound. His phone buzzed as the boots on the ground checked in.

"Whoa," Audra breathed as she tapped the television screen. "Tell the group to watch themselves."

He leaned forward, his eyes narrowing. The guards lining the steps of the police station had activated their UV lights, the beams moving in sync toward the sky and the ground like a warped lazar show. "Rhys must be on his way," he muttered, unwilling to look away from his brother's arrival.

Buzz.

He glanced down, reading Mickey's message before relaying the information to Audra. "Looks like two helicopters have arrived on scene and they're scanning the crowds. Two vamps have been outed by UV lights. Neither one was Louis."

Audra's lips pursed. "Is there any way to get Mick and Dominic off the rooftops and into a top level office?"

"Too late," he grumbled, pulling up Jagger's drone

footage. "Looks like they're a few dozen meters off the scanning zone, though. Nine minutes."

The pair watched the live feed as the camera zeroed in on the entrance to the station. Audra took in a deep breath, her shoulders shaking slightly.

He frowned at the screen when Rhys appeared, dressed in low-slung baggy jeans and a faded INXS tee. "What the hell is he wearing?"

CHAPTER THIRTY-EIGHT

Rhys made no outward indication he was hit as a stray UV beam caught his bare feet. His attention was wholly focused on Lis's back while he walked the gauntlet toward the Deepfryer. The chanting had grown louder and cruder while he strode through the light display, his hands in the pockets of Heisner's faded jeans. Blocking out the hollers toward him, he kept his eyes locked on the long brown hair and chiffon skirt standing motionless in the glass enclosure.

"Hey, sweetheart," he greeted casually when he entered and the door was secured behind him.

"Do you think they're here? Your brothers?" she whispered, keeping her back to him. "I've been looking, but—"

He peered out into the throngs of people filling the streets. Species Purifier shirts and hats created a sea of red spanning the middle of the raucous crowd, with the equally vocal pro-vamp humans flanking the sides.

"I think if they are, they're doing their job by staying out of sight," he replied quietly, not willing to commit to the idea his hauntmates could be close.

Or in danger.

Lis continued to stare out the glass wall.

Continued to stare at the *Satan's Whore* sign in the hands of a pleasant-looking elderly woman. The *Burn For Eternity* sign being pumped up and down by a young man in skinny jeans and sunglasses. The *God Purges the*

Evil sign a pretty woman was pulling out of reach of the toddler on her hip.

"Turn around," he ordered, refusing to allow her last visions to be ones of damnation. "Now, Lis."

Three minutes.

Behind him, he could hear their sentences being read through a microphone, the speaker reduced to yelling to be heard over the din of protestors and supporters. As she turned to face him, he smirked and reached up to push her hair from her face. "If you reeked of weed and pulled a few threads out of the hem of that shirt, you'd look exactly as you did when I got on that fucking bus."

Her forehead fell to his chest, her shoulder heaving as she began to sob.

Two minutes.

"Aw, baby," he murmured, wrapping his arms around her. He dropped his head into the crook of her neck and extended his fangs behind the curtain of her hair. "I wanted so much more for you. So much better. I wanted—" He closed his eyes. "What I wanted doesn't matter when this is the best I can do for you now."

He eased into her jugular gently, tightening his grip to still her.

"No!" she hissed, futilely pushing against him while the crowd began to quiet down. "You'll burn longer!"

One minute.

"Don't do this," she whimpered, her heart rate racing as he pulled her blood from her body. "You'll die alone. Rhys, please."

The snap of the electrical current warned him milliseconds before the Deepfryer lights were activated. With his fangs still embedded in her throat, he arched over her and used his body to shield her from the scorching rays.

****

Nichol's finger hovered over his keyboard, his teeth clenched as Molly's voice rang over his speaker.

"Oh God," she sobbed. "He won't let her burn. Nichol, you have to do it now!"

"Dominic!" he barked into the phone, pulling a tearful Audra's attention from the television. "Is your mate capable of fulfilling her job?"

Dom's voice was tight. "Molly will be fine. Just make it soon, okay?"

"Everyone's in place," Audra said softly, staring at the live video footage. "He won't last much longer in there."

His fangs sliced into his lip as the camera zoomed in on Rhys's body, his broad form crouched tight around Lis, using his body as a shield against the Deepfryer rays. His bare arms were already blackened, small tufts of smoke rising from his back. "Fucking incompetent government. One goddamn minute early," he hissed, watching his younger brother's muscles ripple against the pain. "I need thirty-seven more seconds. I know he has that in him."

****

Two more pints.

Lis was limp, her body held off the floor solely by Rhys's charred arms and his stubborn refusal to release her. The constant whisper of her existence in his head became muted eighteen seconds ago, just as her pulse stuttered for the first time.

Fucking Lis and her fucking obstinate heart.

The massive intake of fresh blood was keeping his body from igniting under the UV rays. Lis's potent blood worked to heal the damage only to have the constant streams of light reopen the wounds. He adjusted his grip on her when his legs began to give way, keeping her hidden from the beams when he dropped to his knees.

****

12:01.

"NOW!" Nichol bellowed into his phone when the clock turned and his finger slammed against the keyboard. He and Audra stared at the television, their ears tuned in to the cellphone speaker as the Deepfryer emitted a final blinding pulse and went dark.

The unmistakable sound of gunfire echoed through the television and phones.

"Molly got it!" Dominic shouted over the mayhem of the city streets. "Top right, three holes. That should weaken it enough for the others to shatter it."

He and Audra leaned in closer to the screen. "There!" she called out, pointing to a large blond blur barreling through the crowds.

"Top right, west side," he barked into his phone, hoping Boy had left his speaker on. The mute vamp adjusted his trajectory slightly, his shoulder pummeling the weakened Deepfryer glass and shattering it as a flood of UV flashlights zeroed in on him. Jagger's hoodie appeared on screen while he followed hot on Boy's heels.

"Why aren't they leaving?" Audra screeched, grabbing his shoulder.

He knelt in front of the television. "Motherfu… Rhys isn't releasing her. They can't get her out of his arms and they can't move them out together. GODDAMN IT!"

The throng of human observers was in chaos as the

guards began shooting into the Deepfryer. Through his phone speaker, the screams of the mob drowned out Jagger and Mickey.

"Louis!" he hollered, swatting Audra's hand off him. "Location?"

"Thirty yards south," Louis called back, his voice muffled. "Mick's twenty away…fifteen."

He sat back on his haunches, rubbing his temples as Mick's blond head appeared in the corner of the video feed. "Permission to start taking out the guards," he ordered. "Boy, contain Rhys through any means necessary. Get Lis to Bianca. NOW."

He and Audra watched helplessly as the UV lights and gunfire continued to descend on their hauntmates, his fingers flexing when Jagg broke Lis free of Rhys's hold.

"Jagger. Northwest to the alley on your left," he muttered as he texted the order, pulling up an aerial view of the area on his laptop and comparing the spread of the crowd with the view on his computer.

"On it," Jagg called out over the speaker with a grunt.

"Mickey, two on your left," Audra suddenly called into the phone. "Louis, three to your right."

He scanned the screen and watched as Boy hefted Rhys over his shoulder. "Boy, head northeast two hundred yards. Back alley access to the low-rise roofs. Go high for five blocks and drop at the gas station." He sat back and ground his teeth when his hauntmates disappeared from the television, leaving the injured bodies of fifteen humans behind. "Dominic, you and Molly get your asses back here now."

"On our way," Dom replied tersely.

"Bianca?" Audra called over. "Any visual on Jagg?"

The phone went silent outside of the din of chaos.

"Bianca?"

"I see him," she breathed. "He has Lis. We'll be there in five."

****

Jagger was first to stumble into the tiny bolt hole, Lis's lifeless body slung unceremoniously over his shoulder. "She's not going to make it," he grunted, kneeling to lay the woman out on the floor.

Her skin was pristine, completely untouched by the UV lights of the Deepfryer.

Pristine, and grey.

Nichol tuned into her vitals, silently agreeing with Jagger's assessment. "Bianca, see to Jagg. Audra, keep watch for the others."

He stared at his own wrist, debating the lengths he was willing to go for a traitorous Tender when the door burst open, and Boy lurched forward onto the floor with Rhys.

"Oh God," Audra gasped, stepping back from the charred body on the ground.

"Audra," he barked, "Start lining the blood bags up. Don't worry about type, just get them prepped."

He tore into his wrist and brought it to Rhys's mouth, tilting his head back gently to force the blood into his system.

His brother was unrecognizable, his facial features completely altered by the damaging lights, deep holes where his fangs had been before Boy removed them to free Lis. "Rhys," he muttered, meticulously scanning his brother over for any undamaged part and coming up empty. "We're on this. We got you. You're out."

Lis's heart rate hiccupped, freezing the vampires in the room.

He glanced at his phone. "Audra? Could you text Mick?"

"I already did," she said softly. "Louis, too."

Rhys's charred body struggled to sit up, his irises white from light blindness and his face unrecognizable.

"Down," he ordered, unwilling to touch his hauntmate for fear of causing more pain.

When Rhys's head slowly turned toward Lis's motionless body, he ran a hand through his hair. "Jagg? Are you okay to haul Lis over here?"

Jagger released Bianca's wrist instantly and crouched beside Lis, gently easing her toward him and Rhys before returning to Bee.

"This is going to hurt," he warned as he brought Rhys's arm to his mouth and sliced his veins. He guided the arm to Lis's mouth. "Boy, I'm going to need you to hold him there."

Blood bag in hand, Boy crossed the room and complied silently. Holding Rhys's blackened wrist to Lis's lips, he massaged her throat to encourage her to swallow.

Five minutes passed.

Ten.

He glanced to his phone methodically every thirty seconds while Rhys fed. "Audra, can you pass me a few more of those bags?" he asked into the quiet of the room.

She tore her attention away from the door and absently handed him two bags of O-positive. He tore into the first one, staving off the worst of the blood loss he was experiencing through Rhys's feeding. "Boy, are you healing up?"

The blond nodded.

"Jagger?" he inquired.

"I've got most of the bullets out," Bianca replied, her tiny body straddling her mate's back. "But this stubborn one is already healed into the bone. I think I'll need plicrs."

Audra moved robotically to Nichol's bags, rifling around until she found the tool. "Keep them out," she said, glancing at her phone. "I might need them for Mickey."

Nichol reopened his wrist, staring at the back wall as he listened for any more signs of life or death from his orders.

CHAPTER THIRTY-NINE

"It's Dom and Molly," Audra announced, her voice hollow when she opened the door.

Nichol craned his head to check over his youngest hauntmate. "List your injuries," he growled, tearing open another blood bag to keep up with Rhys's demand.

And Lis's.

"Not a scratch," Dominic replied, eying Rhys hesitantly and instinctively guiding Molly away from the visual. "Is…he'll be okay, right?"

"Sure," he grunted, reassessing Lis's color. "What's the blood bag situation sitting at?"

Bianca moved over to the coolers, squeezing Audra's arm gently as she passed. "Eighteen left."

"Time?"

"Just after one."

He ripped his wrist open again. "Audra, you, Molly, and Bianca pull the vehicles up tight to the door. I want all three hatches open, all left running. Seats flipped down in the last one." He glanced around the room. "Jagger, you and Dominic are in charge of packing this place and loading up. I want five blood bags in each vehicle. Leave three out so I can keep Rhys and Lis going."

Audra remained still as the others began following orders. "What if they're hurt?" she asked. "They might—"

"Then we heal them up on the move," he stated.

"We're sitting ducks here. As soon as Louis and Mick arrive, we're heading for Vegas before the city's exits are sealed off."

If Louis and Mick arrive.

He rolled out his neck, pushing the thought from his mind. "I'll ride with Rhys and Lis. Jagger and Bianca, Louis will ride with you so Bianca can tend to Louis if he requires it. Audra, you and Boy are together and will haul Mick in when he arrives. Dominic, you and Molly will be with me. We'll caravan. If there's any trouble, you two will hop in with Boy and get the fuck out. Yes?"

He gingerly placed a hand on Rhys's blackened chest, pulling back when his prone hauntmate arched in pain.

Pain.

Too much pain.

Fuck.

He dropped his head, realizing he'd made a grave error. "We need to map out Mick and Louis's path. Get me my laptop and everyone needs to start calling out every visual we had of them."

****

"Take a right here," Nichol called to Dominic, clenching his hold on Rhys's charred wrist while he hovered it over Lis's lips.

The headlights of the 4x4 behind them were almost blinding as Audra remained tight to their asses.

He straddled Rhys awkwardly in the cramped space, trying to balance above the burned body while the vehicle rounded the city streets. Lis's color had moved from grey to white, her heart pumping slowly but steadily.

"We'll fan out from here," he ordered when they

slowed, creeping through the streets and winding through the back alleys. Scanning for any signs of Mick and Louis, he refreshed the news app on his phone in case they'd been caught.

Audra's voice came over the speakers. "I think I see something."

"Stay put," he ordered. "Audra, I'm not screwing around here. Keep your ass in the car. Boy, you and Jagger check it out. Ladies keep the doors unlocked and stay tight in the driver's seat. Keep your foot on the brake, keep it in drive."

His hauntmates disappeared down a long alley and he reopened his wrist for Rhys, biting into another blood bag to stave off the weakness he was feeling.

All contingencies.

He'd planned for every possible scenario. Every possible angle.

Everything except the impact Rhys's time in the Deepfryer would have on Mikhail and his empathic skills.

Now they were sitting in a darkened street in a city gunning for vampires with one injured human, one injured hauntmate, and two missing vamps.

He ground his teeth and scanned the area the best he could with his limited movement. "Are we still on speaker?" he asked Dominic as he spat a piece of plastic from his mouth.

"We're here," Audra called, drowning out Dominic and Bianca's replies.

"Make sure those doors are unlocked," he instructed. "Boy and Jagger are halfway down the alley and they have cargo. Dominic, you and Molly get out and help get those hatches open."

Molly and Dominic scrambled out of the car and popped the doors open on the other two vehicles. Craning his neck to watch Boy deposit Mickey unceremoniously into the back, he continued to bark orders. "Boy, you're driving. Audra, get Mick fed ONLY if it's safe. Maximum speed to Vegas and we'll establish a scattered return schedule to separate Rhys and Mick as soon as possible."

Boy tore out of the side street and blasted from view as he turned his attention to Louis's status. "Bianca, will bagged blood hold for Louis until we hit Vicente's?"

"I'm good," Louis said over the speaker as Dominic began pulling onto the road. "Mick was able to lock onto me until we got outta there. It's only been the past forty minutes he's been deteriorating."

He lifted Rhys's wrist from Lis's mouth. "Good. You two will be a required pairing from here on out since he can hide in your stream."

Ignoring Bianca's fussing over Louis, and Jagger's mutterings for Louis to 'just comply and she'll back off quicker', he focused on his immediate charges.

Lis was close to becoming an accidental turning, her intake of blood dancing dangerously near the limit. Her heart was weak but steady, her breathing more labored than he preferred.

But Lis was faring better than Rhys.

Externally, Rhys showed no sign of improvement. With so many of his burns going bone-deep and without Kaius or Mickey to provide an assessment of his internal condition, he had no guarantee he hadn't moved too late.

****

"We have several AB-negatives available," Wolfgang offered, pulling Nichol's attention from

Rhys's charred form. "I can send two or three in here."

He shook his head and spared a glance at Lis who lay motionless beside Rhys. "Thanks, but no," he muttered, straightening his back. "Rhys won't be feeding on his own for a while."

Vicente chuckled. "For you, Nichol. A weakened leader can be more detrimental to a haunt than an incompetent one."

Grinding his teeth, he stepped between his brother and his host. "Your offer is appreciated, but unnecessary."

The younger vampire grinned, his fangs on full display. "I assure you, it's necessary. Leave the tall, silent one with these two and we'll have a chat over dinner."

****

Nichol crossed his arms and cocked a brow at Vicente. "Where are the others?"

"The rest of the hauntmates fell to my own weak will," Wolfgang replied, hanging his head in feigned shame. "I'm afraid immersion in the hedonistic pleasures of the Strip have whittled away at my impulse control. Though, in my defense, there were only two others left in the line."

Fallon Derry spat at Nichol from his position on the wall, heavy chains restricting his movements.

"I suppose transporting him to Colorado would be more effort than it's worth," he mused aloud. "It's a shame Rhys couldn't get in on this."

Vicente moved closer to the rabid vampire. "Although I despise manual labor, I could assist you in bringing him to the guest suites."

He hesitated at the offer. "Perhaps this isn't a

decision I should make for the others. Would you be willing to stand guard at the entrance of our rooms while I consult with my hauntmates?" he asked, stepping back when Fallon spat again. "Why is he silent?"

Wolfgang smiled cheerfully. "I removed his larynx an hour ago. Again. Poor impulse control and all." He motioned toward the exit. "I will personally guarantee the safety of your injured and your women. Will you require any supplies?"

****

Nichol held back while the others entered the small cement holding cell. They spread out across the wall, arms crossing and eyes narrowing in sync.

"Go on in," he ordered Boy when the mute vamp paused. "Everyone gets their pound."

Fallon stilled as he took in the visual of the Kaius hauntmates standing shoulder to shoulder and Nichol smirked. "The camera's catching this from three separate angles," he stated, aligning himself with the others. "For posterity's sake, of course. And for Rhys's viewing pleasure. He was unable to make it tonight."

"Prior commitments," Louis chimed in, widening his stance.

He glanced over at the red-haired vampire with approval. "You fucked with the wrong haunt, Fallon. A simple execution order carried out in the privacy of your cells would have sufficed, but you got greedy."

"Deadly sin, man," Mick interjected, subtly keeping one hand on Louis's shoulder to stay centered in Louis's flat affect.

Fallon's frantic eyes scanned the group, settling on Jagger.

Boy moved over slightly while Jagg pushed his

320

hood off and ran a tongue over his elongated fang. "We'll be forwarding this movie to every haunt across the globe. Smile, fucker."

Flicking on one of the UV flashlights Vicente had generously provided, Nichol took a step forward, careful to avoid the beams of the other lights flickering to life. Fallon writhed in his manacles, a strange guttural groan echoing in the chamber as the rays lifted to his body.

"Seven minutes, eighteen seconds," he stated, starting the timer on his phone. "You only need to hold on for seven minutes, eighteen seconds, and you'll be free to go. I recommend you go far." He caught Fallon's eye and flashed his fangs. "I doubt Rhys will take it this easy when he comes for you."

CHAPTER FORTY

Lis lifted her head from the damp grass and smiled up at Audra. "Five more minutes?" she implored, not quite ready to leave the fresh air and moonlight.

Mick's partner glowered with feigned sternness. "Five and then straight inside for a snack before bed."

She lay back down, closed her eyes, and breathed in deep, her thoughts returning to her first conscious night back in the Kaius haunt.

"Where am I? Boy? Boy! Where's Rhys?"

She watched while Boy fumbled with his phone, his large form blocking the exit from the unfamiliar room. He held out his phone to her.

"Who's Audra?" she demanded after reading the text, swinging her legs over the edge of the bed, and rising before her knees gave out and she found herself being held up by the elbows. Boy eased her back onto the mattress and returned to his post, crouching slightly as though preparing for an attack.

The door opened a crack and Boy's stance relaxed instantly when a woman in stiletto heels marched into the room, her black hair pulled up in a sleek ponytail and dyed a brilliant turquoise at the tips.

"It's about time you woke up!" she announced, smiling over at the intimidating Boy. "Honey, could you go ask Nichol to meet me here? I want a full assessment done as soon as possible. And let Bianca know we'll need a selection of easy snacks made up."

She shrunk back as Boy, the most reclusive vamp of the Kaius haunt, nodded and disappeared down the hall to obey the woman's orders.

"Audra Verdi," the woman said, approaching her bed slowly and extending her hand. "I'm the resident psychologist here. And Mickey's partner."

Hesitantly, she shook Audra's hand. "How is Rhys?" She stopped short when Audra's name clicked. He mentioned that name a lot at the McConaughey haunt. Unfavorably mentioned that name. The Wicked Witch of the Haunt.

"Rhys is resting," Audra replied, pulling up a chair and gracefully lowering herself into it as she held up a small notepad and pen. "Our concern right now is with you. You've been out for three days, and I want to make sure everything is healing up as it should. Can you tell me your name?"

"Time's up," Audra called over from the garage. "Let's get down to the kitchen before Molly and Bianca polish off the charcuterie tray without us."

She brushed the grass from her clothes and joined Audra, listening half-heartedly while the woman called down to Nichol to report their whereabouts.

****

"You shouldn't be in this hall."

Lis startled as Jagger came up behind her. "I was just lost," she stammered, accepting his arm, and allowing him to lead her back toward the halls of the main haunt.

Five weeks.

For five weeks, she'd been living in what she came to learn was Rhys's official room in the vampire wing of the haunt. Boy stood guard throughout the day, his mere presence ensuring she wouldn't even attempt to open her door until the sun set.

Nichol assessed her vitals every evening at dusk, a quick once-over before he hid out in the com room for the night. Audra always arrived shortly after, often escorted by Mickey as he passed down the hall and joined Louis in his bunker. A full breakfast followed, with Bianca and Molly bickering playfully over the final slices of whatever salty meat was featured that evening.

It was nice. Almost normal.

Nichol placed high restrictions on her movements during her first days, his amber eyes watching her every move while she slowly gained the strength to walk the halls. She suspected it was Audra who pushed for a laxer perimeter, allowing her to go freely throughout the haunt at night provided she was accompanied by a hauntmate.

And provided she stayed away from the Tender quarters.

She glanced back at what she'd always thought was Rhys's room, the door at the end of a long hall in the Tender training area where she'd spent countless nights curled in the doorframe.

She squeezed Jagger's arm lightly. "When will I get to see him?"

Shrugging off her question, Jagg guided her toward the sounds of Mickey and Louis arguing loudly over a video game, Bianca and Audra's laughter punctuating the slough of insults streaming from them.

****

Lis's eyes snapped open as a soft knocking on her door resumed. Rolling out of bed, she cracked the door open and smiled. "Hey, Moll! What's up?"

Molly with her sniper precision was definitely one of her favorite people.

The brunette shoved her thumbs into the loops of her jeans. "Care to help me unload a few boxes from the mail run?" she asked. "Everyone's asleep except Boy and he still gives me the willies a little."

She peeked out the door to see Boy standing off to the side where he'd been for seven weeks straight—well within hearing distance—and then glanced down at the oversized shirt she had taken from Rhys's closet.

"You're fine," Molly grinned. "You should've seen the get-ups some of the other Tenders walked around in around here. T-to-the-R-to-the-aaaaassshhhy."

Molly talked nonstop while they made their way to the garage, her ramblings about a new band she'd discovered perking Lis's mood up.

"I have to run these three to the weapons room and unbox them," Molly huffed as she balanced the stack precariously on her hip. "If you could take those ones down to the pantry, that'd be awesome."

Carefully piling the boxes in her arms, she followed Molly down the stairs and veered off toward the kitchen in the open Tender quarters. Selecting a knife from a drawer, she sliced the boxes open carefully and began packing the dry goods away.

"That shirt looks familiar."

She froze, a can of lentil soup clenched in her hand.

"A concho belt and some faded Daisy dukes would make it work, but this look just screams 'I raided my trainer's closet'."

Visions of Rhys's arms blackening while they tightened around her came into crystal clear focus.

The odor filling the Deepfryer when he began to burn.

The blissful lightheadedness overcoming her before

325

everything went dark.

"Holy fuck," Rhys groaned in exasperation. "If you faint, I'm draining you for good this time. Scout's honor."

****

Rhys braced himself for Lis's assault, keeping his expression neutral when her arms wrapped tight around his healing chest. He instinctively assessed her condition, comparing the view walked in on against her vitals.

"Are my Neanderthal hauntmates taking decent care of you?" he asked, scenting her to determine if any of them were being especially attentive.

She nodded, mumbling incoherently into his chest, and squeezing tighter. When he flinched, her arms released instantly.

"Oh God!" she gasped, shooting away from him. "I'm so sorry."

He rolled his eyes and grinned, flashing his regenerated fangs. "It's fine, angel. Just a few stubborn areas on my back." When she eyed him warily, he rolled up one sleeve and turned his arm over slowly for inspection. "See?"

Her concern ricocheted through his mind as she approached him, her fingers tracing over the lines of his tattoos. "Do they still itch?"

"Like a bastard," he replied, stepping out of her grasp, and pulling his sleeve back down. "What was it Dr. Winestar said? Localized blood poisoning, confirmed by Nichol."

"We could try removing them," she suggested, her brow knotted.

"We," he said, striding past her to put the rest of the

cans away, "need to get to your room before anyone notices you're missing. I'll finish up here."

He kept his back to her while she hesitated before walking down the hall toward the main haunt. Once her footsteps disappeared, he turned and leaned against the counter to keep himself upright before his legs buckled from exhaustion.

Slumping into a chair, he ran one hand through his hair.

He'd known she was alive the second he regained consciousness two weeks ago, her existence in his mind a quiet, content hum tinged with worry.

But seeing her?

He hadn't been prepared for the hit to his chest he took when she turned to him, those green eyes looking up at him. His head exploded with an emotion he couldn't deal with right now.

Even now, he felt the ghost of her fingers on his freshly healed skin and could still smell the scent of his blood coursing alongside hers in her body.

Pushing himself slowly to his feet, he prepared himself for the long walk down the hall and the solitude of his bedroom.

She had to go. Soon.

****

Rhys strode into the com room three weeks later.

"Look who's back from the dead," Nichol grumbled without tearing his eyes off of his monitor. "Keep your feet off my goddamn table."

Straddling his chair, he craned his neck to look over Nic's shoulder. "Jagger says my continued tortured existence is on your head, Nicky."

"Unfortunately."

"He showed me the news feed. And the special Fallon Derry episode."

His brother leaned back in his seat and looked over at him. "You going after him?"

"Maybe in a few decades. I'll let him sweat it out for a bit." He booted Nichol's chair. "You kicked ass."

Dodging Nic's elbow as it barreled toward his head, he called out to Dominic and Molly who were barreling down the hall. "Molly, sweetheart, how is it you can channel Annie Oakley from a rooftop in the dark but can't match lipstick to your skin tone?"

Her piercing shriek was met with a withering glare from Nichol as Molly raced into the room and wrapped her arms around Rhys's neck. "I hate you so much," she squealed. "So, so much, you creep."

"Ho. Ly. Fuck."

Unhooking Molly from his throat, he grinned at Mick. "Daddy's home."

Audra's lips pursed as she tried not to smile. "You have issues," she stated, patting his shoulder when she passed him to talk to Nichol.

Louis paused in the door, his grey eyes scanning him before he entered the room, Boy in tow. "You're good?"

He flashed him a glimpse of his forearm.

"Good."

Nichol rolled over to the table and smacked his hand down. "Welcome orgy's over. Jagg and Bee will here in a bit. They're oiling up a few more weapons Molly brought in today. There's nothing pressing tonight. Just stay the fuck outta my way and don't screw up the balance on any of the sound systems. Questions?"

He rose to his feet, still moving a slower than usual, his strength nowhere near where it once was. "Wait for me in the hall, Boy. I need a minute."

The others filtered out, Molly happily smacking his arm when she skipped past.

Glancing over at Nichol, he closed the door. "Jagg told me Kaius walked out."

"He did."

"Because of the rescue mission."

Nic hesitated before picking up a stack of papers from the printer. "His disappearance isn't on you. It's on him." The faint sound of Nic grinding his molars filled the room. "He'll return."

Crossing his arms, he cocked his head. "He will or you hope he will? Because from where I'm standing, it looks like you're the new king, Nicky."

"Fuck off."

Knowing it would do no good to agitate his already stressed brother further, he switched gears. "I want you to get a message to someone. A VEA officer by the name Andrew Heisner."

Nichol sat at his computer, pulling the man's info up moments later. "Am I destroying credibility, having him arrested, planting evide—"

"You're depositing two million into an offshore account for him with the message 'You're a decent guy, Andy. Hope this makes up for ruining your INXS shirt.'"

Nichol's fingers paused mid-stroke of the keys. "Serious?"

Smirking, he shrugged. "Heisner is one of the good ones. He did right by Lis. And by me."

Leaving Nic to complete the request, he opened the door to find Boy standing there waiting. "Is Lis in her room?"

"She's technically in yours," Nichol interjected as

Boy nodded. "We needed her secured in a wing where she could be monitored easily."

"Good. Nichol, put Louis on call. Boy, I need you to come with me."

Nichol gave him a long, hard look. "You once agreed to push my ass into a Deepfryer if I ever became connected," his oldest brother said slowly when Rhys turned to leave. "If being shoved into a Deepfryer for over seven minutes didn't cure you of what you feel for her, nothing will."

CHAPTER FORTY-ONE

Rhys lolled his head back as Mahjong downloaded slowly onto his new phone. "What the fuck is taking her so long?" he muttered to Boy. "Slowest. Eater. Ever."

Boy continued to stand in the corner of Lis's room, his blue eyes locked on the door until he cocked his head and took a step back.

Stretching his arms across the sofa, he smirked as Lis entered.

"What are you doing in here?" she asked, glancing over at Boy, and recoiling slightly.

He scanned the corner of his mind where she still resided, ignoring the glowing warmth and focusing on the justified wariness building. "Well, baby," he began, swinging his bare feet onto the coffee table, "I'm going to give you two choices."

She paled, her hands reaching behind her to close the door tight. "So soon?"

"The sooner, the better," he said, motioning toward the sofa and disregarding the jolt of regret slamming through him. "I made a few calls, and we have the opportunity to utilize two haunts in Europe. Isolated areas, minimal risk of recognition. Both masters are willing to overlook your past behavior in exchange for a suitably trained companion."

She sat slowly. When she didn't look at him or reply, he pressed on.

"Door number two is a little more complicated, but

doable," he stated, reaching over absently to run his fingers through her hair. When she flinched away from him, he folded his hands behind his head. "We would have to link you to Boy to ensure you're monitored. Once that's done, we have Louis, our resident hypnotist, ready to jump into action. He'll do his razzle-dazzle and his damnedest to erase the past five decades from your memory while Nichol plays on his computer and sets up a new life for you. The hypnosis may not hold across the board, but I'm sure we can identify the biggest areas and focus his attention on those." He shifted as his stomach tensed. "I can give you the next forty years or so to live out your life, vamp-free. If that's what you want, I'm willing to let you go. It's the best I can do for you, sweetheart."

****

Lis looked over to Boy, who stood motionless in the corner of the room, his attention on the floor at his feet. "Number two."

Rhys didn't want her.

He never had.

He was—would always be—Rhys.

And she couldn't survive losing him again, even if she had never truly had him in the first place.

Her heart seized in her chest.

"You'll age," he warned, dropping his feet to the ground with a thud.

"I know."

"Grey hair. Illness. Guaranteed death within a few decades," he pressed, leaning forward on his elbows. "Wrinkles."

Her mind made up, she stood and walked to Boy. "I'm okay with those."

"The past fifty years will be erased from your memory completely," he stated, his voice growing tense.

She laughed drily, refusing to look him. "And I'll be erased from your conscience. Sounds like the deal of a lifetime for both of us."

****

Rhys forced himself to lean back on the sofa while Boy moved in on Lis, his wrist held to his fangs.

Deal of a fucking lifetime.

The scent of Boy's blood filled the air of the bunker when the vampire scored his skin.

Lis took a small step back.

Fucking Lis.

Boy's body hit the wall as Rhys launched into him, sending a shower of sheet rock down on their heads. He got in two hits before he was thrown back across the room to the sound of Lis's screams puncturing the quiet haunt.

"What the FUCK, Boy?" he snarled, righting himself and widening his stance while Boy stood and prepared to battle.

"You're bleeding!" Lis cried out, scrambling across the mess to him. "What the hell are you thinking?"

Boy remained still in the corner, his blue eyes ovaling. "I'm good," he muttered, dodging her hand when she reached for the gash on his head. "Boy, you can go."

The blond left without hesitation, leaving him alone to dodge Lis's interrogation.

"Isn't he older than you?" she demanded, her hands on her hips. "You could've been hurt bad. This place is a mess now. What were you thinking?" She waved one hand around the room. "Unless Louis is doing his thing tonight, this will have to be cleaned up before bedtime. What on earth is WRONG with you?"

He ran his hands through his hair, groaning when he saw the amount of blood on them. "I really need you to shut the fuck up for a second," he grumbled, wiping his hands on his cargos.

Her green eyes narrowed as she crossed her arms.

"Option three," he said, locking his attention on the extremely interesting, closed door. "You stay here. In here. With me. Until…to be decided at a later century." When she didn't respond, he heard himself begin to spew the stupidest shit his mind could string together.

"We could make it official. Contract, purchase price, the whole nine yards. Maybe leave this room as yours alone like we write into the standard agreements and use mine downstairs for…things. After I fix the walls in here, of course." He could feel her glare boring into his skull. "We could even add a sex clause. Once a year or some shit so you know that's, you know, not all I want." He trailed off, frowning.

"You want to purchase me," she stated, her voice significantly flatter than the torrent of anger swirling through his head from her corner of his mind. "And have obligatory annual sex."

Anger, and a hint of humor.

Regaining his footing, he hooked his thumbs into his cargos and rolled his shoulders. "If that idea doesn't appeal to you, we could just shack up and take it from there," he offered, chancing a glance at her.

"Why?"

Because I fucking want you. "Because I'm a masochist."

She cocked a brow expectantly.

Because I fucking need you. "Because I don't dislike you as much as most humans."

"No deal," she replied flippantly, walking past him toward the door. "You'll need to do better than that."

His jaw tensed. "That's the best I can do for you, baby. If you choose option three, I definitely come out the winner. And you get this." He held out his arms. "You know what this is. You know what I am. And everything I'm not. Personally, I'd hold out for a better bargain if I was you."

He tore his eyes off her retreating figure and stared at the Boy-sized hole in the wall.

"Do you even like me?" she asked suddenly, turning to face him.

I fucking love you and always have. "You're tolerable. But you talk way too fucking much," he responded, scratching at his arms and shrugging off the stray thought looping through his head.

She scanned him thoughtfully. "Tolerable. You're offering to shack up with 'tolerable' for at least a century? That's very altruistic of you."

He took a hesitant step forward. "The offer I'm laying at your feet is the one I should have laid out decades ago. The one I wanted to lay out decades ago," he said, the admission drawing his arms in a fraction. "If you decide to take it, this deal benefits me immensely. Probably the best deal I've ever swung. Deal of the millennia."

Lis pursed her lips. "And I would be saddled with a self-indulgent, obnoxious, ego-driven narcissist with questionable morals and a penchant for exploitation."

"Pretty much."

His fingers twitched as she closed the distance

between them and put her forehead on his chest. He unhooked his thumbs from his belt loops and shoved his hands into his pockets to keep them contained.

"Meh," she muttered, wrapping her arms around his waist. "I suppose we can renegotiate the terms in eight or nine decades. Option three it is."

"This is a pretty extreme case of caveat emptor," he cautioned. "I come as-is. No returns, repairs, or refunds."

"Deal."

"I can be a real asshole sometimes."

She looked up at him.

"I'm a real asshole," he amended.

"You really need to learn when to stop talking," she suggested, raising up on her heels and bringing her lips to his.

He eased his demanding hands out of his pockets, taking care not to crush her to him as he gripped her waist. "I'm an old dog," he muttered against her lips. "I don't learn new tricks."

"Shut. Up."

He was vaguely aware of a low, possessive growl overtaking the room as his tongue dove into her mouth and traced the metal piercing. Her hands flew to his chest.

And pushed.

Hard.

Releasing her immediately, he took a step back and ran his hands into his stiff hair in confusion.

Changed her mind. Call Boy back. Louis. Nichol needs to get on the new ID.

"You're all gross and bloody," she stated, wrinkling her nose. "Ew."

A wave of relief washed over him, and he dove back

to her lips, backing her toward the bathroom where he hoisted her onto the counter. "Don't. Fucking. Move."

"You swear a lot," she called over to him while he turned on the shower and tested the temperature.

"No refunds or repairs," he muttered, adjusting the shower head. "And no trade-ins for another model from the same line." He yanked his shirt over his head, tossing it into the corner as he stalked back to her.

She leaned back on her arms, her green eyes assessing his remaining injuries with concern. "Are you sure you're oka—"

"Very. Fucking. Okay," he growled. "No exchanges."

"Maybe some tweaking," she said slowly, tearing her attention off his scars. "Like a swear jar, where you have to put a dollar in every time you curse."

He tugged impatiently on the hem of her shirt, glaring when she refused to move. "I'll have Nichol set one up online," he relented. "Two hundred a day should cover it." When her only response was a raised brow, he ripped the tee up the middle and pushed it off her shoulders. "Holy fuck," he muttered, trailing his fingers over the black lace of her bra. "This is more like it. Up my swear jar donation to three hundred a day. Fuck."

He lowered his head to her cleavage, tracing the soft fabric of her lingerie with his tongue.

"You're still ew," she breathed out, shoving his shoulders back.

"For fuck's sake," he grumbled, fumbling with the clasps of his cargos. "Fine. Get those pants off."

She hopped off the counter and shimmied out of her jeans. His fingers froze on the button of his cargos when he got distracted by the view of her ass in the mirror.

"Oh for…let me do that," she huffed, kneeling down to pop his fly. She sat back on her heels and looked up at him. "So the commando thing isn't a prison thing. It's a Rhys thing."

Any smart-ass reply he might have thought up disappeared into oblivion when her hands wrapped around his erection and her tongue made an appearance.

Her tongue with that goddamn metal ball.

The goddamn metal ball traveling up his shaft and teasing the head of his dick.

The contrast between the heat of her tongue and the coolness of the metal sent his eyes rolling back in his head.

Fuuuuuuuuuck.

He reached down to tangle his fingers in her hair while she wrapped her mouth around him and was rewarded with a swat as she leaned away.

"Your hands are still all gross from your valiant attempt to take Boy down."

Not trusting himself to speak, he lifted her into the shower and stepped in behind her. When her head dropped back into the spray, he ran his fangs lightly down her throat, unhooking her bra and lowering her panties to the floor while he licked and kissed his way down to her hips.

"Is this our annual mating?"

He fixed her with a dead stare. "I don't want to answer that."

"Tell you what," she murmured, running her fingers through his hair. "If you impress me, I'll consider removing that clause."

No pressure.

He refocused on the water trails sluicing down her

body, his tongue tracing the paths leisurely. "What the hell are you doing?" he mumbled into her inner thigh when something wet dropped onto his head.

"Washing your hair," she replied, massaging his scalp. "As you were."

The shampoo pooling at his knees ran pink and he lifted her leg over his shoulder, steadied her, and froze.

You've done this thousands of times.

You know what the fuck to do.

Don't be a fucking newbie.

Annual. Sex.

No pressure.

As his tongue hit her core and swirled up to her sensitive nub, her hands tightened in his hair and sent a jolt of satisfaction through him. He ran his tongue through her folds leisurely, savoring her taste and memorizing every move hitching her breathing or earning a moan. When she released his head and braced herself on the tile, he flattened his tongue, increased his speed, and pushed two fingers inside her.

"Ohmygod," she panted as he sped up. "I'm gonna… ohmygod I'm gonna come!"

He sat back on his heels, lifted a brow, and nuzzled her thigh. "That's kind of the point."

When her teeth clenched and she fixed him with a cold stare, he dove back in until her body tightened around his fingers. She gripped the back of his head and held him tight to her. "Don't you dare stop," she moaned, her nails digging into the back of his neck as her walls began to flutter.

He briefly debated disobeying, considered pulling her back from the edge just so he could push her back toward it over and over until she was an incoherent mess.

His aching hard-on wasn't fond of the idea.

When the first shudders of her orgasm passed through her, he slid his fangs into her inner thigh. Her heel dug into his spine as she slammed her hand against the wall and arched into him, her body clenching around his fingers while he tortured himself with the aphrodisiac of her blood.

By the time she began to go limp against him, he was teetering dangerously close to insanity. He held her thigh tight to him and rose to his feet, wrapping her other leg around his hips while he pushed inside her.

Holy fuck, that's warm.

"Don't slip," she warned breathlessly, lacing one arm around his neck, and running her other hand through his wet hair.

The small part of his brain still functioning past his baser urges stilled his thrusts. "You're kidding me, right?"

She nuzzled into his neck, running her tongue along his jawline. "It's wet and slippery. I don't want us to get hurt."

"I'm the God of wet and slippery," he grinned, thrusting deep into the warm body wrapped around him. He adjusted his grip on her ass, angling her back into the heat of the shower water before he resumed pumping into her.

"You're so full of yourse…ohmygod."

Bingo.

Gritting his teeth, he doubled his tempo and held the slightly awkward position until she let loose a string of curses even he found impressive. When her nails dug into his shoulder blades deep enough to draw blood, all control he had snapped. His fangs dove into her throat, and he released inside her with a growl echoing in the tiled shower.

Don't fucking drop her.

She was still clinging to him while he fumbled them out of the shower and hastily wrapped a towel around her back.

"We should do that again," she murmured, her eyes closed as he carried her to the bed.

Lowering her onto the mattress, he resumed slowly rocking inside her heat, reaching up to push her wet hair from her eyes. "You're positive option three is what you want?"

"Hmmmm," she smiled lazily, stretching her arms to the headboard. "If you can walk into a Deepfryer for me, I suppose I can give shacking up a try for you." She opened one eye and looked up at him. "I kind of foolishly still love you."

He dipped his head into her neck. "I can feel it in your corner of my mind. It's nice."

She smacked his tattoos. "Nice?"

Keeping his head down, he lowered his chest to hers. "You know saying it back isn't who I am, right? You're going to need to be okay with that. I'll prove it every fucking night and I'll do anything I can to make up for lost time, but words aren't my thing."

She wrapped her arms around his back. "In your seven centuries, how many Tenders have you wanted to shack up with?"

"One."

"How many have you taken an imprisonment for?"

"One again."

"And how many have you taken a Deepfrying for?"

"That would also be one."

"Yeah, I'm okay with it."

CHAPTER FORTY-TWO

"Looking good, Lis!" Mick called out as Lis and Molly crossed the field toward the sparring match.

"Says the guy who wants his testicles removed, rolled in salt, and shoved down his throat," Rhys growled, placing himself directly in Mickey's line of sight. He glanced over at her, distracted momentarily by the exposed skin peeking out from under her sheer peasant top when she waved over at them. "Look away, little man."

Grinning, Mick waved at her over Rhys's shoulder and backed up a few steps. "What is it you always remind Jagger? Hey, Jagg! What does Rhys always tell you about Bianca?"

"They never forget their first vamp," Jagg smirked.

"Ah, yeah," Mick smiled cheerfully, winking at Lis. "They don't, do they?"

He could feel Nichol's weight hurling him to the ground before he could strike the Cheshire grin off Mickey's face.

"You two dumbasses head back inside," he barked to Jagg and Mick. "Rhys, payback's a bitch. And you have centuries' worth coming. Enjoy."

****

"Tonight, you have to do everything I say."

Rhys grinned at Lis's words. "Sounds intriguing. What brought this on?"

She pulled her shirt off, revealing an emerald lace

bra his body responded to on cue. "Audra says role reversal can be an effective way to better understand your partner."

"Yeah, we should have a little talk about that," he muttered, rolling onto his back, and grabbing his erection unhidden beneath his boxers. "See this? If you want this to disappear completely, possibly forever, use the words 'Audra says' in this bedroom again."

Shimmying her jeans off, she crawled onto the bed and straddled him. He relaxed back while she ran her fingers along his ribs and up his arms, gripping his hands and extending them over his head. She flicked one of his fangs with her tongue piercing before kissing along his jaw line to his earlobe.

"Audra said you'd say that," she smiled, hopping off the bed and bending to grab something out of the pocket of her jeans. Producing a small pen knife, she took a step back. "Tonight," she said, spinning it between her fingers, "you're going to walk for me, talk for me, bleed for me, and—" Pausing, she licked her lips. "Beg for me."

A low growl rumbled through his chest, his fangs lengthening as he stood. "I'm not wholly against this brand of therapy."

"Uh-uh," she scolded, her hands on her hips. "I don't believe I asked you to move. Hands behind your back."

He obeyed with the lift of a brow, bowing his head a fraction while his senses heightened with her command.

She strode to him and raised the small blade to his chest, slowly scoring his skin and biting her lip when a trickle of blood dripped. With the flick of her tongue, the blood was gone, the cut already healing.

He could feel his irises ovaling, the predator in him rising up. "I don't think that was the punishment you hoped it would be."

Sliding the blunt edge of the knife along his hardened length, she smiled. "This is exactly the punishment I hoped it would be." Backing away until she reached the far wall, she crossed her arms. "Spin for me, pretty boy."

Extending his arms out, he turned on the spot. "Yes, mistress."

His response earned a sharp inhale, her green eyes darkening to a wicked shade of emerald matching the bra he was aching to remove with his teeth.

"Boxers off."

When he grabbed the waistband to tug them off, she shook her head.

"Uh-uh. Slow and steady. A good show isn't rushed."

Running his tongue along one fang, he let his gaze linger on the juncture between her thighs until she shifted on her feet. He hooked his thumbs in the elastic and inched them down his hips enough to give her a full view of the V-cut he knew she was hot for. When her heart rate sped up, he tore them off and tossed the destroyed plaid on the floor between them.

"That," she stated, her voice as strong as her pounding heart, "was intentional disobedience."

Striding toward him with the fluidity of a huntress, she brought the knife to the V-cut he'd enticed her with and sliced, sank to her knees, and rolled her tongue piercing between her teeth.

"Lis," he growled in warning, his vision narrowing

dangerously.

With a long, slow lick, she erased all sign of the cut and stood. "We need to work on your ability to follow directions." Backing up to the wall again, she leaned against it. "Now walk for me, angel."

He stalked toward her, his fangs laying long over his bottom lip as the low rumble in his chest amplified. Stopping within her reach, he towered over her.

"I don't know," she breathed. "Something was missing. Let's try it again with a little more finesse and a little less snarling."

With a smirk, he backed up slowly, catching her gaze as it drifted to his length. "My apologies, mistress."

Keeping his eyes locked on hers, he sauntered over again, stopping only when he was flush to her, his erection pressed against her belly. "Better?"

She flattened her palm on his shoulder and pushed down gently with a nod. "Much. On to linguistics."

Lowering himself to his knees at her unspoken command, he gripped her thighs. "*En français?*"

"*Oui.*"

Hitching one leg up, he swiped his tongue over her panty-clad sex. "*Le lion mange la petite souris.*" A small hand tangled in his hair, holding him to her. "*Regardez le prédateur attraper la proie.*"

"Roll those Rs," she panted.

"Yes, mistress," he growled, repeating the sentence twice more. Met with nothing more than a breathy moan, he unhooked her leg from his shoulder and sat back on his haunches. "Better?"

She blinked, her cheeks flushed as her balance wavered and the pen knife dropped from her fingers. "Game's over." Reaching back, she unhooked her bra and eased it off, draping it around his neck. "Take the reins back, baby. I don't want to think anymore."

It was all the invitation he needed.

Spinning her on the spot, he grabbed her hands and bent her over the sofa before gripping her hips and sinking to his knees. Hooking his fangs into the delicate lace, he tugged her underwear off, scraping his teeth along the smooth skin of her ass. With a grunt of appreciation, he sat back on his heels to admire the view. The urge to take her in a single swift motion, to pound into her until her knees gave out and she was screaming his name was relentless in its demand.

But the sweet torture of anticipation was greater.

The longer he sat without touching her, the heavier her breathing became, her skin flushed while she stayed draped over the sofa, ready for him.

He pushed himself to his feet and stepped closer, a hair's breadth away from the smooth skin calling to him.

Giving in to the need to touch her, he trailed his thumbs along the inside of her thighs, inching his way to her ribs and smirking when she arched her spine and pushed back against him.

Lying across her body, he brought his lips to her ear. "Uh-uh," he murmured, nibbling her lobe. "I don't believe I asked you to move." She wiggled her hips and looked over her shoulder at him, the sensation of her ass pressing on his erection speaking directly to his instincts. "Beg for me," he growled, his control precarious.

With a laugh, she reached back and gripped his thighs. "I think not. I'd rather hear *you* beg for *me*."

He shoved one hand into her hair and tugged gently as he bent over her and grazed her throat with his fangs. "Let me fuck you."

"No."

With a smirk, he nuzzled her neck. "Please let me fuck you."

"Nope."

Growling low, he ran his tongue along the shell of her ear and gave her what she wanted. "Please," he murmured, sliding his arm under her hips to position her. "Let me make love to you."

Contented, she reached back and ran her hand through his hair before dropping her hands to the sofa frame and tightening her hold. "Only if you do it hard enough to collapse this couch."

Challenge. Accepted.

EPILOGUE

Nichol banged on Rhys and Lis's door as he passed, smirking when there was a loud thump sounding suspiciously like furniture breaking. "I want silence in this wing in two hours," he called out when Rhys let loose a string of curses and Lis giggled.

"Three," Rhys barked back. "No. Three and a half."

Rolling his eyes, he made his way to the sanctity of his com room, closed the door, and collapsed into his chair. He rolled lazily over to his monitor, tapping the mouse, and watching the screen fire up.

Highsteaks1403: — U up —

Nichol glanced at the clock before replying.

587OriginalNK: — What r u still doing awake —

He opened his browser and began scanning the anti-vamp sites, noting any new logins.

Highsteaks1403: — Worked the nightshift —

Highsteaks1403: — I'm booooored —

Slouching back in his seat, he dragged the chat to the center of his screen and pulled his keyboard onto his lap.

A word about the author…

Katja Desjarlais is a teacher by day and a paranormal romance writer by moonlight. She is an unapologetic music addict and has an obsession for bad Bach puns despite her irrational aversion to Baroque. Her favorite words include 'plethora' and 'dapper', and she is physically repulsed by the word 'moist'. Katja's interest in the paranormal can be traced to her early childhood film choices and to the revolving book collection on her phone.

Desjarlais lives in the Okanagan Valley with her husband, three children, and three cats. Her ideal summer vacation is spent traipsing through the United States with her family and attending heavy metal concerts.

katjadesjarlais.wordpress.com

Thank you for purchasing
this publication of The Wild Rose Press, Inc.

For questions or more information
contact us at
info@thewildrosepress.com.

The Wild Rose Press, Inc.
www.thewildrosepress.com